Mere Enchantment

Alicia Rivoli

Alicia Rivoli Books
http://www.aliciarivoli.blogspot.com

Cover illustration by Danijel Firak
http://danijelfirak.com

Copyediting by Christine LePorte
http://www.christineleporte.com

ISBN-13: 978-1475145533
ISBN-10: 1475145535

Copyright © 2012 Alicia Rivoli

First Paperback Edition: April 2012

To my wonderful
husband Chad for all his hard work and patience
these many years. Also to my sister and muse, Colette.

Contents

1

Nebula's Attack

"Nebula has been defeated, Sire. We must get you out of here immediately!" said a tall, muscular man.

The King looked up from his throne, the signs of exhaustion clearly visible in the dark lines surrounding his pale, blue eyes.

"Is there no other way?" he asked the man.

"No, Sire, we must leave now," the man repeated. "Jacan is nearly at the gate."

The King rose quickly and walked toward the front entrance of the grand hall. He turned to give his beautiful castle one last look. A boy of no more than three ran up to the King, his father, and jumped into his arms. A beautiful woman holding a baby girl followed the boy, stopping at the King's side. The tall, muscular man, who was dressed in a bright red robe, black pants, and a white V-necked tunic, raised both hands above his head, and the family disappeared.

The kingdom in the clouds, that's what it was named after. Nebula was a beautiful city full of happy people, marketplaces, gardens, and one of the most beautiful castles

ever built. Each stone changed color depending on the way
the sun shone on it that day. Each spire looked as though it
was spun delicately on a loom, and the dark blue color made
it even more enchanting. The five turrets were around ten
stories tall, each one encircled by a golden ring. In the center
was a lush garden full of wildflowers, daisies, and bluebells.
The water features trickled down stone-cut designs, and soft
benches were placed strategically around for any extra
relaxation one might need. However, this kingdom was
different than any other; it was a kingdom that was built
literally on top of the clouds. It went wherever the wind blew
it, never staying in one place for too long.

　　Unfortunately, the once beautiful city was now being
devoured by Jacan and his army of Umbra. The houses that
had been built meticulously by the hands of their previous
owners were now either being lived in by the terrible black-
clothed beasts or simmering ash from the recent raid. Jacan
had won over the entire Kingdom of Nebula. The King and
Queen, along with their children, had sounded the retreat
and disappeared.

　　Jacan was furious that they got away and vowed that
he would find them, if it was the last thing he did. You see, he
was once the Duke of Calidity, a prosperous city in the
Kingdom of Nebula. The King trusted him and considered
him his right-hand man. When the King received the news
about Jacan's betrayal, he was furious and put a warrant out
for his arrest. However, the man he once thought a friend
was nowhere to be found. The kingdom was told of a possible

attack, and nearby kingdoms were informed of the betrayal, but no one expected the nightmares that had haunted them as children would become real.

Jacan discovered a way to gain power over the Umbra, dark fearsome creatures that lived and strived in the shadows. They were nearly impossible to kill, only able to die from the poison of a bilian plant. These plants were only found in the waters of the Todswan River, but you have to ask a very strange creature to get it for you, because if a human were to pick the plant, he would have bad luck brought upon himself. They have bright blue petals and prickly stems. Once you have the plant, you rub the thorns up and down the sharpened sword until the blade glows blue. One thorn will cover an entire sword and also the tips of the arrows in a quiver.

Once Jacan had these powerful creatures, he knew that he had the power to defeat Nebula and someday the entire Kingdom of Mere. He planned his attack carefully, finding the smallest towns first, destroying them, and getting even more recruits from captives. He would threaten the stronger men to fight with him, or he would destroy their families. The smaller cities in the kingdom were very weak and had only a few guards, so destroying them was no difficult task. Jacan's army grew larger and larger and soon his army was so large, you could see it from miles away.

People in the kingdom became frightened of their own shadows, and would only leave their homes at noon day when few shadows were cast amongst them. The King called

3

together his army to go out and meet them, to fight for their homes, their land, and their families. He himself mounted his horse and suited in armor. Wizards were called to assist and thousands of arrows were made, hundreds of swords were forged, and tunnels were dug through the clouds to protect the women and children.

The King's army rode forward, not knowing if they would live to see their families again. Fear showing on their armored faces, they marched on. Soon it was time to fight; the army of Jacan was only a hill away. Their numbers were scarce compared to that of their enemy, but they were ready. The King raised his sword, and the archers stepped forward and aimed their arrows at the enemy. With a movement of his sword, the archers released their arrows and they went whizzing toward the beasts in black. Jacan did the same and the arrows of his men flew straight toward the good people of Nebula. The arrows hit their targets, many of the King's soldiers fell, and many more were injured. However, none of the arrows of the King's warriors killed their enemy. They were simply thrown aside, and Jacan sent forth his army.

At the time, the King knew nothing of the special poison needed to kill the black beasts, and with each slash he made with his sword into his enemy, the wound inflicted would immediately heal. The wizards set up guards around the King's army, protecting them as much as they could, but the forces were too strong. By the time the King called for retreat, he'd lost hundreds of his men, and not a single enemy had been destroyed by their swords. The wizards did manage to kill a few dozen of the enemy with magic, but magic is very draining, and without rest, will kill the person using it.

The survivors, including the King, returned to the city of Nebula, and the King called for immediate evacuations. He informed his people that the Kingdom of Nebula was no longer safe and they needed to seek refuge among the other kingdoms in the world. The people quickly packed their valuables and began their descent toward the kingdoms on the ground. It wasn't easy to get there; you needed a wizard to make the clouds go lower to the ground, creating fog so you could easily get on land.

The wizards began working together to get the people down, but Jacan's army came too quickly. Few escaped; most that did retreated to other kingdoms with their families. Some hid themselves in the lowering clouds. The King and Queen knew it was time for them to retreat as well. Nevertheless, the King promised that one day he would find a way to defeat Jacan's army and gain control of his kingdom once more. He vowed he would save his people from captivity, and destroy Jacan.

The wizards transported the royal family to the Kingdom of Mere, where they were looked after by the King and Queen of Mere. Immediately, the entire kingdom became a target for Jacan's army. All the wizards of both Mere and Nebula called a counsel to search for ways to defeat the army of Jacan and protect the Kingdom of Mere. Hours went by, and nothing had been established. The wizards talked

5

well into the night and through the next day. Each hour they talked, Jacan grew closer to the entrance of the kingdom.

Finally, after two days of debate, they found a solution to protect Mere and also possibly defeat Jacan. It wasn't going to be easy; they would have to put a protection spell over the entire kingdom. No one would be able to come in or out unless they held the key to the gateway. Only four people would have that key, and no one except those four would know how to get in and out. They also sealed a marriage between the two kingdoms. The King of Nebula gave his eldest son, while the King of Mere gave his only daughter. Once they were married, the two…

"Dad, why are you telling me this story again? I'm not a child anymore," Preston said as they sat by the fire in their log cabin.

Preston's family had lived here since Preston could remember. He had grown up here. They lived on the banks of a large lake in the Rocky Mountains—Mirror Lake. It was so beautiful. The water was so clear you could see the fish swimming through the dead logs at the bottom.

Preston loved it here. His dad had told him they moved here after his grandparents passed away and left them the two cabins. One was where they lived. The other was across the lake and was always made up for anyone who might want to visit, although Preston couldn't remember any visitors ever staying there. He would occasionally use it as his fortress when he was a small boy, where he would pretend to fight off the evil Jacan and his army of black soldiers from his father's stories.

He had no idea why his dad brought up this story again. He had heard it many times before, along with many others about the wonderful creatures that lived in his fairy tale of an imagination. Each time the story became longer and more detailed.

"I just thought we might enjoy a blast from the past. It's been awhile since we've had time to sit around the fire together," his father responded.

Preston's mother rose from her favorite armchair and walked to the kitchen. She placed a tea kettle on the stove and heated up some water.

"I love your stories, dear, they make me feel so young," she replied.

"I'm just too old for these stories now," said Preston. "I don't want to sound ungrateful, I had a blast as a boy playing the King of Nebula and fighting the fearsome Jacan, but I'm almost eighteen now. Isn't it time to grow up?" He couldn't keep the sarcasm out of his tone.

His father smiled at him.

"Well, you never know when my stories of war might be helpful," he said jokingly.

Preston laughed and took the cup of hot chocolate out of his mother's soft hands.

"Oh, we forgot to tell you, son, the other cabin is going to be occupied for two weeks. We've decided to rent it out during the summer," his mother said.

Preston nearly choked.

"Really?" he asked. "I've never seen anyone else up here, except of course a few hikers that come wandering out of the woods completely lost and looking for water and food."

Jennifer, Preston's mother, laughed. "Yeah, that cabin has been empty far too long. They should be here tomorrow sometime."

Preston blew on his hot chocolate and took a large sip. He couldn't help but wonder what it would be like to have someone else around for two whole weeks. He wasn't really around people that often. Only when he and his parents drove the two hours out of the mountain to a nearby city once every couple of months to restock their food supply had he ever even seen other people.

"We need to go and make sure that the beds are made and there's plenty of firewood for them. I figured we would go right after lunch," his father said. "I also want to make sure that they have a boat. Would you mind letting them borrow your canoe for a while?"

Preston nodded. He couldn't wait for tomorrow. He only hoped that they had kids around his age. It would be great to take them hiking or swimming and show them all the cool caves. And maybe they would have one of those handheld Nintendo things that ran on batteries. He had always wanted one, but his dad said they were too expensive. He saw one in a magazine in the city once and had wanted to at least have a chance to play one someday. He could even remember the game that was being sold with the system:

"Zelda." He couldn't believe they had games that would let the characters use swords.

"Preston, are you ready to work?" his dad asked, bringing him back to reality.

"Uh, sure, are we going to get more firewood?" he asked, clearing his throat and setting his empty cup of cocoa on the small coffee table.

"Yeah, we are running a little low, and the wind is telling me there's a storm coming."

Preston was always amazed at how well his father predicted the weather. He was nearly always right, but sometimes some weird storm would blow in and they would be caught completely off guard and have to bunker down under the staircase in case a tree blew down.

He quickly put on his boots and a light jacket. His father opened the door and walked out into the bright sunshine. It was a beautiful day; the sun was warm. Preston always enjoyed being outside. Ever since he was a little boy, he loved playing near the water, hiking, going fishing, or even just lying in the warm sand along the beach of the lake.

His father handed him an ax and Preston quickly went to work chopping wood, his thoughts never leaving the excitement that was only twenty-four hours away.

2

The Meeting

Looking out the car window, you would never be able to guess that it was the middle of June. The windows of the Clister family Jeep were slowly beginning to collect frost and there was no sunshine to be seen. Chloe and her little brother, Jason, were getting anxious to arrive at the lakeside cabin in the Rocky Mountains. Chloe was a beautiful sixteen-year-old girl with flowing brown hair, green eyes that sparkled in the sunshine, and a smile that would brighten up your worst day. She and her family were on their first family vacation in six years and had been driving for what felt like forever to Chloe. They had begun their journey at their small home near the Oklahoma border. The entire trip was about a nine-hour drive and by now the whole family was ready to get out of the car.

Her father, Michael, slowly turned the car down a dirt road toward a beautiful lake.

"What is that lake called?" Jason asked his father. Jason was fourteen, with dark brown hair that matched his sister's. He had a mischievous look in his big brown eyes as he turned to his sister.

"I believe if this map is correct, that is called Mirror Lake," his mother, Aimie, answered. "The brochure says that our cabin overlooks Mirror Lake, so we must be getting close."

"Ow, Jason, don't throw your book at me," Chloe squealed. She quickly picked up the book and began lifting it to throw it back when her mother gave a loud sigh. Chloe swiftly put the book down and peered out the front window.

"What is it, Mom? What do you see?" asked Chloe.

Chloe followed her mother's stare out the window of the car and saw a log cabin that looked as though it were completely encompassed by large trees. Chloe thought it looked absolutely beautiful. The family pulled their car into a weed-infested driveway and began piling out. Jason ran to the front door and began to open it when his mother grabbed his hand and pulled him back.

"What's the matter, Mom?" he asked. "Why did you do that?"

"Jason, you need to help your father unload the car before we go in."

Jason sighed, and they slowly walked back toward the car to unload their luggage. As they pulled the last bag out of the trunk another car pulled up behind them. Michael, Jason and Chloe's dad, made his way over to the car and shook the hand of a tall, skinny man Chloe knew very well by the name of Jackson. He was wearing a worn-out old pair of jeans and a red and blue plaid collared shirt. There was also a very short skinny woman in a flower-colored shirt and jean shorts named Misty, a short young boy named Zach, with blond hair and an overgrown brown and gray T-shirt with a wolf on the front, and to Chloe's surprise, her best friend, Megan. She was a pretty teenager with long flowing red hair that shone brightly every time the sun's rays hit it. Her eyes were also an intense green and she was always dressed as if she were going to a party. Today she was wearing name-brand jeans, a bright orange short-sleeve shirt, and an expensive diamond necklace tied around her neck with matching stud earrings. It was their family friends, the Pearsons. Chloe's father looked at her and gave a big smile.

"Dad, why didn't you tell me that the Pearsons were coming?" Chloe said, squealing with delight that she wouldn't have to spend the next two weeks with her geeky little brother.

Her father gave her a big hug and kissed her softly on the cheek.

"We planned this trip months ago," he said. "We didn't tell any of you kids that the other was coming."

They all grabbed their luggage and began the short walk to the front door. Chloe's father turned the doorknob and pushed open the door to reveal the inside of their cabin. At first glance you would have never guessed it to be as small as it seemed on the outside. It was actually large and spacious. The families made their way in and began looking around their home away from home.

The cabin was at first very dark, but Jackson pulled a red shiny lantern out of his backpack and a match from his shirt pocket, and soon the whole cabin was filled with a warm light. They soon saw that it was lined with old wooden rockers and big comfy couches. There was a big rock fireplace that rose to the top of the ceiling and seemed like it would go on forever. Beneath the fireplace lay a big black bearskin rug. In the kitchen they found a beautiful hand-carved dining table surrounded by eight wooden chairs. There was no refrigerator, there seemed to be plenty of cupboard space. There was a big farmer's sink in the middle of the countertop with a long metal faucet with a large handle on the back side of it. It reminded Chloe of the old-fashioned well pumps. Aimie lifted the handle and pushed it down; to their relief fresh clean drinking water poured out. Aimie opened the curtains of the six big windows to let in any light that might come through the clouds and exposed the beautiful picturesque lake. The sight was so beautiful it seemed almost like someone had painted it there.

Chloe and Megan decided that they should see what the second floor had in store for them, so they borrowed the light from Megan's father and climbed the wooden staircase to the second floor. Jason and Zach, Megan's fourteen-year-old brother, went with them. As they reached the top of the stairs they found four different doors, two down the hallway to the left, and two down the hallway to the right. They decided to open the first door down the hallway to the right. As they pushed it open and held in the lantern they saw a beautiful four-poster queen-sized bed. The linens were a bright yellow fabric with big white fluffy pillows, and a mosquito net pulled back around each wooden pillar. The wooden floors were an oak finish, well worn but in beautiful

13

shape. The room was decorated with beautiful paintings of rivers and mountains. Behind the door they found a full-length mirror that was encircled by stunning purple and yellow flowers. On the far wall there was a big picture window with drapes in the same shade as the linens on the bed. Chloe opened up the curtains to let in the already setting sun that had peeked, for a moment, through the clouds.

Megan walked over to the open door and peered at herself through the full-length mirror.

"I hope that tomorrow is a lot warmer," said Megan. "It is freezing outside, and if it stays like this we won't even be able to go swimming in the lake."

Chloe nodded in agreement.

They made their way to the door and left what they decided to call the sunshine room. They turned to their right and headed for the next door down the small floral-lined hallway. Zach slowly turned the knob and pushed open the door. Megan entered the room with the lantern and made her way to the window. She put her arms out in front of her and drew back the curtains to expose yet another view of Mirror Lake.

"Look at it," Chloe said, "isn't it gorgeous?"

"I can't believe that it is so clear," said Megan.

"I feel like I've been here before," said Chloe, "But I think it's just because of how many times I looked at the brochure my mom had."

"Yeah, I know what you mean," Megan replied. "I feel the same way."

14

The two girls turned to look around. They saw that the room they were in had two twin beds, one on the left and another on the right. It also had beautiful cotton linens; this time they were a baby blue with dark blue pillows and white embroidered lilies on the pillow cases. The drapes matched the linens on the bed also and had the same old oak floors. The room had beautiful photographs of ice-capped mountaintops reflected in a lake, with trees and grassy meadows all shimmering as well. The pictures were all so beautiful.

"Look," said Zach, "they are all of Mirror Lake."

"You're right," said Megan. "I can't wait to get outside and see it!"

"Come on, guys, lets go to the other rooms," stated Jason. "This is getting boring."

They turned to go to the other two rooms on the other side of the house. While walking they passed two more beautiful mirrors that were lined with dried flowers. They reached the next door and pushed it open. They found another four-poster queen-sized bed but instead of yellow linens, these were an amazing purple hue. A purple that none of them had ever seen. It was a mix between a lilac and plum color, and there were matching drapes, a matching flower-enclosed mirror, and again the most stunning photographs of Mirror Lake. All Chloe could think about was getting outside and seeing it up close. They continued on to the final room in the house and found it like the blue room, but this time

15

everything was light and dark green with still more photographs.

Back downstairs, they found that their parents had already begun unpacking the food and putting it in cupboards.

"Mom, you should see the rooms," said Zach, "they are so cool."

"Yeah, Mom, wait until you see them. You are going to love yours and Dad's room," added Jason.

"I'm sure they are very nice," Aimie said, smiling at her son.

"When can we go outside?" Jason asked, jumping from one foot to the other.

"We are going to have to wait until morning, I'm afraid," his father replied. "It's getting too dark to go anywhere now."

"Can we go swimming tomorrow?" the girls asked in unison.

"Well, if the weather is nice tomorrow, I don't see why not. After all, that's why we are here," spoke Misty.

"However, let's get some dinner ready and get our things unpacked," said Jackson. "Then we can all get some sleep."

The two families began setting the table with the dishes that were provided in one of the cupboards, warming up some canned soup on their propane grill in the kitchen, and getting some water from the old-fashioned pump. During dinner the children explained the rooms to their parents and how amazing the photographs on the walls were. After everyone had their fill of beef stew, they grabbed their luggage and headed upstairs.

"Dad, I have to use the bathroom," Jason complained, "but I don't know where it is."

"Well, Jason, the bathroom isn't like the ones that we are used to," his father explained. "It's called an outhouse."

"What do you mean, an outhouse?" Jason asked.

"An outhouse is a restroom that is outside. There is no electricity here so there is a little building just outside the back door that you can use," Michael explained to his son.

"Oh, okay," Jason said. "Hey, Zach, do you want to come outside with me to the bathroom since you have our lantern?"

The two boys went back down the stairs and headed toward the back door. A few minutes later, both the boys were back upstairs heading for what they had decided was going to be their room. They had chosen the green room, across the hall from Misty and Jackson, who were in the purple room because it didn't have the flowers on the pillows. There was no way they wanted to stay in a flowery bed. The two girls started to get settled in their room and had just turned down their beds when Jason came running in.

"Hey, Chloe," he said, "wait until you have to use the bathroom. It stinks in there and the toilet doesn't even flush."

"What did you expect?" she replied. "There's no electricity here. Now go back to bed, Jason, we'll talk in the morning."

17

Jason sighed as he turned quickly around and headed back down the hall to his room.

The girls climbed into their beds and began talking about all the fun that they were going to have tomorrow.

"I'm going to get such a great tan!" Megan said. "I can't wait until Tommy sees me again."

Tommy was Megan's boyfriend. They had only been dating for a short while, but that seemed to be all that Megan could think about. Tommy was her first boyfriend, but they only saw each other at school.

"Megan, what's it like to have a boyfriend?" Chloe asked.

"Well, Tommy does stuff for me; he carries my books to class, he bought me a rose and gave it to me after school, and he even said that we would go on a date when I got back from vacation." she answered.

Chloe got really quiet for a minute, and began thinking about what it must be like to be Megan. She was perfect. Beautiful hair, glowing green eyes, perfect body, and a boyfriend.

"I can't wait until I get a boyfriend," Chloe whispered through the dark.

Megan smiled at her friend and quickly fell asleep.

The next morning the smell of pancakes drifted under their door and woke them up.

"Man, I really have to use the restroom," Chloe said.

"Yeah, me too," Megan replied. The girls got up, made their beds, and put on some jeans and T-shirts and headed down the stairs.

"Good morning, girls," said Aimie, "did you sleep well?"

"Yeah, we did," said Chloe, "but I really need to go use the restroom."

"Well, I'm afraid that you are going to have to wait. Jason just went outside to go," her mother said. "Why don't you sit down and have some pancakes while you wait."

They sat down at the table and Aimie brought them some big hot pancakes.

"Wow, Mom, these look great!" Chloe said.

"Yeah, Mrs. Clister, these are really good," Zach said from the other end of the table.

"Thank you very much." she said, "I'm afraid I've never made them on a propane stove before and I was a bit nervous."

"Well, no need to be nervous, hon," her husband said as he leaned forward and kissed her on the cheek. "They are delicious."

Soon everyone was full and Chloe and Megan ventured out to use the restroom. They went out the door expecting a cold draft to hit them in the face but instead they got a blast of warm sunshine. They could hear the birds singing in the trees and the sound of water nearby.

"Oh, it's a great day!" squealed Megan. "I will definitely be tanning today."

19

"You are so funny, I can't believe that you are worried about tanning. We are going to be here for two weeks and we are going to be doing stuff on that lake most of the time," Chloe said.

"Well, I have to look good for Tommy when we get back. I don't want him to think that all I did was stay inside," answered Megan.

They both finished using the restroom and turned to go back inside to get some things from their room.

"Look," Chloe burst out, "there is a boat on the beach. Let's go boating!"

The two girls carefully climbed into the canoe and were about the push off from land when Jason and Zach ran down the embankment.

"Wait for us!" shouted Jason. "Mom said that we could come with you."

They swiftly climbed into the boat with Chloe and Megan and helped push off the sandy beach. There was only one paddle, so each person took turns paddling around on the water.

"Look at that," Zach said, "you can see all the way to the bottom of the lake."

"Yeah," said Megan, "look at the dead logs and all of the fish, and the plant life."

"You can even see the reflection of the sun and those mountains," Chloe added. "I wonder why it is so clear."

"I don't know," said Megan, "but isn't it the most beautiful thing that you have ever seen?"

20

They continued paddling the boat when Megan began staring at one spot and pointing her finger towards the far shore.

"What is it?" Jason asked.

"It looks like there is a dark cloud or something right there." Megan didn't have time to finish what she was saying, before a strong burst of wind hit them and began pushing the boat further away from shore.

"What is going on?" Megan shouted at them. "Why aren't we paddling back toward the cabin?"

"I'm trying but the wind is too strong, I can't hold on to the paddle," Jason yelled through the howling wind.

The paddle was ripped from his hands as the boat moved farther and farther away from shore. Chloe heard the thunder in the background and then they all saw a big bright flash of lightning that looked like it was only a few hundred yards away, followed by an ear-deafening boom from the thunder that followed, startling them all.

"There's another boat right there," Megan shouted.

"Yeah, look, it has two people in it," Jason said. "I think we should try and get their attention."

"No way, we don't even know who they are. They could be dangerous and we are already too far from the cabin."

"We have to try or we are going to get lost out here," Zach said.

The two boys began yelling loudly in the direction of the boat.

"What are you doing, stop!" Megan yelled.

"Come on, Meg, don't be scared, I'll take care of you," her brother said.

They finally attracted the attention of the other boat after what seemed to be ten minutes of all four of them yelling for help. They saw the boaters turn around and start heading straight for them.

"Hi," said Jason.

As the two boaters caught up to them Chloe noticed that one of the boaters seemed to be her age, and was a spitting image of the man sitting next to him, with light brown hair and eyes so blue they seemed to glow. He wore a light blue shirt that made the color of his eyes all the more brilliant, and he also had on a pair of blue jeans tucked into some galoshes. Chloe realized that she must have been staring because Megan reached over and elbowed her in the ribs.

"Can you help us?" Chloe said loudly, trying to talk over the thunder. "We lost our paddle when the storm blew in."

"Of course," said one of the boaters. "Here, take this rope and tie it to the ring in the front."

The young boater tossed a rope into their boat and Zach tied a quick knot around the silver ring on the front of their canoe.

"My name is Jason and this is my sister Chloe and our friends Megan and Zach. What are your names?"

"I'm so sorry," Chloe said as her cheeks turned a shade of pink, "my brother can be so pushy sometimes."

"Don't worry about it," the boater said. "My name is Preston Minnow and this is my father, Jack. We were just out enjoying the sunshine. What are you four doing out here on the lake?"

"We were doing the same," said Zach. "We are here on vacation and we are staying at the cabin over there."

"Oh, you must be the Clisters and the Pearsons," Jack said loudly. "Hang on, we will try and pull you to shore."

They all held on the side of the canoe as the two men began paddling their own canoe and pulled them slowly to shore. When they finally got to shore, they quickly pulled the boats up on the sand, and everyone climbed out.

"We own that cabin, and just decided this year to rent it out for two weeks a month for families such as yourselves." Jack said. "My son and I live with my beautiful wife Jennifer in a cabin just there on that hill."

They looked toward where he was pointing and saw a cabin that looked almost identical to the one that they were staying in.

"Wow," blurted Jason, "you live up here year round? That must be amazing to see this lake in the winter."

"Why don't you all come and meet my wife and have some lemonade?" Jack suggested. "The weather changes very quickly here and it has become a very stormy day. My wife would love to have some new company around, especially some women company."

23

Without an answer Preston and his father began walking toward the cabin. Zach and Jason followed as quickly as they could, the girls right behind them. They finally reached the cabin and found that it had a big deck with a lot of patio furniture.

"I hope that my dad didn't scare you. He can speak so loudly at times that all the birds will fly from the trees, and if there was any wildlife around it would surely go the opposite direction," Preston said. "He is just a loud talker and always has been."

"No, he didn't scare us," Megan said in almost a whisper.

"Megan, why are you whispering?" Zach asked his sister. "We aren't in a library; we are in the open woods."

"I don't want to scare the birds and other animals," she answered, this time a little more loudly. The others laughed, and they soon arrived at the back door of the cabin.

"Hello," came the sound of a woman's soft voice. "I'm so happy that you could make it here. Jack and I were so worried that yesterday's chilly weather might have scared you off. Did you have a nice trip?"

Chloe quickly turned around to meet the voice, but was unable to answer. Jennifer Minnow might have been the most intimidating but gorgeous woman she had ever seen. She had shoulder-length silvery hair, almost white, with the same piercing blue eyes as her son. She wore a beautiful yellow summer dress, with bright red flowers and a pair of

24

white sandals that complemented her tan skin so perfectly it almost seemed unreal.

"Yes, we had a good trip," Megan answered. "I'm just so happy that your husband and son were out on the lake or we might have gotten lost."

"I'm sorry," Chloe began. "My name is Chloe Clister, and this is my brother Jason and our friends Megan and Zach Pearson."

"Oh, what a beautiful name," Jennifer said to Chloe. "Are you named after someone special?"

"I don't think so," Chloe answered. "My mom said that when she was a little girl that she had a doll named Chloe and I guess that's how I got my name."

"Well, please come and sit down in the living room. Jack is bringing out some lemonade. Preston, dear, could you please get some cookies from the cupboard?"

"Sure, Mom. Oh, would you guys like anything else?"

"No, thank you," Megan replied. "The lemonade and cookies sound delicious."

Preston hastily disappeared behind the doorway, leaving them with his mother.

"So, how long have you and your family lived here?" Jason asked.

"Well, this was my father's cabin and he left it to us when he passed away. The cabin that you are staying in was my grandmother's and she left it to my father who then left it to us," Jennifer replied.

25

"Mrs. Minnow, maybe you could tell us why the lake is so clear," Jason said as he stared out the window at the lake.

"Oh, please," she said, "call me Jennifer; however, I'm afraid that I don't know the answer to your question, Jason. The lake always looks clear no matter what happens. Even in the winter time when everything is covered in snow and the rivers have begun to form ice, the lake will freeze over but you can still see all the way to the bottom."

"That's amazing!" Megan said loudly. "But no one knows why?"

"Well, I'm sure someone knows, but it's not me," Jennifer said with a chuckle.

"Ah, here we are," Jack said, "a nice cold glass of fresh lemonade, and a batch of chocolate chip cookies."

They each took a glass and a cookie and began eating and drinking and talking about their trip to Mirror Lake. They were having such a great time that they didn't realize that the storm had passed and the sun was shining brightly again.

Megan looked at her watch and gasped.

"Mom and Dad are going to kill us. We have been gone for four hours—they are going to think we fell in the lake!"

"You're right," Chloe said. "Mr. Minnow, is there a faster way to get back to the cabin from here?"

"Sure," he answered in his booming voice. "Preston and I will take you in the truck, that way you don't have to leave the canoe behind."

Jack and Preston walked out the back door down to the lake and hoisted the canoe up over their heads and slowly began walking to the truck just on the other side of the cabin.

"Thank you so much for the lemonade and cookies," Chloe said to Jennifer. "They were very good."

"Oh, you're welcome, sweetheart. You all come and visit again while you are here, okay?" Jennifer responded.

"You bet," Jason said. "I love it here."

The foursome climbed into the truck as Jack and Preston finished tying the boat in the back. Then they got in and Chloe found herself sitting next to the cutest boy she had ever seen, and they began their drive back to their cabin.

3

The Hike

The truck slowly pulled up the driveway of their cabin and they all climbed out. As Preston and Jack untied the canoe, Jason ran in to let their parents know that they were home.

"Hey, Mom, Dad, we're home," Jason yelled throughout the house. "Mom, where are you?" "MOM! We're home!" he yelled as loudly as he could.

When he couldn't find them inside the house he decided he had better go look outside. He soon found them down by the lake looking toward the way that their children had previously rowed.

"Hey, Mom," Jason said cautiously.

"Where have you been?" Aimie said hysterically. "We have been worried sick. I can't believe that you would stay away so long. We thought that you got lost or your canoe tipped and you had drowned. Where are your sister and the other two?"

"They are helping Mr. Minnow and Preston unload the canoe out of the truck," Jason answered.

"Mr. Minnow? You mean the people who own this cabin brought you home?"

"Yes, they only live just over there and when we realized how long we had been gone they brought us home," he answered quickly.

Aimie, Michael, Jackson, and Misty followed Jason to the front of the house, where Jack and Preston had just unloaded the canoe.

"Oh, hello," Jack said as he wiped his brow with a cloth. "You must be Mr. and Mrs. Clister and Mr. and Mrs. Pearson. I'm Jack Minnow and this is my son, Preston. I'm sorry if you were worried about them. We took them to the house during the storm and they stayed to have some lemonade and we lost track of time. Please don't be mad at them, it's our fault."

"My name is Michael Clister and this is my wife, Aimie. This is Jackson and Misty Pearson. It's a pleasure to meet you both. The cabin is so beautiful. We appreciate you letting us stay here for a couple of weeks."

"Not a problem at all. I hope that you found everything you need inside," Jack replied. "I know that there isn't any electricity or a working bathroom but we can't seem to convince the people in the city to come hook it up for us."

"Actually," Jackson began, "I'm glad that we don't have any of that, it makes it feel more like a mountain cabin, and we don't have to worry about a television, a radio, or a telephone."

"Yeah, that's why our family stays here also. We don't know anything that is going on outside of these mountains and we never want to. It's so peaceful up here that

29

we don't want to ruin it with the bad news you always hear on a television" Jack said.

"Yeah, there are a lot of problems going on in the world and everyone seems to be so caught up in it that they can't even take time for a family vacation anymore," Misty replied shyly.

"The world is a hard place to live in, but living here makes it all worth it. Doesn't it, Preston?" Jack said, glancing toward his son.

"Yeah, it is really nice being able to go out on the lake or hiking whenever I want to," Preston said with a half smile toward Chloe.

"Well, Preston and I better be getting back home. I'm sure that Jennifer will have made lunch by now. It was a pleasure meeting you all, and don't forget, kids, you are welcome back anytime." The Minnows shook hands with everyone and got into their truck.

"Well, they seem like nice families, don't they, Dad?" Preston said. "And I have a feeling that Chloe might have a little crush on me."

"Well, what do you expect?" his father asked. "You are a strapping young boy and your mother is absolutely beautiful."

"Yeah, Chloe's not so bad herself, is she?" Preston replied.

"No, she is very pretty," Jack said, "but don't get your hopes set too high. Don't forget they are just visitors and will be leaving in two weeks."

"I know, but she is really cute, and she looks to be just a little bit younger than I am," Preston replied. "Anyway, it wouldn't matter if she were staying here forever, it's not like I have a choice of who I date."

"Now, don't start on this again, Preston, we've talked about this over and over and I thought that we had an agreement. Lillie is a bright young girl and would make a wonderful bride and a terrific mother to your children," Jack said with a stern tone.

"Dad, don't you get it? I've never even met Lillie. How can I marry someone I've never met?"

"Your mother and I had an arranged marriage, and look, we love each other very much and we had a terrific son," Jack replied as he gave a wink to his son.

"I don't care what tradition we have, Dad, I don't want to marry her. She may be a bright and beautiful girl, and maybe she has a lot of money, but I want to marry for love, not because it's tradition," Preston said, his face darkening in anger

"Look, Preston, I really don't want to talk about this right now. You'll be eighteen in three weeks and then you will marry Lillie, that's the end of the discussion!" Jack said loudly.

They drove the rest of the way to their cabin in silence. Preston opened the door, jumped out, and slammed it shut. He walked angrily to the house and was greeted by his mother. Her smile dimmed when she saw his face.

"Preston, I have a feeling that you are angry about something. Do you want to talk about it?" Jennifer asked her son.

"No, Mom, I'm just going to go sit out back and cool off for a minute okay?" Preston kissed his mother softly on the cheek.

"Okay," she said. "Lunch is just about ready; I'll bring it to you when it's done."

"Okay, Mom, thanks," Preston almost whispered. He made his way past his mother and walked around to the back of the house. He sat in the chair that Chloe had been sitting in only a short while ago.

Why do I have to marry Lillie? he thought to himself. *I don't even know who she is; I've never even talked to her.*

As Preston sat there thinking about the conversation he had just had with his father, he became angrier, so he decided that he would go down to the lake. When he got there he found himself looking in the direction of the other cabin, and it made him think of Chloe. He began picturing her in his head with her brilliantly long brown hair. Her eyes, he contemplated, were stunning.

His mother joined him with a tray full of sliced apples, a pork chop with mashed potatoes, a hot roll, and a cold glass of water.

"Thanks, Mom," Preston said.

"Let's go up and sit on the deck," his mother said softly.

The two walked back up the sand bank and sat in two chairs opposite each other. As his mother began searching him for answers, Preston slowly began eating his lunch.

"Mom," Preston said after his first bite of pork chop, "were you excited about getting married to Dad?"

"Oh, that's what you and your father were arguing about on the way back from the other cabin. Well, to tell you the truth, I wasn't happy at all. Getting married to a complete stranger wasn't my idea of a fun marriage," she said with a smile. "I didn't even get to see your father until after the ceremony was performed. The women in my day had to wear black veils over their faces during the ceremony so we couldn't be seen, and so we couldn't see our husband. We had to have people help us walk to the altar and then assist us during the entire ceremony."

"But why, why didn't they want you to know who you were getting married to?" Preston said abruptly. "I don't understand why they wouldn't want you to know."

"Well, son, it was tradition, it made it more exciting. The tradition has changed now though. Instead of a black veil, the brides wear white so you can meet your bride at the altar before the ceremony," Jennifer answered quietly. "I know that you don't want an arranged marriage, Preston, but that's how things work in our family. I'm sure that Lillie will be a wonderful bride. What brought all this up again anyway?" Jennifer asked her son.

Preston quickly looked away from his mother, hoping that she couldn't read his mind.

"Oh," she said quietly, "it was that Chloe girl, wasn't it? I could tell that you found her attractive when you couldn't keep your eyes off of her."

"Well, can you blame me?" Preston blurted out loudly. "I mean she was beautiful and she seemed so normal. Why can't I choose who I want to marry?"

"I just told you, Preston, this is how things work here, and that's just the way it is. The parents choose your bride," his mother said with a frown forming on her beautiful face.

"Thanks for the lunch, Mom. I really enjoyed it. I don't want to talk about this anymore, okay? I'm going to go out on the lake and think for a while. I'll be back around dinner time, all right?" He stood and wiped his mouth with the napkin that was on his lap.

"Okay, dear, but be careful and stay close." His mother began clearing off the table near the chair they were sitting in.

"Okay, Mom, I love you," Preston yelled as he took off for the lake.

Preston wasn't really excited to go back out on the lake because he knew that all he would think about was Chloe.

Why don't I just go to their cabin? he thought to himself. *My parents wouldn't know where I was and I could just be back by dinner time. I would love to talk to her again.*

Preston had made up his mind he was going to take the boat to the other cabin and see Chloe. He knew that he would have to be careful because if his dad knew what he

34

was doing, there would be trouble when he got home.

I'll just canoe out to where they can see me and stay there for a little while then I'll start paddling toward the cabin. They'll never know where I'm going, I do this every day.

He pushed the canoe out into the lake and began paddling a little ways from shore. Soon enough he was where he wanted to be and stopped. He lay back and acted like he was just relaxing in the sun and thinking. He looked toward his cabin and saw his dad looking out at the lake from the deck. He waved at his son and then turned around and went back inside. Preston decided that he would stay there a little longer before making his move. About a half an hour after his dad waved from the deck he decided to try to leave. He picked up the paddle and began rowing toward the other cabin. He was finally out of sight of his cabin and began to relax as he rowed.

What am I going to say when I get there? he wondered.

"I'll just tell them that I got bored and decided to come and visit to make sure they have everything they need. Yeah, that sounds good, I'll just say that. They'll never know," he said out loud.

Preston finally made his way across the lake to the cabin where Chloe was staying. He rowed to the dock and climbed out of his canoe and pulled it onto the shore. He was walking up to the door when he heard something near the lake. He spun around and glanced at where he thought that he heard the noise, but nothing was there. He decided that it was just his imagination and turned around and began walking again to the door. When he reached the door he put his hand out to knock, but was knocked completely off his feet as the door flew open and Jason came bolting outside.

"Oh, I'm sorry; I didn't know that anyone was out here. We were just playing hide and go seek and I was running to hide," Jason said as he pulled himself up off the ground and held out a hand to help Preston up as well.

"That's all right, Jason, don't worry about it. I just wanted to stop by and see if you all had all you need," Preston answered.

Just as Preston got to his feet he was again knocked off his feet, this time by Chloe.

"Oh my gosh, I am so sorry. I didn't know that you were out here. I was running after Jason and he…"

"It's okay, don't worry about it," Preston said as he cut Chloe off in mid-sentence. "I guess I'll use the front door next time."

Chloe's face was bright red as she pushed herself off of Preston and got to her feet. She held out her hand to help him up and he took it and hoisted himself up for the second time.

"How about we move from the doorway?" she said. "I'm sure that Zach and Megan will be right behind us soon."

Sure enough, just as they moved away from the door the other two came running out at full speed.

"Hey, it's Preston," Zach said as he tried to catch his breath. "What are you doing here, man?" Zach put his hand in the air and waited for Preston to give him a high five. Preston slapped his hand and smiled brightly and laughed.

"I was just telling Jason before I got knocked over that I came by to see if you all had all you need," Preston repeated.

"Knocked down?" Megan asked as she too tried to catch her breath.

"Yeah, I was just about to knock on the door when I got ran over by Jason, but just as I got up Chloe ran into me and knocked me down a second time," Preston answered with a smile. "I wasn't expecting to get quite a welcome, but I guess that's what happens in a game of hide and seek, you find the person that's hiding, but next time let me know that I'm the person, okay?" He laughed.

Chloe's face turned even redder at his response but she laughed with everyone else.

"Preston, we are so sorry, I feel horrible that we knocked you over. Can we get you anything?" Chloe said hesitantly.

"No, thanks, I just wanted to say hello and see what you all were up to."

Chloe, Megan, and the boys moved toward the picnic table and sat down to talk.

"No, Mom and Dad weren't too mad at us when they found out where we were," Jason said, "but we aren't allowed to go out of sight of the cabin anymore."

37

"Oh man, that's harsh," Preston said. "There's so much to see out here. We have berry bushes just over there to the right that have the best berries around, and to the left there are caves full of hieroglyphics and lots of fossils. We could go on a hike and see all of it if you could go. It's only about a mile hike from here," Preston said with an adventurous look in his eyes.

"I bet Mom and Dad would let us go if you took us and Chloe asked," Jason said. "She always gets whatever she wants."

"I do not Jason, you are the baby of the family and you are so spoiled, you would get away with anything," Chloe retaliated. "I'll ask, though, I think that it would be fun."

Chloe stood up and urged Megan to come with her. When they were out of earshot of the boys Chloe let out a big sigh of relief.

"What?" Megan asked as she eyed her best friend.

"I can't stand it, Megan, he is so cute, and I get embarrassed about everything. I feel so dumb for knocking him over. I landed right on top of him. I was completely devastated. I bet he thinks I'm so stupid," Chloe said as she began to frown.

"No way," Megan said. "He can't take his eyes off of you. Haven't you noticed?"

Chloe's face went red again. "He's staring at me?" Chloe whispered.

"Yes, he has been watching you ever since we met him on the lake," Megan said with a smile on her face.

"You are such a liar. He has not been watching me," Chloe said, smiling back.

"Whatever, girl, he totally likes you," Megan said as she laughed at the look on Chloe's face.

Chloe had never had a crush on anyone before, but Preston was different from anyone she had ever met. He was a gentleman. Most of the boys Chloe knew from high school were jerks and didn't care one bit about anything but sports or cars or who their next target for their new prank would be.

When Chloe and Megan reached the door to go in Chloe glanced back to see if she could see Preston, and sure enough he was looking right back at her.

They opened the door and found that their parents were all sitting around the dining room table playing cards.

"Hey, sweetie, are you guys having fun?" Aimie said as she kissed Chloe on the cheek.

"Yeah, it's so nice here. We were wondering if we could go on a hike with Preston? He said that he would take us to some caves to see some hieroglyphics, it's only a mile from here," Chloe said with a smile that she knew all too well her dad would have a hard time saying no to.

"I don't know, sweetie, we really don't know them all that well. Anyway, I would hate for you to go back across the lake and ask him," Aimie answered with a worried look on her face.

"Oh, we don't have to go to his house, Mom; he is in the back yard with Jason and Zach. He stopped by to make sure that we had everything we need," Chloe said as she remembered what had happened only moments ago.

"Just let them go, dear, they don't get to get out very much. We might as well let them have some fun," said Michael. "Anyway, it will give us all time to ourselves to continue our game of cribbage."

"Oh, all right," Aimie said with some reluctance. "But I want to talk to Preston first and find out exactly where you are going."

"Thanks, Mom, thanks, Dad, I promise we'll be careful," Chloe squealed as she kissed them both on the cheek.

Chloe and Megan went outside to get Preston and to tell their brothers the good news while their parents began packing them some snacks and water.

"Hey, guys, they said we could go!" Megan said as soon as she was out the door.

"But they want to talk to you for a minute, Preston, so they know where we are going."

"Really?" Jason asked with a big smile. "They said that we could go?"

"Yeah, but we have to be careful," Chloe answered, trying not to look at Preston.

"All right! I've never been on a hike before," Jason said as he jumped up from the table. They all went back inside to talk to their parents about where they were going.

"Chloe said that you wanted to go see some hieroglyphics," Jackson said. "Are they very far from here?"

"No, it's only about a mile's walk. I've been there tons of times," Preston answered.

"Well, just be careful and try to be back before dinner," Misty said as she kissed her children softly on the cheek.

"We went ahead and packed you some snacks and water in case you get hungry or thirsty, okay?" Aimie said as she handed them each a small bag of pretzels and a bottle of water.

They gave their parents a hug and then they were all out the door. They glanced toward the sky to make sure that there were no more clouds that were going to come through, and then they started walking toward a patch of trees just off to the left of the cabin.

"Well, it will take us about an hour to get to the caves," Preston said. "Then we can explore inside for a while, but we have to leave there by three o'clock."

"Why do we have to leave by three?" Zack asked curiously.

"I don't have time to explain that right now, but it will give us time to go to the lake before dinner," Preston replied.

Chloe glanced over at Megan and shrugged her shoulders.

"I wonder why we can't stay past three," Megan whispered to Chloe.

41

"No idea, but I'm sure he has his reasons," Chloe said without taking her eyes off of Preston.

For the next few minutes the group walked quietly without making any noise except for their feet cracking sticks or an occasional cough.

"Make sure you stay really close," Preston said, breaking the silence. "I don't want you to get lost out here. I may live here but I still don't know the land all that well."

They kept walking closely with Preston, and every time a breeze came by, Chloe could smell the cologne he was wearing.

"What is that smell?" Jason said as he plugged his nose.

"That's sulfur from that small pond over there." Preston explained. "No one really knows why, but that pond has always smelled like sulfur."

They all glanced in the direction of the pond and saw that it was completely gray. It didn't seem that there was anything living within twenty feet from its outer banks. It gave Chloe the chills looking at it so she hurried along to talk to Preston.

"Do you like living here?" Chloe asked as she tripped over a rock.

"Well, I do like it, but it does get kind of lonely up here all by ourselves."

"Don't you ever have family come visit?" Chloe said.

"No, you are the first people to ever come here," Preston responded, and Chloe could tell that he wanted to change the subject. She looked back to see if Megan and the others were still behind her and Megan gave her a smile and winked at her.

"So do you like it here?" Preston said, catching her off guard.

"I think it's so pretty here. The lake is almost like a dream," Chloe said dazedly as if she were dreaming of it. "I can't help but think that I've been here before, but it's just because of the brochure that my mom has."

Preston stopped and looked at her as if her were trying to remember something but then turned around and kept walking in the direction of the cave.

"We should be getting there soon," Preston said more quietly than usual. "We need to be really quiet around here, okay, no one say a word and please watch where you step."

Megan, Jason, and Zach all caught up with Preston and Chloe and they continued walking very slowly around a giant boulder.

"Preston, why do we have to walk so quietly?" Zach whispered.

But Preston didn't answer; instead, he put his hand back and waved them forward. They turned around the corner of the boulder and saw one of the biggest caves that any of them, except Preston, had ever seen. Chloe's mouth dropped and apparently so did the others' because Preston began to laugh out loud.

"You should see your faces," he said with a grin. "It's okay, you can talk now."

43

"Why did we have to be so quiet?" Zach asked again. "Is there something here that isn't supposed to know that we are here?"

"Well, legend has it;" Preston began, "that this cave is home to some of the strangest creatures ever known to walk the earth. They are supposedly part human, part fish, and that pond that smells like sulfur begins somewhere in this cave, and that's how they get in and out. I'm always hoping to catch them, but to this day I've never seen one."

Megan and Chloe gaped at him in disbelief, but his face showed no sign of joking around.

"You can't be serious," Megan said as she let out a quiet laugh. Chloe elbowed her in the stomach and glared at her.

"Would you be quiet?" Chloe whispered to Megan. "You are embarrassing me."

"Don't worry about it, Chloe, that's why I couldn't explain why we needed to be out of here by three o'clock. The path going back gets flooded over and runs down almost to the lake and we would be stuck here."

"Oh, okay, that's fine. Um, are we going to go in there?" Chloe asked.

"Well, of course we are," Jason said, "that's why we are here, to see the hieroglyphics inside the cave."

Preston looked at Chloe and, seeing how scared she looked, smiled at her.

"Don't worry," he said, "nothing is going to happen." Preston held out his hand for her to take.

44

Chloe looked at him and saw that he was smiling at her. She reached out her hand and grabbed his and then he led them all into the cave.

"Jason, did your mom pack a flashlight?" Zach asked. "I've searched through our bags and we don't have one here."

"I don't think so," Jason said, searching his bag, "I can't find one either."

"You won't need one once we are inside," Preston said. "You'll see."

They walked further into the cave and then saw a small patch of light just ahead.

"What is that?" Megan asked.

"That's where we are going," Preston answered, still holding on to Chloe's hand. They kept walking and the light kept getting bigger and brighter until finally they were at the source.

"We need to stop here," Preston said, letting go of Chloe's hand and holding out his arms to stop them from going further in. "That light is coming from the water just ahead but we can't get any closer to it because of the hole right there."

They all looked at where he was pointing and saw not a small hole but what seemed to be a cliff that dropped off into pure darkness.

"But what is making that light?" Megan asked.

"I'm not sure," Preston said. "I've never been able to get there, and to tell you the truth I don't really want to. Here

45

are the hieroglyphics," he said, pointing to a cave wall.

They walked toward the wall and saw beautiful drawings of people, and what seemed to be the lake. They could see the drawings clearly because of the mysterious light that was shining on them from somewhere beyond that cliff. They saw a series of drawings that resembled a doorway, and what seemed to be buildings.

"What do they mean?" Chloe asked Preston.

"I don't know, I just think that they are really cool, and I thought that you might like them."

Chloe looked at Preston and then turned around to look at the drawings again. They walked back and forth looking at every drawing they could find, and there were a lot of them. Chloe stopped at one particular drawing of what seemed to be a young girl in a room full of mirrors. As she looked at them she felt someone behind her and turned to find Preston looking at the drawings over her shoulder. He smiled at her and slowly slipped his hand into hers and pulled her to another wall of drawings. Chloe wasn't sure if he grabbed her hand because he liked her, or if he just wanted to show her the other drawings, because as soon as they got to the drawings he let go of her hand and pointed at a drawing on the wall. She looked at the drawing and could barely see what he was pointing at. It seemed to be so old it was starting to fade away. What Chloe could see of it was what seemed to be some sort of long car, but it only had two wheels. At least, all she could see were what looked like two wheels. She kept looking around at the drawing and saw more pictures of doorways and more pictures of the lake.

"How did you find these?" Chloe asked Preston as she continued to walk back and forth from drawing to drawing.

"My father brought me here when I was really young. He used to make up stories and tell them to me here in the cave."

"Hey, come look at this!" Jason shouted. "It's a drawing of the cave."

They quickly found their way over to where Jason was kneeling down looking at some drawings closer to the ground.

"You're right," Megan said. "Look, there is the cliff and it looks like someone started to draw what is beyond the cliff but it's scribbled out."

"Sorry, guys," Preston spoke, "but we really need to get out of the cave now. It's getting really close to three."

"How can you tell?" Zach asked with a curious look on his face.

"Because I looked at Chloe's watch," Preston answered as he gave a small chuckle and then helped them up off the ground. Preston started walking toward the direction from which they had come in and the others followed, whispering quietly about the drawings.

When they arrived at the entrance again, the warmth of the sun was a welcome feeling. The cave was damp and cold, and Chloe shivered from the change in temperature.

"That was so cool!" Jason said as he jumped down off a rock that was in front of the cave.

"Yeah, those hieroglyphics were really weird. I wonder what they mean," Zach said as he too jumped off a nearby rock.

"We can get back to the lake if we follow this path right here," Preston said. "Then maybe we could go swimming or something."

"Yeah, that sounds great," Jason said. "It's so hot out here right now."

"I bet I could get a great tan right now," Megan whispered to Chloe.

Chloe wasn't really listening to what everyone was saying. All she could think about was why Preston grabbed her hand and about those drawings.

"Hey, are you okay?" Megan asked Chloe. "You look like you're going to be sick."

"What?" Chloe said as she looked at Megan. "Oh, yeah, I'm fine. I was just thinking about the drawings." She looked over at Preston, who was looking at her with a concerned look on his face.

"Why don't you guys walk on ahead. I'll stay back here with Chloe and make sure she's okay," Preston said to the others.

Megan glanced down at Chloe and looked as if she were going to say something.

"It's okay, we'll be right behind you," Chloe said, trying to smile at Megan. Megan didn't say a word but she turned around and began following her brother and Jason down the trail.

"Are you okay?" Preston asked Chloe as soon as they were out of earshot from the others.

"Yeah, I'm fine. I just can't stop thinking about those drawings," Chloe answered.

Chloe hadn't realized that she was sitting down. She grabbed a branch of a nearby tree and began pulling herself up off the ground. Preston reached down and grabbed her other hand and helped her the rest of the way. Chloe looked up at him and began wondering whether or not he was trying to help her or if he just wanted another excuse to hold her hand. Preston must have read her mind because he returned her glance and smiled at her. Chloe couldn't help but smile back.

"Look," Preston said, breaking the silence, "I think you and I both know that I like you, but I can't figure out what you think of me."

Chloe looked at him in surprise, not believing that he just said that he liked her.

"Chloe, you are the most beautiful girl that I've ever seen. I know that we've only known each other since this morning and that's why I keep pulling my hand away. I don't want you to think that I'm crazy or something."

"No, I don't think you are crazy," Chloe said, a smile forming on her face. "The truth is I like you too, but we are only here for two weeks and then I probably won't ever see you again. I've never had a boyfriend or even held hands

49

with anyone so I'm not very good at this stuff. I've been trying to figure out if you were just trying to show me stuff or if you really wanted to hold my hand since you led us into the cave, but I was to afraid to ask you."

"I've wanted to hold your hand ever since we sat together in my father's truck," he said, "but I was afraid I would be moving too fast and I would scare you away."

Chloe realized that he was still holding her hand from when he helped her up, and she wished that he wouldn't let go. Preston must have again read her mind because he looked toward the others, who were still walking just a short way away.

"Come on, lets get going or we will lose the others," Preston said as he started walking down the trail, but he didn't let go of her hand.

Chloe followed with a smile on her face. "I think that this will work," Chloe said as they walked hand in hand down the trail.

"You think what will work?" Preston asked as he took a quick look down at her and smiled.

"You and me. I know that I'm only going to be here for two weeks, but that's okay because I can probably talk my parents into coming here next summer too."

"Well, I'm glad that I have your blessing to continue courting you," Preston said, laughing.

"Courting?" Chloe asked in surprise.

"What, is that the wrong word?" Preston asked. He stopped quickly and looked at her, then started walking again. "You know, um, holding hands, dancing, things like that."

"You mean dating?" Chloe asked him, trying to refrain from laughing.

"Yeah, dating," he said, laughing, "isn't that what I said?"

"No," Chloe laughed, "you said courting."

"Well, what's the difference?" he asked her more seriously but still smiling at her.

"Courting is something you do when you are trying to get married, dating is something you do, well, for fun, I guess," she answered thoughtfully.

"I don't know about you, but I'm not looking to get married anytime soon."

Preston stopped again looked down at Chloe and sighed.

"Yeah, I don't want to get married anytime soon either."

They continued walking down the path, holding hands and talking about what they could do for the next two weeks. Soon they were back down at the lake, and the cabin where Chloe and the others were staying was only a few hundred feet away. They released each other's hands and walked to the cabin.

"What took so long?" Megan asked Chloe when they reached the cabin.

"Nothing, we were just walking more slowly than you were," Chloe said as she winked at her friend, letting her know that she would tell her all about it later. They spent the

51

rest of the afternoon swimming in the lake and relaxing in the sun.

"I had better get going," Preston said. "I've got to get back before dinner." He stood up and slowly walked toward his canoe.

"Hey, thanks for taking us to see that cool cave," Jason said as he ran toward the lake. He jumped in, came back up out of the water, and said, "It was so cool."

Megan and Zach both thanked Preston and went back to swimming and sunbathing. Chloe, however, followed Preston to his canoe.

"When will I see you again?" Chloe asked him.

"Well, hopefully tomorrow if that's okay with you and your friends, and I can get away from the house," he answered smiling at her.

"I don't think that they will mind too much. I think Jason and Zach love having another guy around, and Megan doesn't mind," Chloe said, smiling back at him.

"Then I'll see you tomorrow." He bent down and kissed her softly on the cheek, climbed into his canoe, and pushed off the bank. Chloe watched him head toward his cabin and couldn't help but smile. She returned to where Megan was and sat down next to her.

"Well, what happened?" Megan asked her friend.

"I'll tell you about it later when no one else is around. Let's go swimming," Chloe said as she jumped up and grabbed Megan's hand and pulled her up.

They both ran and jumped in the lake with their brothers and played around until they were called in for dinner.

4

The Storm

As Preston traveled home in his canoe he couldn't stop thinking about Chloe and the progress he had made in one day.

I can't believe that I have a girlfriend, he thought dreamily to himself. *I can't wait to see her again. She is so beautiful. I can't wait to tell Mom and Dad.* As Preston thought this his heart sank and he remembered his arranged marriage to Lillie in three weeks' time.

I can't believe this. I finally found someone I really like and I have to marry some girl I don't know, because of some stupid family tradition! I don't want to marry her. I want to be able to choose for myself, he thought angrily to himself.

Preston realized that he was paddling rather hard and he was starting to breathe very heavily and was starting to sweat. He decided he had better slow down so that his parents wouldn't think that he had been to the cabin. He started paddling slower and began to relax as he came closer to his home.

When he reached the outer banks of the shore he saw his father out on the balcony of their cabin. Preston waved and found that his father was not waving back. He had a very stern look on his face and was chewing a large piece of jerky and staring at the far side of the lake and not looking at Preston at all. Preston knew that face and he knew that he was in trouble. He slowly pulled the canoe to the shore and tied it to the dock. He walked slowly to the cabin and onto the back porch, where he was met by his mother. She looked at him with her big blue eyes and smiled slightly. Preston noticed that she had been crying.

"What's the matter, Mom?" Preston asked as he gave his mother a big hug. "Why have you been crying?"

"Preston, you need to go and speak with your father right away. He has something to talk to you about," his mother said softly as she returned the hug and kissed him gently on the cheek.

"Mom, what is going on? Why is Dad so angry and why have you been crying?" he said.

Instead of answering, his mother pulled open the back door to allow her son into the house.

Preston began to feel angrier than he was only moments ago in the canoe. He wanted to know what was going on. He wanted to know why his mother had been crying and why his father wouldn't look at him when he waved and why he looked so angry.

Preston ran up the stairs to his parents' bedroom. He opened the bedroom door and crossed the floor to reach the door to the balcony. Before he could open it he heard his father stand up from the chair that he was sitting in and walk toward him. Preston froze and waited for his dad to open the door. However, the door didn't open. He could still hear his father walking out on the balcony, but he sounded as if he were pacing back and forth, trying to figure something out. Preston slowly opened the door and found his dad still looking at the other side of the lake and pacing around the balcony.

"Dad, what's…"

Before Preston could finish his sentence his father pointed to a chair and motioned for him to sit down. Preston obeyed his father and sat down at the far end of the balcony in a white wicker patio chair.

"Preston, where have you been?" his father said quietly. "We have been looking for you for hours."

"I went hiking up to Lightning Cave," Preston answered, watching his father.

"Your mother and I were worried sick! I went crazy running around the lake searching for you."

"Nothing happened, all I did was go to the cave," Preston said a bit more cautiously now. "Why were you so worried? I've been gone all day alone before, and it wasn't a problem then!"

"That's not important!" his father answered, still staring at the lake.

"Why isn't it important?" Preston yelled.

Jack looked right at his son and sat down in the chair next to him.

"Did you go to the other cabin this afternoon?" his father asked angrily.

56

"Yes, but…"

"But nothing, Preston, we told you that you were not to go there. Why did you disobey me? I can't believe that you would do this, Preston. What has gotten into you? You have never disobeyed me before."

"I went over there because I think that she is the most beautiful girl I've ever seen," Preston interrupted. "I think that I have a right to choose who I want to be with, and I don't think that you or anyone else has the right to tell me who I'm going to marry." Preston blew out a breath in anger.

"Preston, this is our family tradition, why don't you understand that?" his father shouted.

"This is America; this is the land of the free. Why can't I be free? Why can't I choose? You keep telling me that it is family tradition, and that is why I have to be married to this Lillie girl and I don't have a choice. Well, I'm not going to do it; I'm not going to throw my life away just because of some tradition!" Preston shouted back.

Preston immediately knew that he had gone too far. His father shot up out of his chair and it flew across the balcony.

"I forbid you to ever see that girl again, Preston. If you ever go over there again I swear you'll spend the rest of your so-called 'freedom' chopping wood!"

With that last burst his father grabbed the door to the balcony, flung it open, and disappeared behind it.

Preston was so angry he could feel his heart pounding in his chest. He didn't understand why his father wouldn't listen to him. He slowly walked to the edge of the balcony and looked toward the cabin, where Chloe was probably eating her dinner. He couldn't see the cabin but he knew exactly where it was.

A sudden chill of wind made Preston look in the other direction, and he saw that another storm was blowing in. He grabbed the patio chairs and put them closer to the house to try to prevent them from blowing over the edge. He looked up again at the dark clouds that were forming over the mountain and started to walk toward the balcony door that led inside the house. Before he reached the door he realized that the cloud looked a lot different from the other storm clouds that he had seen here many times. The clouds seemed darker than any that he had ever seen. He also noticed that they were moving slower and seemed to be heading only toward Chloe's cabin and were going to completely blow over his own house. He didn't understand why they looked so different and he really wasn't in the mood to try and figure it out. All he wanted to do was to see Chloe again, but he knew that he would have to find some other way to do it without letting anyone know that he was gone.

He grabbed the door and flung it open. Before he went inside he took one last look at the clouds and decided that it was only his imagination and they looked exactly like every other storm that blew through there. He turned around and walked inside, carefully closing the door behind him and making sure that it latched correctly so it wouldn't blow open in the high winds that would surely come with the oncoming storm. He walked through his parents' bedroom and began his descent down the stairs to the living room.

Preston settled down in a large overstuffed arm chair that was near the fire and began thinking of all that had happened that day. He thought of how wonderful it had been to spend time with Chloe and how great she was. He also thought of the light in the cave and began trying to figure out a way to get across the ravine as he had many times before. His mind was almost back to Chloe when he was brought back to his senses by his mother's voice.

"Preston, will you come help me set the table for dinner?" his mother asked kindly.

Preston got up and walked toward the kitchen; he glanced up at his mother and saw that she no longer looked like she had been crying but looked more beautiful and radiant than ever.

"Mom, you look great. What's the occasion?" he asked her, smiling.

"It's your father's and my anniversary today. We are going to have dessert out on the lake," she answered, smiling back at him.

"Oh yeah, I totally forgot. Where is Dad anyway?" he asked, walking over to get the bowls from the cupboard.

"He is out getting more firewood for the fire. He'll be back in a minute," she said, tapping the spoon on the side of the pot that she had been stirring.

"Well, it smells great in here. What did you make?" he asked, trying to peer into the pot.

"We are having beef stew with rolls and then coffee cake for dessert," she answered.

"That's one of my favorite things that you make," he said as he began walking toward the table.

"I know, I decided that you deserved it," she said. "I know that you have had an adventurous day."

Preston stopped and looked at his mother, who gave him a little wink and then returned to stirring the stew. Preston smiled back and then turned around to set the table. He couldn't help but wonder what his mother knew, but he decided that he would ask her a little later.

Moments later Jack made his way into the house carrying a large load of wood. He walked toward the fireplace and sat it down in the wood box that sat next to the hearth. He looked over at his wife and gave a big smile and walked toward her. He wrapped his arms around her and gave her a big hug followed by a long, soft kiss.

"I love you, Jennifer," he said, pulling back and smiling at his wife.

He reached into his vest and pulled out a beautiful black velvet box and handed it to her.

"Oh, Jack you shouldn't have gotten me anything," she said, a big smile forming on her face.

"Don't be silly. What kind of husband would I be if I didn't get my wife an anniversary gift?" He chuckled.

Jennifer slowly opened the box and found a beautiful gold necklace with a pendant attached that looked like mountains. At the bottom of the mountains was a small blue stone.

"That stone represents Mirror Lake," Jack explained to his wife. "I had it specially made to always remind us of our home here."

Jennifer threw her arms around her husband and gave him a kiss. "Thank you," she said after pulling away. "I love you too."

Preston watched his mother and father exchange looks of love and began wishing that he were with Chloe right now rather than watching his mother and father fall all over one another. He slowly pulled out a chair from the table and sat down, trying not to look at his parents. A few moments later his father sat next to him. Jack looked at his son and smiled.

"Preston, I'm sorry about earlier. I was just scared, that's all," he said, still watching Preston. "I know that it's hard for you to understand this now, but you will thank us later."

Preston didn't answer; he just continued to stare at his empty bowl. His mother was soon by his side with the pot of beef stew and she slowly scooped some into his bowl. The smell of the beef stew was so great that he couldn't remember anything else that was bothering him. He grabbed his spoon, thanked his mother, and began eating. They ate their dinner in silence except for the tinkling of their spoons on their bowls. Soon they were all full and they began clearing the table.

"Preston, the coffee cake is on the counter in that bowl. I've already got your father's and my piece, go ahead and help yourself," Jennifer said. "We probably won't be back until late so we will see you in the morning."

She kissed Preston on the cheek gave him a hug and walked toward the back door. Preston looked over at his father, who was staring back at him. "I'll see you later son," he said. "We'll talk in the morning." The next thing Preston knew he was being bear hugged by his father.

"You two have a great time, Happy Anniversary," Preston said, returning his father's hug. They withdrew from each other and his father turned and followed his wife out the back door.

"Finally," Preston said out loud, "I never thought they would leave."

He walked over to the counter and took out a knife. He cut himself a large slice of warm coffee cake, poured himself a large mug full of hot cocoa that his mother had also made, and found his way back to the armchair near the fire. Just before he sat down he heard a large rumble of thunder outside.

I forgot all about the storm, he thought quietly to himself. *They will be back any minute. They will never go out on the lake now.*

Just then he heard another loud rumble of thunder, and it was followed by a bright flash of lightning. Preston began to wonder if his parents were okay. He put down his cake and cocoa and made his way to the back door. He pulled

it open and glanced down toward the lake. The canoe was
gone and he couldn't see his parents anywhere on the water.

They are probably just around that bunch of trees, he
thought to himself.

He quickly shut the door and walked back to his cake.
He sat back down and began eating. He listened to the rolling
thunder and watched the flashes of lightning for a few
minutes then got up and lit the lantern on the side table. He
put some more firewood in the fireplace to keep the fire
going and began walking around the living room and
glancing toward the back door.

Soon it began raining very hard and he could hear the
wind howling through the trees outside.

They should have been back by now, he thought. "*I
wonder where they are.*

Preston put on his rain coat pulled on the hood and
his galoshes and walked toward the back door. He quickly
pulled open the door, grabbed the nearest lantern, lit it, and
ran outside, pulling the door closed behind him. He ran down
to the dock and to the very end, where he could see just
around the bend. He pointed the lantern across toward the
lake but he couldn't see anything, it was raining too hard. He
ran back to shore as the lightning and thunder crashed down
behind him. The wind was blowing so hard that he could
barely keep his balance. The rain poured down and hit him in
the face. He ran toward the house and pulled open the back
door. He ran inside shut the door behind him and ran into the
kitchen. He grabbed his father's keys from the hook near the

sink for the truck and took one last look at the back door, hoping that his mother and father would come in. But when they didn't he ran for the front door, pulled it open, and ran out, slamming the door behind him. He ran as fast as he could toward his father's truck. Just then, a bolt of lightning struck a tree fifty yards to the right of Preston, knocking it down; it missed him by only a few feet. He finally reached the truck, climbed inside, and started it. He pulled the truck out of the driveway and began driving toward Chloe's.

I need to see if I can see them, he thought. *I need to get closer to the lake*. Preston turned the truck down a small side road that he and his father used to go down to go fishing sometimes and began driving toward the lake. He pulled up on the bank and put the lights of the truck on bright so they would shine out across the lake. He still couldn't see his parents or the canoe anywhere. He backed up the truck and turned it back toward the other road. He turned back towards Chloe's, feeling like something was terribly wrong. He arrived at the cabin a few moments later and threw the door of the truck open just as another rumble of thunder sounded throughout the sky. He got to the front door and knocked loudly, but there was no answer. He opened the door and ran through the house, trying to find someone, anyone. He ran up the stairs and saw a small light coming from one of the bedrooms. He ran toward the door and threw it open. He was met by a loud scream and Michael jumping from the bed to grab anything he could to defend his family. Preston saw to his relief both families sitting in the middle of the floor between Chloe and Megan's beds playing card games with the light of their lantern and the blinds pulled open to expose Mirror Lake and the storm outside.

"What is going on?" Michael shouted above another rumble of thunder.

"I can't find my parents!" Preston shouted back, running toward the window to see if he could see any sign of their canoe.

"What do you mean you can't find your parents?" Chloe said, looking worried and trying to recover from being scared half to death by Preston barging into her room.

"Today is their anniversary and they always take the canoe out and have dessert on the lake. Well, just as they left this storm blew in and now I can't find them anywhere," Preston said, trying to catch his breath.

Michael ran across the hall and grabbed his raincoat that was hanging on a hook near the door and put on his galoshes.

"I'll come help you look," he said.

Jackson also ran down the hall toward his own room and put on his rain gear as well. The three men made their way down the stairs and out the back door toward the lake. Chloe, Megan, and everyone else ran down the stairs behind them and watched them from the large windows in the living room. Jackson and Michael had both grabbed their flashlights from their bags as well and were shining them out on the lake looking for any signs of life. The rain and wind were so strong, however, that they couldn't see a thing beyond a few feet in front of them.

Preston was beginning to get very worried. He began to go over in his head the fight that he had previously had with his father and how mean he had been. They all went back inside the house and Zach was already lighting a fire in the fireplace. Preston sat down in a chair and stared down at his feet.

"I know they are out there," he said. "I need to go back home and wait for them."

"I don't think that's a good idea," Jackson said as he sat down in a chair next to him. "I think you had better wait out the storm here."

Chloe felt her stomach jump as she heard what Jackson had just said.

Preston is going to be here with me! she thought to herself. *This day couldn't get any better!*

"No, I have to go home; you don't understand, I'm not supposed to be here. I could get into a lot of trouble." Preston jumped up from his chair and headed toward the front door.

Another flash of lightning could be seen from out the window, which was followed by a loud rumble of thunder.

Chloe's heart sank. *What does he mean he's not supposed to be here?* she wondered. *We had such a great time today.*

"Well, if they aren't back in few hours I want you to come back and we will go look for them," Michael said, following Preston toward the door.

"Okay, thanks, Mr. Clister, I appreciate it," Preston answered.

Michael opened the front door and Preston glanced back at Chloe. With a sigh he turned around and headed back outside into the storm. Michael followed him out and they ran quickly toward the truck.

"Now if they aren't back, don't forget to come get us, we will come help you, okay?" Michael shouted over the wind and thunder.

Preston gave a quick wave, jumped into the truck, and started backing away from the house.

He watched as Chloe's father ran back inside the house and shut the door. He began his drive back toward his own cabin and arrived just as the storm began letting up. He pulled into the driveway and turned off the truck. He got out and ran toward the door of the cabin, having to go around the large tree that nearly hit him only a short while ago. He pushed open the door and found to his surprise his mother and father soaked completely through sitting next to the fire.

"Mom, Dad, I was so worried. I went out and…" Preston was cut off by the look in his father's eyes.

"What is it?" Preston asked.

"I thought I told you not to go there again!" his father shouted loudly.

"But," Preston began but was quickly stopped by his father staring in his direction.

67

"I don't care what the reason is that you went over there, I gave you a strict order never to go over there," his father said angrily.

"I went over there looking for you!" Preston shouted back. "I can see more of the lake from there so I went to see if I could see you. I ran to the dock and I couldn't see you anywhere so I jumped into the truck and followed the lake looking out hoping to find you. I stopped there just to make sure they were okay and to see if I could see you."

Jack stared at his son and then sat back down near his wife, rubbing her back trying to get her warm. Jennifer had a look of awe on her face as she stared at her husband and then at her son.

"I can't believe you two," she said as tears formed in her eyes. "You haven't stopped fighting for weeks now. What is wrong with you? If it's not this, then it's that. I've had enough!" she shouted, jumping up from where she was sitting but still staring at Preston and her husband.

Jack slowly stood up and wrapped his arms around his wife.

"I'm sorry, dear," he whispered. "I'll try and hold my temper."

Preston couldn't believe it. He was out searching for his parents because he thought something terrible had happened and found himself in trouble again.

"Where were you?" he slowly asked his mother and father, who were now sitting back down near the fire.

68

"We were out on the lake," his father answered. "Then the storm came and it blew us to the embankment just down the road where we go fishing."

"I went down the small road to the little beach and I couldn't see you anywhere."

His father shot him a questioning look and then shuffled in his seat.

"We were near there; you must not have been able to see us through the trees," his father said a little more timidly. "We are okay, why don't you go ahead and head up to bed, Preston; we'll talk in the morning."

His mother said good night as she tried not to look directly at her son. She stood up and gave Preston a hug and kissed him softly on the cheek. His father also stood up and gave his son a hug. Reluctantly, Preston turned around and headed upstairs to his room, his mind still full of questions as to where his parents had been.

He went into his room and closed the door, setting the lantern that he took from the living room on a small table near his bed. He could still hear what was left of the storm outside his window. Preston got undressed and climbed into bed.

Where did they go? he thought to himself. *I can see the entire shoreline except for the bend that leads to our house. I know I would have seen them if they were there.*

Preston began going over the conversation in his head but he still couldn't figure out where they went.

How did he know that I went to Chloe's, he would have never known that, Preston thought. He couldn't figure out what was going on anymore. *It seems that the closer I get to eighteen, the worse things get. My dad is on the edge all the time, we argue, and fight, which we never usually do. My mom cries more and more every day. I want to know what's going on.* He kept on trying to figure things out until he slowly drifted to sleep.

Preston was woken the next morning to the smell of waffles drifting up from the kitchen into his room. He quickly jumped out of bed and got dressed, thinking that if he could just speak to his father then everything would make sense. He hurried down the stairs to find his mother drinking hot cocoa and eating a fresh batch of waffles.

"Where's Dad?" he asked, quickly pulling out a chair from the table and sitting down to a plate full of waffles that his mother had just put in front of him.

"He's out cutting that tree that blew over in the storm last night," she said, kissing him on the forehead. "How did you sleep last night?"

"Fine, I guess," he said with his mouth full of waffles. "I couldn't stop thinking of the storm."

As soon as he said this, his mother dropped her cup full of hot cocoa and it shattered on the hardwood floor. Preston jumped up from the table and stared at his mother, trying to figure out what had just happened.

"I'm sorry, Preston, I didn't mean to drop my cup, it just slipped out of my fingers. It must be because my fingers

70

are a little greasy from making the waffles." She quickly got a towel from the counter and mopped up the hot chocolate from the floor, trying not to look at him.

Preston couldn't believe it; his mother had never broken a dish in her life that he could remember.

Something must have happened last night and she's trying to hide it, he thought, sitting back down to finish his waffles.

He hurried and ate the last few pieces of waffle, picked up his dish, and set it in the sink.

"Can I help you with anything, Mom, before I go help Dad?" he asked, trying to get her to look at him.

"No, thank you, sweetie, you go ahead and help your father." She still didn't look up from the floor where she was finishing picking up the broken glass.

Preston gave her one last look and then headed outside to help his father. He walked the short distance toward the tree and found his father sawing away.

"Hey, Dad, can I give you a hand?" he asked.

"Sure, there's another saw in the back of my truck," his father answered, not looking up from his work.

Preston went to the truck and found the saw and returned to the tree.

"Dad, what happened last night?" he said cautiously, trying not to sound pushy.

"I already told you what happened and I don't want to talk about it anymore, do you understand?" his father said, quietly looking up from his work and staring at his son.

71

"I just don't understand, I would have seen you if you were…"

"Preston, I don't want to talk about it. Let's just get this tree finished. You are lucky it didn't hit you." His father continued his work with the saw.

Preston couldn't believe it. How did his father know that he had almost been hit by that tree? He knew, however, that he wasn't going to get any answers from his father so he began sawing the tree.

They worked all morning and only stopped for lunch and quick breaks for a drink of water. They finished the tree just before dinner and decided that they would stack the wood the following morning. For the rest of the day, Preston didn't mention anything to his parents about the night before, but he couldn't help but wonder what really happened. He couldn't understand why his mom and dad wouldn't answer any of his questions. He also couldn't stop thinking about when he would get to see Chloe again. He remembered that he told her that he would see her today, but he knew it wasn't going to be possible. He decided that he would try tomorrow, but he wasn't sure how he was going to accomplish it. His mom and dad seemed to know everything that he was doing and he couldn't figure out how.

"Preston, do you want to come sit over here and play cards with us?" his mother asked as she shuffled the deck of cards and began dealing them out.

"Sure," he answered, hoping this would take his mind off of Chloe and everything else.

72

Preston and his parents played cards until it was time for them all to go to bed. Preston made his way to his bedroom and opened the curtains so he could see the lake and maybe he could see Chloe's house. Then he lay down on his bed and very quickly fell fast asleep.

Preston awoke to a loud noise downstairs. He jumped up from his bed and realized that it was still quite dark outside. He pulled on a pair of jeans and opened the door of his room. He went to his parents' room and found that neither of them was in bed. He then made his way downstairs and found his father kneeling on the floor, his nose bleeding and his mother in the kitchen getting a towel.

"What happened?" Preston said, running over to his father.

"Preston, listen to me, you need to go up to your room and pack a bag of clothes. We have to get you to a safe place," his father answered, getting to his feet now holding the towel to his nose.

"Why do I need to pack a bag?" he asked his father.

"I don't have time to explain it now but I promise as soon as we get you out of here I will explain everything. Now go and hurry," his father said.

Preston knew not to ask another question. He ran up to his room and pulled a duffel bag from the top of his closet and began throwing clothes into it. Within minutes he had his bag full and he was back downstairs. When he came off the last stair he saw that his father's nose had stopped bleeding and there wasn't a trace of blood anywhere on him.

"How did you, I mean what happened to the blood?" Preston asked, now a little frightened.

"Don't worry about it, we are going to take you away and we will come get you when it's safe, do you understand?" his father said, now moving quickly to the front door which Preston just noticed wasn't there anymore.

Preston followed his mother and father outside and found that instead of heading for the truck they were heading in the direction of the cave.

"Where are we going?" Preston asked, trying to keep up with his parents.

"We'll talk about it when we are in a safe place." Jennifer spoke for the first time since Preston heard the noise, which he now knew was their front door being ripped off the hinges. "Just keep quiet and follow your father."

Preston was so confused, he had no idea what was happening. He glanced back at his house and saw to his surprise a large black cloud moving quickly over it. Jack was now running and Preston and his mother were sprinting to keep up.

The trio kept running through the trees and Preston was beginning to get an ache in his side and his legs were starting to throb, but he knew that he needed to keep up with his dad. He looked back to check on his mother and saw that she too was struggling. He reached his hand back and grabbed hers and they ran together. After what felt like an eternity of running they reached the cave. Jack stopped at the mouth of the cave and looked back at his son and wife, who were now on the ground panting and breathing rather heavily. Jack reached down and grabbed Preston by the hand and pulled him to his feet.

"Listen to me, Preston, do you remember all the stories I told you when you were little?"

"Yeah, I guess so," Preston replied, still trying to catch his breath.

"I need you to tell me that you remember them, I don't want an 'I guess so,'" Jack said now with a look of fear on his face.

"Yes, I remember all about them. I used to love those stories, you would tell them to me every night," Preston answered. "Please tell me what's going on."

"The stories are all true. If you truly remember the stories you will know what's happening." His father was now helping his wife up off the ground. Preston couldn't believe what his father was saying. How could all the stories be true? How could there be a kingdom below the lake? Preston wasn't sure what was going on, but he had so many questions to ask his father.

"Dad, the stories can't be true; if they are true then..."

"Listen to me, Preston, you need to stay here until I come for you. I don't want you to ever go outside of this cave. I'm sorry I can't tell you any more right now. You need to run as fast as you can into the cave. If you go as deep as the path leads you, you will find a cliff; off to the far right there's a large boulder that has a rope tied around it. That

75

rope is attached to a large box of food that I put there this morning in case something like this would happen. Remember, do not come out until I come for you."

With that his father and mother gave him a hug and a kiss on the cheek. Preston saw that his mother was starting to cry. Jack pushed him into the cave, but when he turned around they had both disappeared in the thickness of the trees. Confused at what his father had just said to him, he turned around and ran as fast as he could deep into the cave. He knew it well because he had been here many times before.

Preston reached the cliff and found the food that his father had put there, along with matches, clothes, lanterns, blankets, and many other supplies. From the look of everything that was there he was going to be here a long time. Preston decided that maybe he should start unpacking some things so he could make something to eat. He got some firewood from a pile that had recently been stacked and started a fire. Soon the cave was bright with his firelight and also the light from the other side of the ravine. He began cooking a can of soup and decided while it was cooking he would walk around a bit.

Preston picked up a lantern. He walked around and began reading the markings on the wall that he was beginning to be very familiar with. He glanced over at them and then moved over to the other side of the cave and began looking at those. Before long he was caught up in the pictures and for some reason he had no desire to stop looking at them.

He saw what seemed to be a picture of a hand faced to the left with its thumb extended and squiggly lines going across the forefinger. He decided that it looked like a crown and figured that it meant king. Another picture showed a hand faced to the right that looked almost exactly like the first, but it had not only the squiggly lines across the top but also running down the back of the hand, and he assumed that must be hair and it meant queen. They were both standing on what seemed to be a cloud.

Preston heard the bubbling of his soup on the fire and swiftly ran over and stirred it and poured it into a bowl. He then walked back over to the wall and continued to venture his best guess at the hieroglyphics. Preston sat and stared for what felt like hours but was only a short time and finally decided to retreat to bed. He had a very long day and was beginning to feel the effect of the run through the forest to get to the cave. He pulled a sleeping bag from the pile of things he had unpacked and slithered his way into a nice, deep sleep.

5

The Stranger

Chloe couldn't stop thinking about Preston after he made his surprise visit. All she knew was that her stomach still did flips every time she thought about him. She couldn't wait until she would be able to see him again the following morning. The storm had started to clear up and she could almost see the moon peeking through the clouds. She could still hear the rumble of thunder in the distance and the wind blowing quietly outside the living room window. She kept watching out the window, hoping that Preston would return and stay there with them, but she knew that she would have to wait until tomorrow to see him. She began moving slowly from the window when something caught her attention from the corner of her eye. She quickly glanced back out the window and saw a man standing in the trees a hundred feet away staring into the window where Chloe was sitting. Then he disappeared into the thicket.

Chloe couldn't believe her eyes. She quickly jumped away from the window and ran to the kitchen to tell her father what she had seen. As she spoke, she saw the color on his face vanish and he went white as a ghost.

"Stay here!" he shouted.

Michael and Jackson both jumped up from the stools they were sitting on, ran to the door, and threw it wide open. Aimee followed her husband to the door and shut and locked it behind him. Chloe, Megan, Jason, and Zach looked at their mothers in pure shock.

"What is it, Mom?" Zach said, sounding more like his father than a fourteen-year-old boy.

"Listen, you all need to go upstairs and stay together. We will come get you in a moment," Misty answered her son with a slight sense of fear in her voice.

Without an argument Zach helped his sister to her feet and they all four traveled up the stairs and made their way to Chloe and Megan's room.

"What do you suppose is going on?" Megan asked the others as she watched Zach pull the curtains closed.

Jason set the lamp he had been carrying down on the table and pulled out a deck of playing cards from the nightstand.

"I'm not sure," Zach replied, "but I don't think that we need to argue with them about it right now." Zach looked over at Jason, who returned his look of fear, and then back to the girls.

"Come on, let's play cards to help keep our minds off of whatever is going on," Jason said as he started dealing out the cards to all of them. "How about a nice game of Go Fish?"

They all sat down on the floor and began playing and laughing, and soon they were having so much fun that they had forgotten all about the man in the woods and their fathers running outside to find him.

Chloe glanced down at her watch after winning a game of Slap Jack and couldn't believe that they had been playing for nearly two hours. The thought of what happened earlier had now returned and she wondered if their dads had come back home.

"Hey, do you think that they are back?" she asked the others.

They all looked up from their card game and stared at her.

"I don't know, but I'm sure they are," Megan said, yawning and looking at her own watch. "It has been quite awhile."

"I think that I'm going to go downstairs and see if they're home yet," Chloe said, getting to her feet.

"No, you stay. Zach and I will go down and look, and if they are here we'll come get you. That way you and Megan can get into your pajamas and get ready for bed," Jason said, stopping his sister and pointing for Zach to follow him.

"Okay," she said a little anxiously, "but don't be gone long, okay?"

Jason and Zach left the room and began climbing down the stairs. They found their parents sitting in the living room near the fire talking quietly amongst themselves.

"Did you find him?" Jason asked as he walked over to his parents.

Zach followed and they both sat down on the bearskin rug near the fire so they could see their parents.

"No, I'm afraid not, son," Jackson replied with a slight shrug of his shoulders.

"Whoever it was, I think they got frightened when they saw Chloe and ran for it," Michael said. "I think we had better let the Minnows know so they can be on the lookout."

Jason looked over at his mother and saw that her face was white as a ghost and she had tears rolling down her cheeks.

"What's the matter, Mom?" he asked her, slowly getting to his feet and giving his mother a hug.

"I'm okay," she said, "just a little bit nervous. Where are the girls?"

"They are upstairs getting ready for bed. We said we'd come get them if you guys were home," Zach said.

"Well, go and get them then, I'm sure they are both scared," Misty replied. "I'll make us some hot chocolate."

Zach and Jason both ran back up the stairs to the girls' bedroom. Their door was open a little bit so they knocked and were greeted warmly by their sisters, who looked like they had been nervous the whole time they were gone. They followed their brothers back down the stairs and ran and gave their fathers big hugs as Michael repeated the story.

"Well, I hope he doesn't come back," Chloe said. "He looked scary out there in the dark."

81

They all sat down near the fire and told their parents all about the card games that they had just played, and a few minutes later they all had a cup of creamy hot chocolate and were heading back up to their rooms to turn in for the night.

"I wonder who it was," Chloe remarked to Megan as she slipped into the covers of her bed and set her cup on the night table.

"I don't know," Megan answered, "but I hope that he doesn't come back."

The girls stayed up and talked about their busy evening with Preston running into their room, and then the man outside, but soon they were both quiet and were fast asleep.

The next morning came too quickly for the girls. They had only received a few hours' sleep and were exhausted from the previous night's adventures.

"Oh, I do not want to get out of bed," Megan said, turning herself over on her side to see Chloe.

"Yeah, tell me about it," Chloe said. "Last night was brutal."

The girls slowly climbed out of bed put on some jeans and T-shirts and made their way downstairs for breakfast.

"Good morning, girls," Misty said, smiling at them as they walked into the kitchen. "Did you sleep well?"

"I guess," Megan said, sitting down at the table, "but I feel like I haven't even slept."

"Well, that's because you didn't go to bed until after four this morning," Aimee answered, putting fresh eggs and bacon on their plates and filling their cups with orange juice.

"What time is it?" Chloe said through a yawn.

"It's a little after seven," her mother said, kissing her on the cheek.

"Have Jason and Zach gotten up yet?" Megan asked as she poured syrup on her bacon.

"Yes, they went over to talk to the Minnows with your father and Michael about what happened last night and to see if they have seen anyone up here," Misty answered, pouring herself a glass of orange juice.

They all ate their breakfast and were putting their plates in the sink when the boys returned. Aimee quickly started another batch of eggs and bacon and then joined them in the living room.

"Did they know anything?" Aimee asked.

"No, they said that they haven't seen anyone up here in a long time," Jackson replied, hanging his jacket on a hook near the front door.

"They were as shocked as we were. They said that while Preston was out looking for them last night one of the trees near their house fell and they said that seemed rather strange. Those trees have a very solid base and the trunk had a pretty clean break," Michael said.

"Do they think that someone cut it down on purpose?" Aimee said, gasping.

"They aren't sure but they think so, especially now," he answered. "Girls, you need to stay inside today. I don't want you off wandering around, okay?"

They both nodded their heads in agreement.

"Dad, do you think he will come back?" Chloe asked.

"I hope not, sweetie, but if he does we'll be ready for him."

Chloe wanted to know more but could tell that her father didn't want to discuss this any further so she went to the kitchen to help finish making breakfast. After the boys all ate their fill of breakfast they cleared the table and began playing board games that Megan's mom packed in case of a rainy day. Of course, it wasn't raining outside but it was all they could do.

Soon the sun began glowing through their windows and letting in the warmth of the outside air.

"Dad, can we go out to the lake?" Jason asked, hoping for a positive answer.

"I don't know if we should or not…" Michael was interrupted by his wife, who was putting away their card came.

"Honey, I think that we could all use some of that warm fresh air. Why don't we all go out and sit by the lake," she said, smiling.

"Oh, all right," Michael said, returning his wife's smile.

"YES!" Jason shouted as he jumped up and ran for the door.

The others followed and as they walked through the back door they were greeted with a warm fresh breeze blowing off the lake.

"Oh, what a beautiful day," Chloe said, pulling a chair near the outer banks of the lake. "I wonder what Preston is doing today." She glanced over at Megan, who was now next to her and removing her sandals from her feet.

"I don't know, but I'm glad that his parents were there when he got back last night."

"Yeah, me too, I was really worried. Did you see his face when he came into our room? He looked like he was going to be sick," Chloe responded as she too slipped off her sandals.

Chloe looked out across the lake, hoping to see a boat coming around the bend toward their cabin, but only saw the reflection of the sun and mountains shining on the water.

"Look at that reflection!" Chloe cried. "It almost looks as if there really is a sun and mountain right there in the lake."

Megan looked toward the lake and saw the reflection also and they both stared in awe at the beauty of it. After a few moments Chloe glanced around to see what her family was doing. Jason and Zach were playing with a Frisbee that they had brought with them and both their parents were sitting at the picnic table reminiscing about who knows what.

Chloe turned around and looked back out toward the lake and saw what seemed to be a dark figure out on the water. She sat up in her chair to get a better look and saw it was a boat, but it was not anything that she had ever seen before. It was a long, sleek boat with oars that seemed to touch both sides of the lake. It had a large clear dome that

85

went over the top of the boat, making it look like a submarine, and inside were three very tall men. Chloe jumped up from her chair and ran toward her father with Megan hot on her heels.

"DAD!" she said, gasping for breath as if she had just run a marathon. "There's something coming this way!"

Michael leaped up from his seat and ran to the outer bank where Chloe and Megan had just been sitting.

"Aimie, get the kids inside right now!" he yelled from the bank. "Jackson, I need you to join me. Misty, you go with Aimie."

Zach looked at Michael and then back at the others and quickly ran along the path with the others toward the house. They soon arrived at the door, opened it, and ran inside. Misty quickly locked the door behind her and they all found themselves inside the house, once more scared and alone.

"Mom, why didn't Dad come with us?" Chloe asked.

"They need to stay out and make sure that it's safe, sweetheart," Aimie answered, but her voice sounded a bit stressed and nervous.

Chloe sensed her mother's anxiety and quickly looked out the big window toward the lake. She saw her father and Jackson waiting by the shore but saw nothing else except the reflection of the mountains on the lake again. She sat and waited but still nothing happened and her father was still standing and waiting for the boat Chloe and Megan had seen only moments ago. Chloe ushered Megan, Jason, and

Zach over to the living room. They all sat down on the floor in a circle and Chloe began telling the boys what they had seen on the lake. Megan looked over at her brother and realized that he looked like he was very ill.

"Zach, are you all right?" she asked as she grabbed a blanket from the sofa and threw it over him.

"I'm fine, I just need some water," Zach replied but he sounded strained and very tired.

"Mom, something is wrong with Zach," Megan squealed. "He just all of a sudden turned white and started to sweat."

Misty ran over to the sink got a glass of water and quickly gave it to her son.

"Drink this, Zach, it will make you feel better," she whispered and then wrapped her arms around her son's waist and helped him drink the water.

Zach's face almost immediately turned back to its original color and the sweat disappeared off his brow. Chloe and Megan were astounded at his quick recovery.

"What just happened?" Megan asked, still shocked at what she just saw.

"He was dehydrated, Megan, that's why he needed water," her mother answered, still holding onto Zach's waist. She quickly helped him to the couch to lie down, being extra careful not to let him fall.

"Zach, are you okay?" Jason asked, sitting on a large chair near him.

"I'm fine, I just needed some water, but I'm going to be real weak for a while," he replied without looking at him.

Chloe still couldn't believe this and neither could Megan. Neither of them had ever seen anything like this. They were both active in track and field and had seen quite a few athletes get dehydrated and water never worked that quickly on them. Megan stared at her brother in disbelief; she could feel the tears starting to form in her eyes and she quickly got up and ran up the stairs to go to her room. Chloe glanced around the room, hoping that she would get an explanation of what had just happened, but it never came so she went to check on Megan and make sure she was all right.

"Megan, are you okay?" Chloe asked as she walked over to her friend and sat next to her on the bed. "What is the matter? Why did you run up here?"

Megan didn't look at her, but Chloe could tell that she was still crying.

"Listen, if you don't want to tell me what's bothering you, that's fine, I understand, but at least look at me," Chloe pleaded.

Megan slowly turned to look at Chloe and quickly wrapped her arms around her friend and started to cry even more on Chloe's shoulder.

"This has been happening a lot the past year," Megan said between gasps. "I think Zach might be really sick, but no one will tell me anything that is going on."

Chloe sat there feeling helpless as her friend cried on her shoulder. After a moment Megan pulled away from

Chloe to expose her face for the first time since Chloe came upstairs. Her eyes were bloodshot and swollen and her cheeks were wet as tears still streamed down her face. Chloe reached to the bedside table and handed Megan a tissue.

"Look, I don't know what's going on either. This place is really starting to freak me out. I have that eerie feeling all the time that I'm being watched, people keep showing up out of nowhere and then disappear, Zach is sick, there is a storm almost every night that is usually stronger than the one from the night before, and for the first time in my life I find a boyfriend, but it's while I'm stuck in the middle of the lake," Chloe said as she handed Megan another tissue.

"Yeah, I know what you mean," Megan responded, "I always feel like someone's watching me too."

The girls looked at each other and Chloe felt her whole body start to shiver.

"I think we had better go downstairs," Megan said. "I want to check on Zach."

"Yeah, let's go," Chloe answered. They stood up and Megan walked over to the full-length mirror and tried to make it look like she hadn't been crying and then they both headed back downstairs.

When they reached the bottom step they realized that their dads were inside now and everyone, including Zach, was listening to whatever Michael was saying. As soon as they noticed Chloe and Megan they stopped talking and Misty stood up and gave Megan a hug.

89

"Are you okay, honey?" she asked.

"I'm fine, I was just scared that's all," Megan replied.

"Who was it, Dad?" Chloe asked as she looked at her father.

"There wasn't anything there," Michael answered. "Are you sure you saw something on the lake?"

Chloe gave them the explanation of what she had seen again and Megan also told them she saw the same thing.

"I think that we need to stay inside the rest of the day," Jackson said. "I think that the mountain air might be getting to all of you."

Megan looked at her father and couldn't believe what she was hearing.

"You mean you don't believe us?" Megan responded as she shot her father a glare. "I can't believe that you think we are crazy! I thought for sure you would believe us."

Chloe was also hurt by what Jackson had just said and they both ran back upstairs to their rooms. As the girls reached their bedrooms they both plopped down on their beds and stared straight up at the ceiling. There was a knock on the door and Chloe and Megan both turned over on their sides so they were facing the wall. Michael and Jackson came in carrying two mugs each of steaming hot chocolate with some cookies that were left over from the night before. They sat down on the two chairs that were near the girls' beds and put the cups and plate of cookies down on the bedside table.

90

"Girls, we don't think that you are lying, all we said was that it was gone," Michael said. "I don't know where it went but it was no longer there when we got to the shoreline."

Chloe slowly turned over to look at her father and she started to cry. Michael got up and moved over to the bed, sat down, and gave his daughter a big hug.

"Everything is going to be all right," he said. "We just have to be careful."

Jackson watched Michael and Chloe and he decided that he would go and sit next to Megan as well. He stood up and sat down on the bed next to her and began combing her hair with his fingers.

"Megan, please look at me," he whispered. "I know that you are angry with me for saying that but we really didn't mean it like that."

Megan wasn't sure if she wanted to forgive her father that quickly but she decided that there was no reason for her to be angry for too long. She knew that he didn't mean they were lying and so she also turned over and wrapped her arms around her father's neck and gave him a big hug. He returned it and then reached to the bedside table and got their mugs of hot chocolate and a couple of cookies.

"Dad, why are there people spying on us?" Chloe asked as she took a bite of her cookie. "I mean, something has happened every night since we have been here and we never seem to know why."

Chloe looked up at her father, hoping that he would have the answer that she needed to hear.

"I don't know, sweetheart. I hope it's just people out hiking and they turned around and went back to wherever they came from."

This was not the answer that Chloe wanted to hear. She wanted to know that they really did find the person and it was just some of the Minnows' friends or something. Then she remembered that Preston said that they had never had any visitors and she began to feel scared that something terrible was going on.

For the next hour the girls sat up in the room and talked to their fathers about everything they had on their minds. They told them about losing their paddle and how Preston and Jack came from nowhere and rescued them. They told them how cool the cave was and how they thought that they should all go there tomorrow if it was a nice day. Their fathers listened and they laughed with them and then they were all called down for a late lunch.

They got up and went downstairs and found that Aimie, Misty, Jason, and Zach were all sitting on the floor on a blanket with the furniture moved up against the walls. The sun was shining in through the big picture window, and made it look like they were outside because it was so bright.

"I thought we might like to have a picnic," Misty said, smiling.

"That sounds great!" Megan said, running over and sitting next to her brother. "How are you feeling?" she asked.

"I'm great. I was just a little tired, I think, and then we were outside for a while so I just needed to rest for a little bit," he answered.

"I'm so glad, I was so worried," she said, giving her brother a little nudge to the side and smiling sideways at him.

"So what's on the menu, ladies?" Jackson asked as he sat next to his wife and started rummaging around the blanket looking for anything he thought he wanted.

"Well, it's a surprise," Aimie said, getting up and walking to the kitchen. She was followed by Misty and they brought out a large basket, plates, cups, silverware, napkins, and a fresh pitcher of water. They set it all in the middle of the blanket, passed out everything they had brought, and then opened the basket to reveal a wonderful feast. There were slices of roast beef and ham for hoagies, along with the hoagie bread, lettuce, mustard, pickles, and anything you might need for a mile-high sub sandwich. There were also bags of potato chips, cookies, and eight slices of chocolate cake.

"WOW!" Chloe and Megan said in unison.

"This is great, honey," Michael said, helping himself to some of the potato chips.

"I thought you might like it," Aimie said, smiling. "Here, let me get you a sandwich."

Soon they were all laughing and telling jokes and eating a delicious indoor picnic.
When they had finished stuffing all that they could fit into their stomachs, including the chocolate cake and cookies,

they helped clean up and move furniture back into its place. By this time the sun was starting to fall behind the mountains and the moon was just peeking over the top of the eastern horizon.

"Well, I guess we won't need any dinner tonight," Misty said with a slight chuckle.

"Yeah, I think you're right. I don't know about breakfast either," Jackson said, smiling.

They all laughed and Zach pulled another board game from the closet and set it up on the rug.

"Anyone up for a little Scrabble?" he said, passing out the alphabetical tiles.

Just as he finished his sentence there was a knock on the front door. Michael shot up from the chair he was sitting in and Misty, Aimie, and Jackson grabbed the kids by the arms and pulled them into the kitchen. Chloe couldn't believe it. Every time they sat down to have a good time something bad seemed to happen. Michael slowly went to the door. "
Who is it?" he said nervously.

"It's Jack Minnow," came the response from the other side of the door.

Chloe's heart started to race. It's Preston, it has to be, she thought.

Michael opened the door. Jack Minnow stood there with an arm full of firewood.

"I thought you might need some more firewood," he said. "May I come in?"

"Sure," Michael said, "can I give you a hand?"

94

"No, I got it, thanks," Jack responded. He walked over to the fireplace, moving around the game board, and placed the firewood in the wood box. "Hope I didn't disturb your game," he said, removing his hat and walking back toward the door.

"Not at all," Michael said.

"Please, won't you come have some hot chocolate or cookies?" Aimie said.

"No, I'm afraid I must be getting back to Jennifer. Preston and I were out cutting that tree all day and I haven't been able to spend much time with her, but I appreciate it," he replied. "But I would like a word with you, Michael, and Jackson, if it's not too much trouble."

Chloe glanced around at Megan and saw that she looked just as curious.

"Sure, excuse us," Michael said.

Michael, Jackson, and Jack all went outside and closed the door behind them.

"Well, how about that game?" Zach said, breaking the silence.

"I'm in!" Jason said excitedly. "Chloe, Megan, do you want to play?"

"Uh, sure, I'll play," Megan said.

"And set me up too," Chloe said.

"How about you, Mom, and Aimie, do you want to play?"

"Not right now, Zach, maybe a little bit later, okay?"

"All right then, so how do you guys want to play? I thought we might make it interesting this time and only use words with five or less letters," Zach said, turning back around to face the others.

"That sounds fun, but I hope you're ready to lose!" Megan said, laughing.

After Chloe had beat them at their first game and they had just started their second, Michael and Jackson returned from outside.

"What was that all about?" Jason asked as he laid down the word "fool" on the table.

"He just wanted to make sure that nobody came by today," Jackson said, looking a little pale.

Chloe noticed that both he and her father looked as though they had just been told horrible news, but she knew that no matter what she said her father wouldn't tell her anything.

"Well, I hope he gets home okay," Chloe said, trying to break the silence that had fallen over the room. "Come on, Zach, it's your turn."

They turned back to their game and played a few more after that. Soon it started to get late and Megan and Chloe decided that they wanted to go up to bed. They were still tired from last night's adventures and now today was added on top of their already tired bodies.

"What a day," Jason said, yawning. "I hope we can just have a relaxing day tomorrow."

"Yeah, I'm getting really tired of the games that we have. I think we have played them all at least five times each," Megan said with a giggle.

Chloe looked over at her brother and best friend and smiled but didn't say anything.

"What's up?" Megan asked curiously.

"Nothing, I'm just really tired and need some sleep," she answered a little sluggishly.

Megan looked at her friend and could tell that she was not happy, but didn't quite know what to say to cheer her up. She looked over at Jason and Zach, waved goodnight to them, and then followed Chloe into their bedroom.

Chloe walked straight for the window and pulled open the curtains to expose the lake.

I wonder why he didn't come today. He said that he would see me today, she thought to herself.

She turned around and saw that Megan was already in her pajamas and getting into bed, but she didn't want to get undressed just yet. She climbed up on the windowsill and peered out across the lake and could just see the bend where she knew Preston's house was.

"Chloe, what's wrong?" Megan asked, getting up and going to the window and peering out to see what Chloe was looking at.

"I don't know, I just feel like something is wrong, and that's why Preston didn't come today," Chloe said.

97

"I know he's probably fine, but I just can't shake it." Chloe turned around and gazed up at Megan and her eyes began to fill up with tears.

"I'm sure he's fine," Megan said, giving Chloe a hug. "Why don't you get your pajamas on and get into bed and try and get some sleep. We've all had a long couple of days and maybe you're just tired."

Chloe slowly lowered herself off the windowsill and got into her bed without putting on her pajamas. Megan got into her bed and sighed, turned over on her side, and quickly fell asleep. Chloe couldn't sleep, however; she couldn't stop thinking that something was wrong. She lay there thinking about Preston and remembered all that had happened the night before and the tree almost hitting him and she began to get very worried. She looked at her watch and she could just read the time through the moonlight that was shining through her window.

It's already one o'clock, she thought, *why can't I sleep, what's wrong with me?*

She perched herself up on one arm and looked over at Megan, whom she could tell was fast asleep. Chloe got up and went back to the window to have one more look over the lake. She peered out over the water and saw a huge black storm cloud just at the bend. It was swirling around and around and wasn't moving.

"That's near the Minnows' house!" she screamed.

Megan jumped up, breathing hard, and looked at Chloe.

"What is going on?" she asked, looking at Chloe with frustration in her voice.

"That storm, there's a tornado! It's at the Minnows'!" Chloe yelled as she flew past Megan and ran out the door toward her parents' room.

Megan looked at the window. When she saw the dark cloud she turned around and followed Chloe. They burst into Michael and Aimie's room and Chloe ran as fast as she could over to her father, but no one was there. They ran back out and down the hall to Megan's parents' room but no one was there either.

"You get Jason and Zach, I'm going downstairs to warn our parents," Chloe said, sprinting past Megan and sliding down the banister all the way to the bottom floor.

Megan ran into Jason and Zach's room and found them fast asleep on their beds.

"WAKE UP!" she screamed and started throwing them their shoes. "THERE'S A TORNADO HEADED FOR THE HOUSE!"

Zach and Jason jumped up and ran to the window of their room and tore the shades open. They peered out the window and saw the storm; now it was getting bigger and heading straight for them. They put their shoes on and the three of them bolted out of the room. Megan ran right into Chloe and they both flew to the ground.

"Get up!" Zach yelled. "We have to get out of here! Where are Mom and Dad?"

"They're not here! I can't find them anywhere!"
Chloe said as she pulled herself up off the ground and helped
Megan up.

"What do you mean you can't find them?" Zach said.
"They have to be here somewhere!"

"They must be outside," Jason answered.

They all ran down the stairs and found it completely
empty as Chloe had stated. They ran out the back door and
screamed for their parents, but they couldn't find them.

"We have to get out of here!" Zach howled.

"We can't leave our parents!" Chloe yelled back.

"Look, Chloe, that storm is almost here! We have to
run for it. Our parents will be fine!" Zach screeched.

"He's right, Chloe, Mom and Dad will be fine. Let's
go!" Jason yelled as he grabbed Chloe's arm and started
pulling her toward the woods.

They all began to run as fast as they could into the
woods and followed the trail up the mountain. Zach looked
back and noticed that the storm was getting bigger every
minute. It was now engulfing their cabin in strong winds and
rain.

"Keep running, don't look back!" he yelled.

They all kept running and Chloe could feel her arms
and legs getting very tired and her side starting to ache. She
looked back at Megan and Jason and noticed that Megan also
looked tired but Jason kept her going. The next thing she
knew her right leg gave way and she fell to the ground. Her

head came in contact with a large rock and everything went dark.

"ZACH, HELP ME!" Jason screamed.

Zach slid to a stop and turned around. He saw Chloe lying on the ground unconscious and Megan lying a few feet behind her not moving. Zach ran back and bent down.

"They are okay, but we are going to have to carry them the rest of the way. That storm is closing in on us," Zach said, hoisting Chloe over his shoulder.

Jason bent down over Megan, struggled to pick her up, and carried her in his arms. They both ran as fast as they could holding onto the girls, which was not as easy as it seemed. Jason wasn't sure where they were going but he just kept on following Zach, hoping not to lose him in the darkness.

Then Jason smelled something familiar—it was sulfur from the small boggy pond! They were headed for the cave. They turned around the familiar boulder and sure enough, there was the opening of the cave. The dark cloud was only yards away by this time and Zach ran right into the cave. Jason followed and ran smack into Zach.

"Don't stop! It's right behind us," Jason panted, still holding Megan in his arms, which were burning with agony.

"We are safe right here," Zach said, setting Chloe down on some sand and sitting on a rock.

Jason didn't understand the cloud was right there; he tried to keep going but he found he couldn't move. His feet were stuck to the ground and he was sinking in mud that appeared from nowhere.

"I'M SINKING!" he bawled.

Zach jumped up and saw that he was in fact slowly sinking lower into the sand. He grabbed Megan from his arms and laid her near Chloe and then turned around to find Jason waist high in mud. Zach grabbed Jason's arms and pulled as hard as he could and released Jason from the mud. They flew backward and landed on the soft sand that was directly behind them. They lay there for a moment, both panting loudly.

Jason turned around and looked at the opening of the cave and saw that the cloud was now beginning to get further and further away.

"What just happened?" he asked. "We should have all been killed by that cloud, and then I almost get sucked into the mud?"

Zach looked around the cave and then he looked at Jason.

"We need to go further in. We are safe from the storm here, but there is something else here."

Without waiting for Jason, Zach hoisted Chloe back up onto his shoulders again and began walking deeper into the cave. Jason stood up and grabbed Megan and followed reluctantly behind. He was so confused at what was going on. He had no idea how Zach knew they would be safe here from the storm, and how he was almost sucked into the earth by mud that appeared from nowhere. Jason felt himself shiver at the thought of his life almost being brought to an end. He looked forward and saw the same familiar light in the distance that was there only a couple of days before, but there was a new light there also; it looked like a campfire.

No, it can't be, he thought. *Who would be here at this time of night?*

"Zach, is that a campfire?" he asked.

"Yeah, I think so, but don't worry about it, I'm sure it's just our parents," Zach replied nervously, holding onto Chloe.

They continued walking and they saw that the light and the campfire were both getting closer. They turned the last little bend and saw a person lying on the floor of the cave inside a sleeping bag. Zach laid Chloe quietly down on the ground, then turned around and told Jason to wait where he was. Jason began to retort, but Zach had already started tiptoeing quietly toward the body on the floor. He got right behind it and then jumped onto it, holding it down. The person started kicking and yelling, trying to get free, and pushed Zach to the floor. The person jumped up out of the sleeping bag, ready for a fight, and saw to his surprise, Zach lying on the floor trying hard to get to his feet. Zach looked up and opened his eyes wide. "Preston?"

6

The Hidden Path

"What are you doing here?" Zach asked as Preston grabbed his arm and lifted him off the ground.

"My parents brought me here hours ago. There was a storm and they said I would be safe here," he said, still a little shaken from being jumped on in the middle of the night.

"Uh, guys, a little help?" Jason asked, still trying to hold up Megan just in case he needed to run back the other way with her.

Preston and Zach quickly ran over to where Jason was standing and Zach took Megan from Jason's arms. Preston leaned over Chloe, scooped her up in his arms, and walked over and laid her softly on his sleeping bag. Zach laid Megan down in the sand right next to Chloe and then Jason and Zach plopped down in the sand next to her.

"What happened?" Preston said, looking at Chloe in utter shock.

"We had to run away from the storm. As we were running up the mountain I saw Chloe fall to the ground and she hit her head hard on a rock. Megan stopped to help her, and out of nowhere collapsed to the ground," Jason said, still trying to catch his breath and rubbing his arms. "We had to carry them up the mountain and through the cave."

"They need some water, Preston," Zach said, also trying to catch his breath.

Preston got up and moved over to where he had set the water jug and returned moments later. Zach moved over to where Chloe was lying and tilted her head so that Preston could get some water into her mouth. Preston tilted the jug and poured the water into her mouth and then to his surprise she drank it. They did the same for Megan and she also drank some. Preston then passed the jug to the two boys and gave them some cups. The boys quickly drank some water, and immediately Jason felt his strength return.

"Where are your parents?" Preston asked, sitting back down near Chloe and laying her head on his lap.

"We don't know. We tried to find them before we ran here but they were gone. The fire was still burning in the fireplace and their cups were still sitting on the table, but they were nowhere to be found," Zach said. "I'm a little worried about them. Where are your parents?"

"They brought me here and then they took off back down the mountain," Preston answered. "I have no idea what is going on, but all my father said was to remember the stories he told me when I was a kid."

Zach and Jason looked at him questioningly. Preston began explaining what had happened, and all about the stories he heard as a child.

"I've been at the cave since about ten o'clock I think," Preston said after he finished his explanation. He got up and went over and grabbed some of the deer jerky that his father had put in the satchel and handed it to Zach and Jason.

"Here, I'm sure you need something to eat," he said as he sat back down and resumed stroking Chloe's hair.

"Thanks," Zach and Jason said in unison.

They began eating their jerky when they heard a noise coming from the direction of the cave opening. Preston, Zach, and Jason jumped to their feet and grabbed large rocks that they could use as weapons if they needed to. Jason ran over and grabbed the lantern off the rock nearby and lit it so they could shine it in the direction of the noise. He held it up and they saw something moving closer, but it definitely wasn't a person. As it came closer they noticed it was a small round animal, with lots of bushy brown hair and bright green eyes.

"What is it?" Jason asked, backing away a little.

"I'm not sure, I've never seen anything like that before," Preston answered.

Zach moved a little bit closer to the animal and crouched down so he could get a better look.

"I think it's a prairie dog," he said, holding his hand out to try and coax the animal closer with a small piece of jerky.

"That is not a prairie dog, Zach. I think you better back up a little bit and stand up," Preston said a little nervously.

The animal inched its way closer to Zach and slowly it stretched out its little neck and put a paw up and snatched the piece of jerky out of his hand. It stood there looking at

Zach as if in amazement that he was able to get the food without a fight. Then it stood on two feet and bowed low toward Preston and Jason and started walking on its hind legs over to where Megan and Chloe were lying, still unconscious. Preston and Jason, shock clear on their faces that this animal was walking like a human being, watched carefully.

Soon the animal reached Megan and jumped up onto her chest, now back on all fours. Zach quickly moved near his sister, hoping the animal didn't attack her. With Preston and Jason on his heels, he stopped and stared at the animal, which was now gazing at Megan's face. It stretched out its paw and touched her softly on the forehead and then jumped down and did the same to Chloe. After it had done this, it looked up at Preston and Jason, took another bow, and then walked over to the edge of the cliff. Moments later, the animal disappeared right before their eyes and left nothing, not even an animal print, to show it had been there.

"What in the world was that?" Preston said, still in shock.

"Did that thing just disappear?" Jason asked.

Zach walked over to the edge of the cliff and peered down into the darkness.

"Where did it go? There's no way down or across from here," Preston said.

A few moments later another noise caught their attention. The three boys spun around to find that Megan had begun to wake up at last. They ran and sat down next to her

107

and Preston grabbed the water bottle that was nearby.

"What happened?" she said croakily.

"Here, drink this, it will help," Preston said, helping her lift her head to take a drink.

Megan slowly drank the water and peered at the three boys, who were now crowding around her.

"Where's Chloe? Where are we?" she said, a little frightened.

"We are at the cave," Zach said, reaching down and giving her a hug.

"Are you feeling all right?" Preston said. "Can you sit up?"

Megan had to squint her eyes to try and figure out who had just asked her this. She saw Preston holding out a hand to help her up and her eyes shot over to Jason and Zach.

"Megan, what is it? What are you doing?" Zach cried as Megan began pushing Zach and Jason out of the way trying to get away from Preston.

"It's him!" she shouted. "Run!"

"Megan, it's just me, Preston, remember from yesterday?"

Megan stopped and turned around quickly to look at him again. Then she threw herself at Preston and embraced him in a warm, sisterly hug. Zach got ahold of his sister and pulled her away from him.

"Megan, what are you doing?" he asked. "What has gotten into you?"

Megan took another drink and then sat back down on the sand.

"The last thing I remember happening was that we were running up the mountain away from a dark storm cloud," she said. "While we were running I could feel my legs starting to feel as if they were Jell-O, and then the next thing I remember is Chloe falling down...Chloe! Where's Chloe?" she bawled.

"Hey, it's fine, she's right here," Jason said, pointing to where his sister was still lying unconscious.

Megan calmed down again and put her head against Zach and started to cry. Deep long tears ran from her face onto Zach's pajama bottoms.

"Megan, it's okay, everyone is safe now. You need to calm down," Zach said as he slowly rubbed her back.

Zach peered over at Preston and Jason; they were both just as awestruck at what was happening as he was.

"Megan, why don't you lay down and try and get some rest?" Zach said. "Here's a pillow and an extra blanket. You can lay right here next to Chloe, okay?"

Megan looked up at her brother, and Zach saw that she was still very frightened.

"It's okay, we are not going anywhere, we will be right here," he said.

At last she decided that it was okay and she laid herself down next to Chloe, pulled the blanket up near her face, and quickly fell right back to sleep.

"What was that about?" Jason whispered.

"I don't know, but she seemed to think that I was coming after her," Preston answered. "Wait a second, why did that animal thing touch them on their forehead? Isn't that a little bit strange?" Preston jumped up from where he was kneeling and running back to the edge of the cliff and peering out over the edge.

"Yeah, and how did it walk like us?" Jason said, now joining Preston.

They waited for Zach to say something, but he was kneeling over his sister, and his face seemed to be pure white.

"Zach, what's wrong?" Preston asked.

"Nothing, I'm just really tired, that's all," he answered. "I think I'm going to try and get some sleep. Why don't you guys do the same? I have a feeling we are going to have a long day tomorrow."

Preston and Jason looked over at one another and shrugged their shoulders.

"Sure, I guess it's not a bad idea," Preston responded. "Come on, Jason, Zach's right."

Jason couldn't believe it.

How are they going to fall asleep at a time like this? he thought. *There's no way I'm going to be able to sleep.*

Preston lay down next to Chloe on the sand and propped his head on a smooth rock, Zach lay near his sister, and Jason decided that he would lie near their feet. To Jason's surprise Preston and Zach almost immediately fell asleep. Jason lay there staring across the cliff at the light and began waiting for that mysterious animal to come back from wherever he disappeared to. Soon he felt himself slowly drifting off to sleep.

Preston slowly opened his eyes and let out a big yawn. He squinted to try to focus on where he was. He had almost forgotten all about the cave and everything else that had happened last night. He sat up and looked in the direction of the ravine and saw that Zach was sitting with his legs over the edge. His back was faced toward Preston but he could tell that Zach was talking to himself. He got up off the sand and looked at Chloe and Megan, who were still asleep. Jason was also still asleep.

"What time is it?" he asked Zach quietly.

Zach spun around, his face still white as a sheet, and stared at Preston. He quickly pulled his legs back onto the sand and stood up.

"Are you okay?" Preston asked. "I'm sorry, I didn't mean to scare you."

"I'm fine, I just didn't sleep well, that's all," Zach answered, not looking at his watch. "It's six thirty."

"Who were you talking to?" Preston asked him. "I saw your arms moving as if you were discussing something important with the ravine."

Zach slowly walked over to where Preston was standing. He reached down and grabbed the water bottle and took a long drink and then stared down at where the others were still sleeping.

"Preston, we need to leave this cave. It's not safe here anymore and you and everyone else here are in danger," he said, not looking at him.

Preston couldn't believe what Zach just said. *How on earth would he know that we are in danger?* "What do you mean we are in danger?" said Preston out loud.

"I can't explain this now, but we need to wake everyone up and get out of here." Zach still stared at the others sleeping on the ground.

"What about Chloe, she's still unconscious. And you didn't answer my question. I'm tired of everyone telling me that they can't explain..."

The ground started to shake and Preston stopped in mid-sentence.

"What is going on?" he yelled.

Zach's face immediately went even whiter than it was moments ago.

"Preston, you need to get Chloe and the others up, do you understand!" Zach yelled back.

Zach turned quickly around and ran toward the edge of the cliff.

Preston jumped to the ground and shook Jason. "We need to go! Get up right now!"

Jason jumped up from where he was sleeping and didn't even ask why. He ran over to Megan and began shaking her to wake her up. Preston was doing the same thing to Chloe. Megan jumped up and screamed and smacked Jason across the face as hard as she could.

"Get away from me! Don't touch me!" she screamed.

"Megan, wake up, it's me, Jason." At the sound of Jason's voice she opened her eyes and immediately gave Jason a hug.

"What's going on?" she asked.

Just as the words came out of her mouth the ground shook again, a little more violently then before. Preston was still trying to wake Chloe up when Zach returned.

"Let's go! Pick up Chloe and follow me," he said, looking at his sister.

"Zach, what is going on!?" she bawled. "Where are we going?"

Without an answer Zach turned around and started walking right for the cliff. Preston hoisted Chloe up into his arms and followed, and Megan and Jason followed right behind him.

"Zach, I need to know what's going on. We can't get across that cliff, I've tried for years," Preston said now right behind him.

Zach looked at Preston. "You're going to have to trust me, okay?"

Zach said something quietly to himself and a few seconds later the animal from the night before appeared out of thin air. Zach bent down, and the animal stood up on its hind legs.

"It's time, ol' friend," he said to the creature.

Without another word, Zach picked up the animal and threw it across the cliff. Preston couldn't believe his eyes, and neither could Megan or Jason.

"Zach, you've killed that poor animal!" Megan screamed. "He'll never make it across there, it's too far."

Just as Megan said that, Zach extended his arms, said something else to himself, and the animal turned into a beautiful large red bird, with wings that seemed to extend out to about five feet. It spun itself around and Megan, Jason, and Preston all gasped and stared at Zach in utter disbelief.

The new red bird swooped down at Zach's feet and pushed off from the edge of the cliff, and behind him he left a rainbow. Zach put his right foot out and stepped off the edge of the cliff onto the rainbow-colored pathway.

Preston's eyes went wide. "It can't be. I don't believe it."

Zach turned around. "We have to hurry!" he said.

Preston cautiously walked to the edge of the cliff with Chloe and put his foot out. He felt the smoothness of the newly created path and gained his balance. Zach turned back around and began following his red bird across the ravine. Preston followed him. Megan began edging herself along the edge of the cliff and then she too stepped out onto the path, followed quickly by Jason.

They walked along this strange path for quite a while. Preston couldn't understand why they weren't to the other side yet; after all, it wasn't that far. Finally, Preston saw Zach walk off the rainbow and onto a rocky cliff. Soon all three were pulled up onto the cliff and they turned around and saw that their pathway had disappeared as quickly as it had come.

114

Jason turned around and stared at Zach in disbelief, but Zach was already making his way up the rocky pathway toward the bright light.

Preston wouldn't move; he sat there staring at the ravine they had just walked across and couldn't believe what had just happened. The story that his father told him was coming true, but how could that be? It wasn't possible. There was no such thing as magic.

"Preston, we have to keep going! Hurry!" Zach said from a little ways up the rocky path.

Preston noticed that Megan and Jason were already following Zach, so he started moving. Just as he took a step the ground shook furiously and he felt himself falling backward. He knew that he was still very close to the edge of the cliff and he knew he was going to fall over. Zach jumped onto another rock, stretched out both hands, and spoke some sort of strange language. Preston felt something pushing him back to his feet from behind and saw three white glittering puffs of smoke. He held on tighter to Chloe and as soon as he was surefooted again he took off up the path, glancing back to try to see what it was that pushed him back to his feet, but there was nothing there. *I must be imagining this, I need to wake up*, he thought to himself. Preston felt Chloe move in his arms and he looked down at her.

"Hey, Chloe's waking up!" he yelled at the others as he followed them at a sprint down the path.

Zach immediately stopped and Megan and Jason screeched to a stop so not to bump into him. Zach turned

115

around and ran toward Preston. He stopped right in front of
him, said something again in some other strange language,
and Chloe bolted up and Preston struggled not to drop her.
He set her down on a rock and she glanced up into his eyes.

"Preston?" she said quietly.

Zach grabbed a water bottle from thin air and handed
it to Chloe.

"Chloe, you need to drink this water. All of it right
now," he said.

Chloe looked up at him in amazement, but drank the
whole thing without saying anything else.

"Chloe, can you walk?" he asked her. "We need to
keep moving deeper into the cave."

"I…I think so," she answered sleepily.

She reached up and grabbed Preston's arm and he
helped pull her to her feet. She swayed a little bit, but before
she could fall the bright red bird came back down from flying
above them and rubbed his feather across her face. Chloe
took a deep breath, stopped swaying, closed her eyes, and
smiled. She opened them again and looked over at Zach.
"Let's go!" was all she said.

Preston was completely bewildered by her quick
change and was about to ask about it, but Zach just smiled
brightly at her and started to run again. Zach was first,
followed by Megan, then Jason, Chloe, and Preston. They ran
deeper into the cave and the light got brighter and brighter
the farther they went in. Preston could feel himself getting
very tired and knew they would have to stop soon.

116

"Zach, we need to stop for a while!" he shouted toward the front of the line.

Zach slowed down and stopped. He turned around and looked at all of them, and could see the exhaustion running the same on everyone's faces.

"We only have a little bit to go. We are almost there, and then we can stop and have a bite to eat," he said, now pointing in the direction they were running. "Do you see that bend right there? We need to go around it and then up a little hill and down one small one and we will be as far as we can go. Do you think you all can make it?"

They peered down the path and saw a bend curve off to the left. They all shook their heads and Zach started walking quickly in the direction of the bend with his red bird still flying above them. They all followed him and soon rounded the bend and started walking up the hill. Chloe looked around and saw that there were icicles hanging on either side of the path from the ceiling, but it wasn't cold. She also saw large sparkling rocks that looked as if they were smeared in glitter. She could hear birds chirping ahead of her as well. She glanced back at Preston, who also had heard the same thing. Preston moved quickly up to Chloe and put his hand in hers.

"Are you okay?" he asked, not taking his eyes from hers.

"I think so. Where are we?" she said.

117

"We are in the cave. You and the others got here last night, but you've been unconscious all night. They said you hit your head on a rock."

"Shhh, we need to move very quietly," Zach said, looking back at them.

Preston turned his head away from Chloe and stared at Zach, who was still walking quickly up the hill. Preston and Chloe walked hand in hand and followed Jason, Megan, and Zach up the remainder of the hill and back down another small hill that Zach had described. They were about to turn a corner to the right when Zach came to stop. They all caught up with him and sat down on the nearby rocks, breathing hard and sweating.

"Where are we?" Megan asked.

"This is called The Hidden Path. It was made for this exact reason over twenty-four years ago. No one uses it because it's sacred," Zach said, still looking toward the next bend.

They all looked at him in surprise.

"How do you know? We've never been here before," Megan said, a little bit irritated. "This is the first time we have been to these mountains."

Zach looked down at her. "Because I helped put it here. We are almost there, it's just around that last bend; however, we can't go there yet, it's not ready. Kamali will let us know when it's safe to go in."

"What is Kamali?" Jason asked.

"He's my best friend in the whole world. He made Chloe and Megan better last night."

He spoke without looking at them but staring at the top of the cave where the big red bird was sitting on a large tall rock, staring down at them.

"You mean that bird is yours?" Megan said, exasperated. "You have never had a pet in your life. Wait, where did you learn that weird language that you've been so quietly speaking to yourself all this time? And what do you mean you helped put this path here?"

Zach looked away from the bend and stared at his sister. "Megan, there are things you don't know about me. Kamali is a magical bird. If he hadn't touched your forehead last night, you and Chloe would still be unconscious. He gave you his strength. He passed it to you because he knew we were in danger," he said, now joining them on a nearby rock.

"Why didn't you recognize it last night then? You said it was a prairie dog," Preston said, staring at Zach.

"I didn't want anyone to know who he was, because I hadn't talked to or seen him in a long time. He can change shape to any animal that he feels necessary at the time. He's also the one who I was speaking to this morning. He is the one who told me it was time to move deeper into the cave, and saved our lives today," he said, holding an arm out for the large bird.

Kamali extended his big bright wings and flew from where he was sitting and glided down onto Zach's arm. Chloe noticed that Zach's arm gave way under the bird's extreme weight, but his face showed no signs of pressure.

"Wait a second, I need to know what's going on. Why we are on this so-called Hidden Path, and what happened to me? All I know is that we are in some strange part of the cave, and Zach has a pet bird that somehow saved our lives." Chloe spoke while staring around the cave at all the others.

Jason explained all he could remember about the night before and then stopped and looked at Zach and Preston to make sure he didn't leave anything out.

"So you are telling me that Kamali made a path across that big cliff and we walked across with no problems and we trusted it and followed it deep into this cave?" Chloe said, now frightened.

"I know where we are. You all just have to trust me," Zach said, now standing up and looking toward the next bend. "We should probably eat something very quickly and then I think it will be safe to go on."

Preston looked angrily at Zach. "We have nothing to eat. We left in such a hurry that I didn't have time to grab any food."

Zach looked down at him, then raised his arm where Kamali was perched and the bird took flight. Zach opened his mouth, and that same strange language poured out. A table, spread out with food that hadn't been there moments ago, along with five chairs, magically appeared. Preston, Megan, Jason, and Chloe all jumped up from where they were sitting, backed away from Zach and the table of fresh food, and goggled at him. All their favorite foods were placed on the table, including; drumsticks and donuts, fresh watermelon, and hot homemade bread with butter and raspberry jam. There were also large glasses of what seemed to be sparkling water, hot mashed potatoes, and lots more that they had never seen before. They also saw bowls of cold chocolate ice cream for their dessert.

"What—I mean how—what is going on?" Megan said as if she didn't have any air to breathe.

"Please, sit down and eat, we really need to get going, and the food is hot and ready," Zach said, not answering her question.

Zach sat down on a chair near the bend in the path and began eating the food without hesitation. Jason walked over to the table and sat down and he too began eating the food. Preston, Megan, and Chloe were still standing where they were, afraid to move.

"Come on, you guys, it's Zach, you know, your brother, Megan, and our friend. This food is delicious! It's like having everything you could dream about and then they add whipped cream and a cherry to top it off. This is great!" Jason said with his mouth full of what looked like mashed potatoes.

They all glanced at one another and then walked over and sat down on the chairs and slowly began helping themselves to the food. Chloe couldn't believe it; the food really was hot, and it was mouth-watering. She remembered that she hadn't had anything to eat since dinner yesterday and she was really hungry, so she helped herself to everything she could get. After a small time, they found themselves all full to the brim and couldn't eat any more. Zach smiled at them, gave a wave of his arm, and everything disappeared as if it hadn't been there at all.

They all sat back in there chairs that were left behind for them and sighed.

"Zach, why didn't you tell me you were magical?" Megan asked a little cautiously as she leaned back in her chair.

"I can't explain everything right now, but in time you will understand. I'm sorry, Meg, I wish I could tell you everything, but it's not my job."

Megan looked hurt by what he said, and Chloe knew it was because they always shared everything with each other. No matter what it was, Zach and Megan were always like best friends.

Preston was just about to ask what he meant when he said it wasn't his job to explain, when Kamali gave an ear-shattering squawk. Zach looked up at him and the others heard him speak in the same language that Zach had been speaking. Then Zach stood up.

"It's time for us to go," he said. "I need you all to stay very close to me and don't speak or ask any questions. We are going into a very dangerous area and if we speak or make too much noise, the cave could give way. Do you all understand?"

They all looked up at Zach with scared faces but nodded their heads and stood up to follow him. Zach waved his arm and spoke the language again and the chairs were gone in an instant.

"We are about to enter what is called the outer regions of Mere. Remember, if you see anyone or anything, do not tell them your names, okay?" he said again.

They all nodded again, though they were a little bit more frightened than they were a moment ago and wondered why he wouldn't explain this at least. Zach, walking very slowly, turned the bend with the others close behind him.

As they turned the bend Chloe looked up and saw that the icicles that she had seen before, above their heads, were now dripping water down to the ground. The entire cave was full of ice everywhere you looked, except on the path on which they were walking. Zach grabbed Megan's hand and she in turn grabbed Jason's and soon they were all walking together holding hands. Chloe glanced back at Preston. He gave her a faint smile, but she could tell that he was nervous.

They kept walking and then they turned another bend, and right in front of them was a large wall of what looked like water that was bright as if the sun were shining on it. Chloe could see something green on the other side of the wall, but figured it was just her imagination. It glistened and shined with the ice all around it and Chloe found that she was starting to feel light-headed. She felt herself start to sway and her head started spinning as if she stayed on a ride too long at the fair. She felt Preston's and Jason's hands leave hers and she saw them fall to the ground with their eyes closed. Then she saw Megan just ahead of Jason, staring at them all with fear on her face. They both fell to the ground at the same time and Chloe looked up just in time to see Zach walking in front of them and talking to himself. Then she felt her eyes close and she was asleep.

7

The City of Loch

Chloe could feel herself lying on velvety-smooth grass so she sat up and looked around. The sight that she saw was so magnificent that she had to blink a few times just to make sure it was real. There were acres upon acres of green grass, rolling hills, tall mountains, and giant trees. To her left were fields of multicolored flowers. The only ones she recognized were tulips and marigolds; the rest were unfamiliar to her.

Far in the distance she could see snow-capped mountains; they reminded her of the cabin they were staying in. They had the same kind of trees growing up around them and running up and down the sloping hills. She could hear birds chirping, crickets singing, and bees buzzing as they collected pollen to make their honey. It was very warm and sunny with no clouds in the sky. She glanced up at the sky and saw the most awe-inspiring thing she could ever have imagined. It looked shiny, and made a sort of reflection that shone on the ground. She thought this was rather odd, but she didn't say anything.

She turned around and looked to her right. Again there were fields of flowers, but not just flowers; there was also golden wheat and tall stalks of corn. She could see the

125

rooftops of little cottages and smoke coming from each chimney. The houses were spaced out quite a bit, but where she was sitting she could see over all the hills, right down to a narrow valley. She heard the whinny of horses and looked around and behind her, and saw, about fifty yards away, a herd of white, black, palomino, and chestnut horses grazing upon the grass.

She leaned back and began watching the horses. A rustle from behind her made her stomach lurch. She spun around but there was nothing there. She heard someone talking, but couldn't see who it was.

"We need to pack up and get going. It's going to be dark soon and we really need to get a good lead on them," a man spoke loudly.

Chloe recognized his voice, but she couldn't remember where she heard it.

"I'll tell Kamali where we are going and he can stay behind and give the others directions on what they need to do," spoke another man.

Chloe also recognized this voice and she remembered hearing the name Kamali somewhere but still couldn't figure out what was going on.

"She's moving, Zachi, she needs to be put back to sleep," the first man said.

Chloe felt a warm hand touch her forehead. She opened her eyes and realized that she had been dreaming about the grass and horses and now she wished it were real, but as it was she could barely see what was going on and who had touched her head. She also had a splitting headache. She looked over and saw to her surprise what seemed to be the green grass from her dream, but there was also another person lying on the grass only a few feet away, and he looked vaguely familiar.

She looked up and saw a strange man carrying a woman, and then another man carrying someone else but she couldn't quite see who it was. She could feel something forcing her eyes to close again and her mind went back to her dream about watching the horses graze on the pasture.

Chloe felt something grab her hand and she shot up as though she had been shocked by live electrical wires. She glanced around and thought that she must be dreaming again because she could see everything that was in her dream, including the horses grazing in the distance, but it seemed different this time. She turned around and saw the man that was lying next to her was now sitting up with a bright red bird, and then Chloe remembered where she heard the name Kamali.

"Who are you? Where's my brother, and Preston, Megan, and Zach?" she said loudly as she began crawling away.

"Chloe, it's me, Jason," he almost whispered. Chloe stood up so she could run away, but she tripped on the hem of her skirt.

I wasn't wearing a skirt, she thought to herself. *What is going on?*

127

She looked down at what she was wearing, and she saw the most beautiful blue velvet dress she had ever seen. It was an empire style with dark blue velvet on top with long sleeves, and the skirt was a lighter blue shear fabric that was laid over the same dark velvet that was on top. She was wearing light blue stockings, and her shoes were also a blue, but were quite different than anything that she could have imagined. They reminded her of a ballet shoe, but without the square toe, and they came up quite a bit further on her ankle. The bottoms were made of some kind of rubber and they were of satin material. She looked at her hands and saw beautifully manicured nails with a glossy polish over them. She reached her hands up to her hair and felt that her long flowing hair was put up into a braid that was tied off with ribbons.

She glanced back over at the man who said he was Jason and saw that he too was wearing some sort of funny fabric. He wore long dark-green pants that looked as if they were some sort of polyester material and a white pullover shirt that was very loose fitted in the sleeves and was untucked and hung a little past his waist. He had on black leather boots, and his hair was the same as her brother Jason's, except a little fuller and darker. His eyes were the same as Jason's as well as his speech, only it was a little deeper and more mature than that of her brother.

"What do you mean you are Jason?" Chloe now asked with some curiosity in her voice. "And why do you have Zach's bird Kamali?"

The stranger looked at her and his face fell into a very deep frown.

"I hoped that I wouldn't be the one to explain what is going on, but I guess I have no choice now," he said a little reluctantly.

Chloe wasn't sure what he meant, but she quietly made herself comfortable and awaited a long explanation of what was going on.

"Chloe, you weren't born in Oklahoma, you were born here in the Kingdom of Mere. When you were two, a kingdom called Nebula was under attack by the Duke of Calidity. They overtook the kingdom and immediately tried to overtake Mere. Mom, Dad, you, and I all escaped, and the wizards of Mere put a spell over the whole kingdom, including the outer regions of Mere and also the other cities under Mirror Lake, including that of the city of Loch and the city of Avis. We were placed in a home in Oklahoma and that's were we were raised. I never knew what happened to the Kingdom of Mere or anywhere else because I was still too young to understand."

Chloe looked at him in disbelief.

"But I'm two years older than you, how could you know anything about this?" she asked.

He looked over at her and then at Kamali. The big bird flew up in the air and produced a hand mirror out of thin air and then brought it back down to the man. He held it up for Chloe to take.

She looked at his face and was about to ask why she needed it when he spoke again.

"Chloe, you aren't sixteen, you are nineteen, soon to be twenty in only two weeks. As for me, I've just turned twenty-four."

Chloe quickly took the mirror from him and held it out to her face. The reflection that she saw was that of a woman no longer a young girl. Her hair was darker than it had been before and her face seemed to be fair and radiant. She reached up and touched her face, skeptical that the mirror was telling her the truth. Her big eyes looked back at her and Chloe couldn't believe it.

"But how—what—I don't understand, I've just turned sixteen only a couple of months ago." She was now frightened beyond belief.

"When we left the Kingdom of Mere, the wizards put a spell on us that would make us younger than we truly ought to be. Your birthday is actually July fourth. The spell made you two years older than I was. As soon as we returned to Mere, the spell was lifted, and we were returned to our actual ages. The land is different as well as the beliefs. They don't have the modern technology that we had in Oklahoma. I knew that we would have to return sometime, but I never thought it would be so soon. This is your home."

He said that last sentence with a little push as if to make her understand, but she still didn't understand what was going on.

"But where is everyone else? What happened to Megan, Zach, and Preston?" she said.

She could feel big tears starting to form in the corner of her eyes, but she didn't want to let Jason see her cry. She turned her head and wiped her tears and then looked back at Jason, waiting for him to answer.

"I don't know. When I woke up the only thing that was here was Kamali. That's when he showed me a mirror and that's when I understood where we were. I have forgotten almost everything because of another spell that was put on us, but as soon as I woke up I could remember only what I have told you, and I know nothing else about this place." He spoke this time looking as if he were lost and afraid.

Chloe sensed the fear in his voice and she too began to feel even more frightened than she was only moments ago.

"How do I know that you aren't just telling me a story? How do I know that you are truly my brother Jason?" she asked, now trying to make herself sound as tough as she could.

"I don't blame you for being scared, Chloe, but you are just going to have to believe me. Wait, I know, if I weren't Jason, how would I know that when you were twelve you still didn't know how to ride a bike, and I knew how before I was six, or how, when you were nine years old, Mom and Dad thought that they were going to have to hold you back a year in school because you were having problems in math class?" Jason laughed as he said these things and he immediately felt better.

He glanced over at Chloe and saw her give him a slight smile.

"All right then, what do we do now?" she asked, getting to her feet.

Jason also got to his feet as Kamali flew into the air and landed on the ground a few feet away from them. Chloe watched him and couldn't remember him being as big as he actually was. She had only seen him from a short distance when Zach had made them such a wonderful meal. Kamali stood about four and half feet tall, and the red feathers were still as bright as she remembered. His claws were extended to be about the size of a volleyball, and his eyes were the brightest green she had ever seen. People had often told Chloe that her green eyes were the brightest they had ever seen, but compared to Kamali's, they were as dim as dead grass.

Kamali glanced at Chloe, then at Jason. He extended his big bright wings and Chloe and Jason were knocked to the ground with the force of the wind. Kamali wrapped his wings around himself and Chloe saw a mist of smoke appear from underneath them. They heard an ear-shattering squawk, and before them stood a man. They looked at him and then at each other, and before they could say another word, Kamali spoke, not in the weird language he had spoken to Zach, but English.

"We must travel north to the city of Loch; there we'll find your guardian, who is to take you to the Castle of Mere. We must move cautiously, however; there are people and beasts here who would love to lay their eyes upon you."

Chloe watched Kamali, noticing that he still had the green eyes, but was a little taller than Jason, who was now at least six feet, and was dressed in a bright red robe with black pants of the same material as Jason's. He was also wearing a white loose-fitted shirt that had a V-neck style but was more masculine than you would find in a women's clothing store. He now had jet black hair that was wavy and thick and wore the same black leather boots that Jason wore, but a sword hung from his hip and the grip on the sword was also black leather and had green stones all through it that matched his eyes. Jason looked at Chloe in utter disbelief at the sight of Kamali and he spoke again.

"Children, I'm a shape-shifter. Zach already explained that to you, so why do you look so frightened?"

"We aren't used to seeing magic. It is still very new to us and it's going to take some time to get used to it," Jason answered. "Why are we going to the Castle of Mere?"

"It's not my job to explain that to you. The King and Queen of Mere are the only ones that can explain it," the man answered.

Chloe wasn't sure that they were supposed to call this man Kamali. Now that it was a man, she thought it to be a strange name for him, but Kamali seemed to hear her thoughts.

133

"Kamali is my magical name. You both may call me Avery. That is what the people here know me as," he said. "We must be moving; we are already a day behind, I'm afraid."

Avery quickly began walking down the hillside towards the road that Chloe had seen in her dream. They walked for a short distance and found themselves at the bottom of a large hill. Chloe hoped that Avery wouldn't expect them to climb all the way over the hill in the clothes that they were wearing. She was already having a hard time climbing over rocks and avoiding mud puddles. She didn't want to get her new dress dirty, as she was rather fond of it already, and blue was her favorite color. Avery climbed a little way up the hill and then he gave a loud whistle.

Jason thought that he had gone deaf; he couldn't hear anything anymore. The breeze went silent; there were no more sounds of birds chirping, or the sound of the small creek in the distance. He looked around at Chloe and guessed that she was thinking the same thing. She was rubbing her ears furiously as if there was something blocking them. He walked over to her and placed his hand on her shoulder.

She looked up at him and tried to speak but no sound was emitted from her mouth. Jason knew now that it was true, he had gone deaf. What was going on? He looked over at Avery in pure shock, but Avery was glancing at something over his shoulder. Jason felt his sister's body jump, and he whipped himself around. He found that he was facing three of the most beautiful horses he had ever seen.

There was a stallion that was as white as newly fallen snow; he had no mud or dirt on him, and his mane was long and straight. He had on a black side saddle inlaid with silver designing and blue jewels on top of a hand-woven black and white saddle blanket that was made out of the same material as Chloe's gown.

There was also a black stallion; it had a light gray mane and tail and was also extremely well groomed. It too was mounted with a saddle, but it was a western saddle instead of a side saddle. The saddle was white instead of black and had green jewels instead of blue, and was also on a white and black handmade saddle blanket.

The third horse Jason recognized as a brown chestnut mare; it too was very well groomed and had a saddle, but this was just an ordinary brown leather western saddle with no jewels or silver. The horses seemed to be awaiting instructions or a treat for their quick arrival.

Avery quickly walked over to the horses and gave them a smooth rub down their neck, and he gave them each an apple that appeared from nowhere. Chloe quickly walked over to the white horse and began stroking its smooth velvety coat. The horse bent down low to the ground and urged Chloe to mount the saddle.

"It's okay, they are tame. They are also our ride to the Castle of Mere," Avery said, already mounting the mare. Jason looked at him in disbelief; he heard him speak. He could also now hear all the sounds of the surrounding areas.

"I can hear!" he said, bewildered.

Avery looked at him and smiled. "You never lost your hearing, my dear boy. All was still because of the magic that these horses bring. Your voices and hearing were still there, you just forgot how to use them for a brief moment. Your bodies are still adjusting to the magic," Avery answered smoothly.

"Whose horses are they?" he asked Avery as he now stroked the black stallion down its long nose.

"These horses belong to no one. They are free animals and come of their own choice. I can only ask for their help, but it is they who choose to give it. The saddles are only figments of our imagination, and once the horses have completed their task, the saddles will disappear and they will run wild again." Avery spoke with the tone of someone annoyed by these simple questions.

Chloe recognized his tone almost immediately, and so it seemed did Jason. His mouth quickly shut and the questions on his mind were left for a later time. He quickly mounted his horse and beckoned it to follow Avery, who was already starting up the hill on his chestnut mare.

The hill seemed to never end, and the horses that they were riding seemed to be getting tired before they were halfway up. Chloe glanced around and saw that a dark cloud was beginning to form in the eastern sky.

"Avery, should we be worried about that storm?" she asked, never removing her eyes from the dark cloud.

Avery quickly glanced toward the horizon and stopped where he was.

136

"The storm is going to bring a lot of rain and wind, but I wouldn't worry too much, we will be at a shelter soon enough," he said. "But we need to move quickly so we aren't seen or we will have problems on our way to the castle."

Chloe could barely hear his last words as the thunder rumbled in the distance. She looked back at Avery and Jason and they were already moving faster up the hill than they were before. Chloe thought for a moment that the horses understood the danger of the rain cloud, because they were no longer acting as if they were tired, but were moving at such a pace that she could only just hold on. She found that there was no need to use the reins, for the horse knew exactly where it was going. So she just gripped tightly to the leaping head and kept an eye on the two men in front of her.

After a hard ride to the top of the hill they were able to see the other side. Jason and Chloe gasped as they saw a large city in the distance.

"Where are we?" Chloe asked politely.

"That is the city of Loch. That is where we will find your next guardian, who will continue with you until the Artesian Basin, which is quite a long ride across the Barren Land. It is there where you will get a new guardian. You can never remain with the same guardian for long, it's too dangerous. By switching guardians often we hope to confuse the Duke of Calidity so he can't form a deal with any of your guardians to turn you over to him. That would make him more powerful than all the wizards of Mere. You must always stay close to your guardian. If you feel that they have

137

misled you in any way, you need to let your stallions know. They will bring you safely to me, do you understand?" Avery spoke with a stern voice and kept his eyes on the oncoming storm. "I said, do you understand?"

"Yes sir, but I'm still confused as to why we are being guarded by the wizards of Mere. Why can't you explain this to us?" Jason asked, also watching the oncoming storm.

Avery did not answer but urged his mare to continue across the plateau toward the city of Loch. Irritated by the rude gesture, Jason followed bitterly and Chloe was left to tail behind the group. She didn't mind, however; it was really quite peaceful to ride on such an elegant animal and the scenery was absolutely beautiful. She couldn't imagine anything as beautiful as this strange land that they found themselves in. She was still a little curious about the difference in the sky here, though. This one seemed to change all the time, like a ripple in the water. It started out smooth, but then suddenly it's different somehow. She couldn't explain what it looked like and she definitely didn't understand anything that was happening to them. She assumed it was all a dream and she would soon wake up sprawled on the ground of the cave with Preston and her other friends there with her. But this dream felt so real.

Could we really be in a strange land with a bird that turned into a man for a guide?

While she was pondering this, her stallion reared up on its hind legs and came down hard. It bolted across the

138

ground toward the other two horses. Chloe was so caught off guard by its quick departure that she was nearly knocked off her horse and was only saved by having her leg arched around the leaping head of the saddle. It seemed to balance her so she didn't fall to one side. She quickly glanced back and saw that the storm was closing in faster than it had been earlier.

All three horses were now galloping across the plateau as fast as they could to keep ahead of the storm. Avery kept looking back at the two children to make sure that they were okay. When he finally opened his mouth to speak Chloe knew that it would be in that strange language neither she nor Jason could understand, but this time it wasn't different at all, but in pure unadulterated English.

"Quickly!"

As soon as he spoke the three horses seemed to quicken their strides, and soon they were only a short distance from the gates of Loch. A strong wind was at their back now and Chloe was having difficulty staying on top of her horse. It was galloping so fast that the rest of the land seemed to be only a blur. She had no idea that horses could run this fast. Avery shouted at the gatekeeper to open the gate and soon they shot across the threshold of the gate and were inside the city of Loch.

The horses slowed down and began to walk slowly up the road, their breathing deep and quick. Avery dismounted his mare when they arrived at a building called Loch Stables. He was greeted almost immediately by a young boy wearing a pair of long black pants, a black shirt, and leather boots. His hair was a dark black and covered with dirt and straw.

"Avery, I didn't know you were coming to the city," said the boy.

Jason and Chloe dismounted their stallions. Chloe glanced around and saw that the storm was just settling over the city.

"I'm here on business, Daimhin, I need you to give these horses the best you have. We will be staying up the street and will be returning in the morning to collect them," Avery said, handing the reins to the boy.

Chloe and Jason did the same.

"That's no problem at all, sir. Who are your friends?" Daimhin asked, staring with wide eyes at Chloe.

"These are good friends of mine from the city of Mere. We are returning from a long journey up north. We'll see you tomorrow, Daimhin, and remember, only the best for our horses."

Avery handed the boy a handful of bronze coins and then quickly turned on his heel and started walking toward the center of the city.

Chloe glanced around and couldn't believe what she saw. It was like stepping into Camelot. There were old wood houses with wood-burning chimneys, and a blacksmith shop with a fire forge that had horseshoes and swords all over the walls. There were no cars or buses, only carriages pulled by horses; and the street lamps were lit by fire, not electricity. The men were dressed in trousers and fine shirts with swords sheathed on their sides and the ladies were dressed in fine satin gowns with their hair curled and ribbons hanging all over it.

There were guards in armor holding swords and bows and arrows. The streets were cobblestone and dirt, and right in the very center of the city was a castle. Chloe had never seen a castle before and she was taken aback by its great beauty. The walls were high smooth stone and had long drapes of purple and black material with the same symbol on them as was on the horses' saddles. Chloe made it out to be two silver swords overlapping each other with a gold band running around in a circular motion all the way up and down both swords. She wasn't sure what this meant but thought it to be very elegant.

The castle was surrounded by a wide dark moat and had long vines extending around the walls. The flowers were in full bloom all around the edge of the water. There was a drawbridge lying casually across the moat and a high tower that reminded Chloe of the story of Sleeping Beauty. She looked over her shoulder at Jason and saw that he too was in awe of the amazing grandeur of the castle.

She looked back over her other shoulder and saw Avery looking to the left of the castle. She let her eyes fall upon a beautiful white two-story Victorian-style house with a wrap-around porch and black shutters. Avery turned toward the house, so they both followed him down the road. They reached the front gate and Chloe realized that all the grass was dead and there were weeds and wild bushes growing all

141

around the house. The paint was starting to peel and the shutters that looked so neat from a distance were falling off their hinges. Avery opened the noisy gate and the threesome climbed the rickety stairs that lead to the front door just as it started to rain.

They hurried up the steps and onto the front porch, relieved at the shelter from the storm. Avery slowly walked over toward the front door and gave a quick knock and then backed away quickly and waited.

After a few moments they could hear loud footsteps running for the front door.

"Who calls at this hour?" came a man's voice from inside the house.

"Avery, Wizard Guardian, and the two children of the city of Mere," Avery answered without the slightest flaw in his voice.

The door slowly began to open and it let out loud groan as if it weren't ever to be opened and then came to a stop. At the front of the door stood a short, fat balding man wearing a pair of blue jeans and a white T-shirt. He had bright blue eyes, and the little hair that was left on his head was light brown. He had a sword sheathed to his side and another smaller dagger down near his leather riding boots. Chloe thought his attire quite strange for the location they were in, but didn't even have a moment to ask.

As soon as the stranger saw Jason and Chloe his appearance seemed to change almost immediately. His blue jeans and shirt turned to the same style of clothing that was appropriate for the Kingdom of Mere. To Chloe and Jason's disbelief the house began to change as well. Where there were weeds and burnt grass, there was now a beautiful full lawn with blooming flowers. White and red roses as well as azaleas were planted under each window. Blue lilies were in full bloom around the large trees that appeared from nowhere. The house became a bright white and the shutters fixed themselves and were clean. The stairs were no longer rickety but sturdy and looked almost new.

"Avery, my old friend, I was getting worried that you had gotten lost," the old man said. "That was the reason for the disastrous state of my house only a moment ago."

"Aden, you are to keep a low profile and not be seen. What have you done? You have caused too much attention upon this house. What if he saw the display that you just caused?" Avery said angrily. He pushed the man out of the way and pulled Chloe and Jason inside the front door.

Aden quickly shut the door and turned to stare at the two children.

"It's been a long time, hasn't it? The last time I saw either of you, you were only little tykes," he said.

Avery quickly shot him a blank stare.

"We need some food, Aden, please show us to the dining room," said Avery with a little bit of agitation in his voice.

Aden must have sensed his bad temper because he quickly moved past Chloe and Jason and opened a large oak door off to the right of the entryway where they were standing.

The dining room was large and bright. There was a large maple wood table with seating for at least ten people but which could have easily fit more. The table was set with some of the finest silver either of them had ever seen. Chloe slowly walked over to the side of the table and pulled out a large red-cushioned chair and reached for the silver fork lying on the side of the plate. When she picked it up, it felt warm to the touch and very smooth. The design on the end of it was the same symbol that was on the banners on the castle, and the saddle that she had been riding on earlier. She quickly put it back down and turned to see what her brother was doing. Jason had also picked up a piece of the silver and noticed the same design on all of the plates, as well as the napkins and table cloth.

"What is this symbol?" he asked Avery, who had just made himself comfortable at the head of the large table.

"It is the seal of the King. It means 'Combined Strength Will Conquer All.'"

"So is it custom for the symbol to be perched on all silver and other things in the kingdom?" Chloe asked, now sitting to the right of Avery.

"My dear, we are currently located in the dining room of the Castle of Loch. What you saw outside was a magical illusion that your mind thought it saw. When we walked into the house, or the front doors of the castle, the illusion was faltered and its true identity was revealed, but the damage

144

had already been done on your mind telling you that this was only a simple house. If you walk to the window you will see that we have walked across the drawbridge and right into the Castle of Loch," Avery answered without the slightest hesitation. He didn't look at Chloe or Jason, but stared instead out the window that was perched a few feet to the left of the table.

Chloe and Jason jumped out of their chairs and ran toward the window. What they saw was absolutely amazing. Avery was right; down about two hundred feet was the outer wall of the castle that the drawbridge was now suspended on, and over that they could just see the outer banks of the moat. When they turned around to look at Avery, the castle itself was there. They weren't inside a wood wall room, but now a wall of rock surrounded them. The table was large and thick and even more elegant than it was only moments ago. They were standing on a red rug that extended itself under the table and a smaller portion was at the large oak doors they came through earlier. The table was still set the same way and the silver and fluted glasses still stayed where they were.

Chloe felt herself getting light-headed again and Avery quickly grabbed her arms and guided her toward her chair. She sat down quickly and glanced around again. She then let her eyes fall on her brother. He too was as white as a sheet and looked as if he were going to be ill.

"Magic is hard to understand at first, but once you get used to it, you can almost tell it's not real," Avery said with a wink and a smile.

145

"Oh, there you are, Aden. This is Chloe and Jason, and this, children, is your next guardian, Aden. He is very wise and is an earth-shifter. He can make the illusions that you have seen today. These illusions play tricks not only on your mind, but the minds of any who look upon it," Avery said now, shaking hands with Aden as if they hadn't seen him a moment ago.

Chloe tried to stand to meet her new guardian but her legs felt weak and she fell back into the chair and just said, "It's nice to meet you sir."

Aden looked taken aback by her words and looked at Avery with a concern on his face.

"These children are exhausted, they need some rest immediately," Aden said, clapping his hands three times as loud as he could.

"They must eat first. I'm afraid they haven't eaten since they were with Zachi in the Cave of Light," Avery said, looking at Aden, but not a wince of emotion was on his face.

Just as Avery finished his words, three tall men with dark hair and black eyes came hurrying through a side door wearing long black robes, green pants, and white satin shirts. They bowed low to the ground at the sight of the three travelers.

"We need some food for our guests and three guest rooms need to be made up right away," Aden said with authority.

146

"Yes, your grace," came the reply of the three men in unison, and they disappeared through another small door at the back wall.

Before Chloe and Jason had time to think, the great oak doors opened and three different men with magenta robes came in carrying three large trays of food, and set them in front of them. Chloe looked in awe at a large plate of roast duck, with boiled potatoes and ripe steaming corn still on the cob. Jason and Avery had the same dish. Their glasses were quickly filled with a sparkling clear liquid of some sort. They were also being served fresh hot bread that seemed to have come straight from the oven.

Chloe quickly picked up her drink and took a large gulp. It was the most delicious thing that she had ever tasted. It was chilled as if it had come directly from the icebox and was smooth and sweet at the same time. It tasted like the apple cider her mother made at Christmas time, but instead of apple it was strawberry or something like it. They quickly finished eating, and after their plates were swept away without hesitation, a smaller plate was placed before them. The door in the back of the room opened again and the same three men in magenta entered holding three large chunks of chocolate pie dashed with whipped cream. They quickly finished their meal then sat back, looking full and tired.

"Aw...I think you outdid yourself, my dear Aden," Avery said as he patted his stomach and gave a loud sigh.

"Are you the owner of this castle?" Jason asked as he leaned back in his chair and gave a loud sigh of contentment.

147

"No, my young lad, this is the home of the Duchess of Loch. She wanted to be here for your arrival, but was needed elsewhere," he responded quickly.

Jason and Chloe looked at each other and Chloe smiled widely. She was in the house of a royal person. She couldn't believe it.

Aden was watching her intently.

"If you have no more questions for now, I think it's time we took you up to your rooms."

One of the men in the magenta robes quickly clambered to the back of Chloe's chair and helped her back it away from the table. He stuck his arm out for her and, taking it without hesitation, she stood and followed Aden out the oak doors. Jason and Avery were quick to pursue and soon they came to a large staircase made entirely of polished stone and iron. They climbed the steps and turned down a large hallway full of gaslit torches and men in arms.

They stopped a few feet into the hall and a short, skinny woman about the same age as Chloe opened the door, revealing a large room with polished stone floors and a four-poster bed with bright blue linens. A cozy fire was lit in the fireplace in the corner of the room. There was a large window that had been covered by even larger drapes, and a nightgown made of satin lay neatly folded on the end of the bed.

"I hope this room will be suitable, my dear, it's the finest room in the castle," Aden said, leading her inside. "This is Emelia. She will be your attendant during your stay.

148

Let her know if you need anything. Jason and Avery will be
staying in the rooms across from yours, and mine is to the
left. Don't hesitate to ask for anything. If I can get it to you, I
will."

Before Chloe could answer he showed himself out the
door and she spotted Jason's anxious face at the door before
it was shut with a loud clunk.

"Your bathroom is to your right, miss, and there's a
bell on the stand if you need any assistance. Your nightgown
is right here on the bed and I've taken the liberty of placing a
warming plate under your covers. Castles are a bit drafty and
you can get quite cold."

"Thank you, Emelia, I will call if I need you," Chloe
said, but she felt a little foolish. She didn't need all of this
attention. All she needed was a good night's sleep and a
couple of aspirin for that splitting headache she still had.
Emelia gave her a curtsey and removed herself from the
room. Chloe quickly got undressed and into her nightgown
and climbed into her large, overstuffed bed. She found it very
warm and almost instantly fell asleep.

8

Preston's Story

Preston reached up and grabbed the top of his head. For some reason he had the worst headache that he had ever had in his life. His arms were asleep as were his legs, and he felt as if he were hanging upside down. He opened his eyes and saw the ground a few feet in front of him. He *was* upside down, and he was being carried by someone who was running as fast as he could. He gave a loud groan and the person stopped and flung him back over his shoulder and laid him softly on the ground. It was dark, but Preston found himself staring at a tall man with brown hair and green eyes. He wore a long green robe with a white shirt that was untucked and hanging past his waist. The man had a long thin sword sheathed at his side and was smiling at him.

"What's going on?" Preston asked, "Who are you?"

Preston felt the pain in his head sear. He turned over and started pushing on the sides of his head, trying to make the pain subside.

"My name is Cane, I'm a Wizard guardian. I'll be taking you to the city of Rill. How's your head?"

"It's sore, what happened? And what do you mean you are taking me to the city of Rill? That's only a fairytale. My father told me stories of the Kingdom of Mere when I was a kid and…" Hs voice suddenly trailed off. "It can't be true. It's just a story. If they are true, then that would make me the Prince of Nebula. My father used to make up stories and he would always make me the Prince of his made-up kingdom. I never expected them to be true. How is this possible? There's no such place."

Preston's head spun as he listened to his own voice say that he was a prince.

What a joke, he thought, *there's no way I can be royalty.*

"Yes, my Prince, the stories are true. You are indeed the Prince of Nebula, and in grave danger. If you can run, we need to keep moving," Cane said, now quickly standing.

For the first time Preston saw another man standing behind Cane holding a woman in his arms. He was tall with black hair, and he was also wearing a long robe, but it was black with red swords imprinted on it with gold inlaid at the seams. He had on black leather boots and also had a thin sword sheathed at his hip. He wore a white shirt that clinked when he moved and very rough-looking black pants.

"Who are you? What is wrong with that woman? Is she sick?" Preston asked. He tried to stand but his head ached so bad he just fell back on the soft grass.

The man quickly lowered the woman onto the ground next to Preston and urged Cane to sit down on the grass. With some reluctance, Cane listened and planted himself down on the grass next to Preston. Preston looked at the woman and gasped; it was Megan, Zach's sister, but she was older. She looked to be about twenty or so with red hair, now with silver streaks all through it. She was wearing an elegant green velvet dress and black lace-up boots. Her hair was curled and pulled back halfway with ribbons.

"What have you done to her?" He spoke now with fear, but tried to hide it.

"My Prince, it is I, Zach, or as they know me here in Mere, Zachi. I'm one of the gatekeepers, and the High Wizard of this kingdom as well as your own. The woman at your side is indeed Megan, your sister and Princess of Nebula, but her royal name is Hanna and yours is Paden. For safety, however, we will continue to call you Megan and Preston. You know the story, Sire, why do you act so confused? From what I'm told, your father has told you this story many times." Zach spoke with ease, as if he had practiced saying this many times before.

Preston was shocked.

How is this person Zach? And how does he know my father? This can't be true, I don't have a sister, why is he telling me this? Preston thought silently.

"My father told me a story, but in the story I had no…" Preston thought quickly and remembered the little baby at the beginning of the story. "But I thought that she was your sister. Wait, where's Chloe and Jason, and your bird Kamali?"

Preston's head was now so sore that he thought it was going to explode, but he continued to wait for Zachi to answer his questions.

"Indeed, she was my sister in the other world as a disguise, as for her appearance, but she was and still is your sister. When you were a little boy, the Duke of Calidity caused war to come between the Kingdom of Nebula and we had to hide you and your parents in another world where Jacan wouldn't seek you. All the wizards were called to aid in the battle but the kingdom was overtaken by creatures that Jacan summoned from another world. We transformed your features and made you and your parents younger. We put you in a cabin as close as we could get you to the Gates of Mere. If we needed to get you there, it would only take a short time. You and your sister Megan were separated for safety and she was placed with me and two other guardian wizards whom we could trust to raise her until it was time to bring you both together. Well, the time came, and Jacan found out where she was and sent people to find her. We had to move quickly and get her safe from there. That's when we showed up at the other cabin. It was built by us as a safe haven and only to be used for emergencies. Jacan knew that we were hiding you and Megan, as well as the King and Queen, so he sent storms all the time to every gateway to the Kingdom of Mere. When we went into the boat on the lake and you found us, we had been seen by spies that we didn't know were there and they immediately told Jacan our location. He tried several times to destroy you and your sister, but without success."

"So you're telling me that Megan, or…Hanna, is my sister and we are both a Prince and Princess, and 'our' parents are the King and Queen of Nebula? Why was I never informed of my sister before? Surely my mom and dad wanted to know if their daughter was okay?" Preston was shocked at this news and no matter how much he tried to hide the shock in his voice, it came through and gave him away.

Zachi sensed his trouble and lowered his head. He thought carefully before he answered the question, giving Preston time to adjust to his new realty.

"We had to keep her identity hidden to protect both of you. It was for the safety of everyone in Mere as well as Nebula." Zachi spoke with such grace that it was becoming hard to believe.

"But where are Chloe and Jason? Why aren't they here in Mere with us?" Preston asked, still holding his head trying to soothe the pain.

"I'm afraid that when we came through the gateway we were separated from them. Kamali was with them, and one can only hope that they are safe," he said. "Now, how is your head feeling?"

"We left them behind? How could you do that? Do they know anything about Mere or the stories? What if they are in danger? We have to go back for them, immediately!" Preston shouted.

Zachi glanced at Preston and a wide smile formed on his face. He looked over at Cane and he too formed a fierce smile.

Preston became so angry at Zachi that he could feel the blood start to rush to his face. He knew that his cheeks had turned bright red and that he was being very forceful with two men that he didn't know, except for a little about Zachi from the lake. He waited for an answer, growing impatient when the two men did not answer him right away.

At last Zachi spoke. "You will make a fine King once you're trained a little. Your temper suits you. But I ask you again, how is your head?"

Preston's mouth dropped. He never thought that he was the successor to the crown. Of course he always wanted to be the Prince, but it never clicked that he would be the next King.

"It feels as if a bomb exploded inside my head, but that's not what matters, we must go back for them." Preston spoke with more force than he did before so to make them understand that he meant business.

Zachi frowned, raised his hands in the air, and spoke loudly.

"Appear!"

At these words a mirror became clear in his hands and he handed it to Preston.

"You must look in the mirror and see yourself as what you truly are. It will subdue your headache almost completely. You might still have a slight ache, but with some rest it will go away fully."

Preston cautiously held the mirror in his hands and turned it to reveal his own reflection. He recognized his eyes, but the rest of his face was almost completely different. He now had dark brown hair that was wavy and thick. He had dark tan lines around his face and when he looked down and

155

saw his clothes for the first time since he awoke he noticed that he was wearing the same kind of pants that Zachi was wearing, except his were blue. He was also wearing a white shirt in the V-neck style and it had two swords with gold ribbon etched around them with fine embroidery on the right sleeve, and was untucked. He felt like a completely different person.

His headache was nearly gone as he lowered the mirror, but he could still feel it throb occasionally.

"What about the others? You still haven't answered my question about them. And how old am I now?" Preston asked, now trying to be more prince-like with his speech.

"I'm afraid we can't return to the gateway, we must continue toward the castle. Kamali will take great care of your friends. And you have recently turned twenty-two years old," Zachi said, placing his long thin fingers on his shoulder and staring at him in the eye with a grin of excitement.

Preston grimaced at the thought of being twenty-two but knew that Zachi would know if anyone did. Preston tried, but he couldn't get Zachi or Cane to agree to take him back to get Chloe and Jason. He finally gave up, realizing that there was nothing to be done about it now. He could not argue with Zachi about returning to the gateway and decided that maybe he was right. Kamali would take good care of Chloe and Jason; at least he hoped. As Preston began to think about more of his father's story, he realized for the first time that the mirror that Zachi handed him came by English and

not that weird language he heard in the cave and he wasn't
sure how that happened.

"Why did you summon that mirror in English, when
you spoke a different language in the cave?"

Zachi smiled. "My boy, your appearance isn't the
only thing that changed when you entered the Kingdom of
Mere. The language you heard me speaking to Kamali was
the language of Mere, and it's the same language you now
speak. That is why you understand it."

Preston's mouth fell. How could he be speaking a
different language and not know it? He tried to speak to deny
this, but found that he had nothing to say, so he sat pondering
over it for a moment.

At his last thought he heard Megan start to stir. He
crouched down and touched her on the forehead.

"She's extremely warm; I think she has a fever,"
Preston said, now fearful.

"Yes, I'm aware of her condition. Her body isn't
taking to the change as quickly as yours. We need to get her
to Aurora, the Sorceress of Rill. She is the city's Sorceress
and leader. She has the power to help her," Zachi said, now
hoisting Megan back into his arms.

"No, I will carry her She is my sister and my
responsibility; you lead the way and we will follow."

Preston quickly lifted Megan from Zachi's arms and
looked around for the path that they were to take. All he saw
around him was a river to the north and hills and mountains
to the south. The eastern horizon was dark with a forest of

trees, and the west a blank canvas of sand.

"Which way are we to go?" he asked.

Cane spoke for the first time since stopping. "We must travel toward the Todswan River and then take boats the city of Rill."

Without another word Preston followed Zachi toward the river with Cane close behind. Once they reached the river, Preston noticed a long, sleek boat with oars that seemed to extend themselves farther than any he had ever seen. Zachi was already boarding the boat and held out his arms toward Preston so that he could take Megan from him. Preston stood staring for a minute then reluctantly handed Megan to him. Zachi laid her softly on the bottom of the boat and then covered her with a blanket that he made appear from nowhere. Preston stepped in to join them and felt Cane slip the boat into the river and then hop in behind them. Preston reached for two of the oars but Zachi quickly snatched them from him.

"You are the Prince of Nebula, and I will not be made a fool of."

Preston looked at him quizzically and then hunched back on the wooden seat and folded his arms and watched as the river went swiftly by. He reached down and softly touched Megan's forehead. A frown formed on his face as the heat from her head touched his hand. Preston was extremely worried about her. He knew that his parents would never forgive him if anything happened to his sister now that they had been reunited. He tucked the blankets around her more tightly and then settled down for the journey.

The sun was starting to peek from the horizon, giving the land a golden hue, and Preston got a good look for the first time at what surrounded him. What he had seen before were only silhouettes of what was truly hidden amongst the dark. The mountains were similar to the ones at the cabin by the lake and the hills were a green grassy meadow with full blooming flowers. He had never seen such beauty in a landscape and was surprised at the river as well. It was as clear as Mirror Lake and you could also see through to the bottom. There were fish in the water that were many bright colors and strange designs. He could have sworn that he saw a fish with the legs of a frog, but quickly convinced himself that it was just a frog. However, when he looked again there was not only one, but a few dozen swimming along with the boat.

"What are those?" he asked, still awestruck by their strange appearance.

Zachi stopped rowing and looked over the edge of their boat.

"They are the keepers of the river as well as the guardians of Rill. They are called the Todswan. They resemble a trout in the world above, except they have green scaly legs with webbed feet to swim with. They can be in either the water or on dry land for several hours, but need both water and land to survive. They can also take the form of man if need be."

"What do you mean the world above?" Preston asked with curiosity.

"My young prince, do you not remember the stories at all?" Zachi looked at Preston with a tired expression but was concerned with his lack of knowledge of Mere. "We are located many miles below Mirror Lake. If you look at the sky, you will notice that it has a shimmering effect, almost as if it were a ripple of water."

Preston looked toward the sky and saw that it was indeed different than he had thought. It was shiny and seemed to wave as a slight breeze went by. It looked like water that had been dyed to match the blue of a real sky with a hint of a hazy glow.

"You mean to tell me that there really is a city under the water? That part of the story is true also?"

"Indeed, when we entered the cave and crossed the Hidden Path, we started traveling down," said Zachi. "No one noticed because everyone was still a little frightened. We are currently located just to the west of the cabin you grew up in. Every time the sun shines on the lake and something is reflected on it, it becomes real here. Those mountains, for instance, they are identical to the ones above. When the reflection leaves the lake, the image disappears as well, but those mountains have stayed and no one knows the reason why. They never disappear. I believe that when the reflection of the mountains leaves, their image is still there, but no mountain. No one that I know of has ever traveled to the

mountains and returned, so we don't know the truth." Zachi
now smiled at Preston.

"What about the hills and flowers and this river?
They aren't part of the 'world above,' as you call it," Preston
said spitefully.

Zachi looked at him in the eyes and smiled widely, as
if what he asked were humorous. Preston found it rather
irritating. He didn't like the feeling of being mocked.

Zachi spoke this time with finality in his voice.

"We have our own land, we just get new things when
the seasons change. For example, our weather is the same as
it was, and is, at the cabin. If it snows there, it will snow here
because it appears on the lake. We really need to be
extremely quiet around this area. The Todswan are getting
restless and if we agitate them any longer, I'm afraid they'll
destroy the boat and we won't be able to get into the city of
Rill on foot."

Preston was still confused but decided to keep his
questioning for a later time. He wanted to absorb the news
that he just heard and keep Megan's chances of help open.

After what felt like hours in the boat, Preston spotted
a tall wall in the distance that extended itself across the river
and then rounded out along the outer banks of the water.

"Is that where we are headed?" he asked.

"Yes, that's the Gateway to Rill, but there are things
that must be done in order to gain access to the city," Cane
said, not removing his gaze from the wall.

"What," Preston asked, "does that mean?"

161

"It means that we can't just knock on the door to gain entrance into the city. The gatekeepers change what they make you do every time someone wants to enter their city. The last time I came to Rill, I had to sing a song about a goldfish. I'll tell you it was the most difficult thing I've ever had to do. I had never heard the song before so I had to listen to the fish in the river and they gave me the lyrics to the song as well as the tune. I wouldn't be surprised if it were similar to that," said Zachi quietly so not to disturb the Todswan below.

Preston began to feel extremely nervous. *What on earth would the gatekeepers demand them to do? Surely they would see that Megan isn't well and she needs assistance.*

Preston kept trying to figure this out as they slowly approached the gate. It was different than he thought; it was made of wood, but it had many different shapes and designs of fish, mermaids, octopi, and other sea creatures that were formed of wrought iron. The gate itself seemed extremely well built and strong. Preston looked at his surroundings and saw that to each side of the river on the banks were beautiful blue irises and yellow daffodils, white daisies, and many other types of flowers all planted to bloom a form of a mermaid. He looked around, hoping to see the gatekeeper so they would have their test and gain access to this weird city, but saw no sign of anyone. He was about to ask Cane and Zachi what to do next when a large rope came whirling out of the water and held the boat in place. The rope twisted itself around their legs and pulled their arms down to their sides and pinned them there. Zachi and Cane sat very still but Preston wasn't going to give in so easily. He struggled against the ropes and tried to get them off his legs but to no avail.

"Be still, Preston, it's only a precaution in these dark and troubled times," Cane said impatiently. "They are only testing our loyalty to their leader, Aurora. The more you struggle the longer we'll have to sit here tied up like prisoners."

Preston wasn't sure what to do. Finally, he let himself be wrapped up in the rope until the only part left untouched was his upper shoulders, neck, and head. Even Megan, who still lay unconscious, had been wrapped in rope. Minutes passed without any sign of their attackers. Finally the water seemed to ripple of its own accord and four of the strangest creatures Preston had ever laid eyes on came up out of the water and sat on the edge of the boat. It was the Todswan, only they were much larger than Preston thought and they indeed looked like fish in the water. Out of the water, they looked like some strange little men. They were small like dwarves, with long bushy hair that was tied back with seaweed, very dark skin, and pale blue eyes. Their hands and feet were webbed and they had no fingernails or toenails that Preston could see. They had long jagged teeth that looked as if they were filed that way and large rippling muscles all up and down their bodies. They also held in their hands spears made of some kind of lightweight rock. Preston thought that they were extremely frightening, but Zachi and Cane made

163

no change of expression at the newcomers.

"What are thou doing at the gates of Rill?" the largest Todswan said, lowering his spear down at their tied bodies.

"We have come to seek the Sorceress of Rill. We are in need of her healing powers," Zachi said, still not showing any emotion and glancing toward the bottom of the boat at Megan.

"Ah, the lady seems a bit distressed. What's happened to her?" he asked, not moving his spear from where it rested against Cane's shoulder.

"The lady is not your concern, Sir Donaghy of Rill," Zachi said dangerously. "She is only the concern of Lady Aurora and the three whom you have imprisoned."

Donaghy seemed not taken aback by Zachi knowing his name, but more irritated at how he had dismissed his question.

"How dare thee speak to me in that matter, Zachi, you know the law in which we live in Rill. 'The arrogant man may never enter into the friends' lair, but he who is brave and true, but need to ask,'" Donaghy said heatedly as he pushed the spear so close to Cane's neck that blood started to drip from the sharpened point.

"Donaghy, release us and give us your test," Zachi said, sighing. "If we answer it correctly you will know we are all true friends of Rill."

"So be it!" Donaghy bellowed. "If your young friend here, whom I don't know and hasn't spoken, can answer our

164

riddle, you will be allowed into the city. Art thou ready, young lad?"

Preston felt his face grow red with fear. He wasn't very good with riddles and he hadn't expected them to ask him to do anything. He wasn't sure that he was going to be able to answer it, but he knew that Megan would be grateful for what he had done, so with all the energy he could find he pulled himself up straight and looked Donaghy in the face.

"I'm ready if you are."

Donaghy glared at Preston and then turned and dove into the water, with his comrades right behind him. He saw them at the front of the boat huddled around Donaghy and speaking quietly. Preston knew they were trying to come up with a great riddle that would be nigh impossible to answer, but he would give it his best shot. He looked at Cane and Zachi and saw their troubled expressions. He shook his head to try to get them to understand that he could do it.

"Think hard, young master, if you answer incorrectly, we won't be able to save your sister," Cane said nervously.

"I'll do my best," was all that Preston could muster.

He was nervous and scared that he would get it incorrect. Time crept by as they waited for their captors to return with their riddle; finally, Donaghy swam to the side of the boat and came to Preston's side.

"If you solve our riddle, you shall all gain access to Rill, but, if you get it wrong, you are to leave this gate and never return. Is that clear?"

165

Preston looked over at Cane and Zachi and they nodded their heads in agreement.

"Deal, but I need to be untied so I can think clearly," Preston said bravely.

With a wave of his arms Donaghy removed the ropes that bound Preston and then began to speak.

> *"I live in dark and troubled waters;*
> *I come and go at will;*
> *People fear my great defenses;*
> *They can harm or even kill.*
> *I have not one but many heads*
> *And just as many hearts;*
> *I am not small but very large;*
> *Comprised of many parts*
> *Some can see me as their friend;*
> *And others as their foe;*
> *Take a guess at who I am;*
> *Or else you'll never know."*

Preston was dumbfounded at the riddle.

What has a lot of heads and hearts and lives in the water? He had to think about this hard and long so not to get it wrong.

Dark and troubled waters, Preston thought, *that must mean that it's dangerous to be around. If it comes and goes at will then it must not have predators. I know that it's large but what can it be, what has a lot of heads? What if the heads weren't its heads and the hearts weren't this "thing" either. That would mean it carries a lot of people or something else that's alive. It has parts, but does that mean body parts or mechanical parts?*

Preston glanced over at Zachi and Cane and saw them trying to urge him to get the right answer. He knew that they knew what it was just by the look on their faces, but he wasn't so sure. After about a half an hour of pondering over the riddle the boat started to move up and down as the wind picked up and pushed the water around. The boat's rocking gave Preston a great idea.

What if, he thought, *the "thing" wasn't actually alive, what if it's a boat, or...I've got it!*

"I know the answer, but I want to ask you a question first," he said.

Donaghy looked puzzled.

"Ask your question, boy, but be careful not to make it your answer."

"How many chances do I get to answer the question?" Preston asked, careful not to say more than he needed.

Donaghy looked surprised at his question and looked at his fellow warriors and laughed until the tears were flowing down his cheeks.

"You only have one chance and one answer to get it right." Donaghy chuckled.

"Okay then, at first I thought of a school of fish, but after thinking about it I knew that wasn't the answer and I pushed my mind to the limits trying to read your thoughts, and I've come up with the only other possible answer, a submarine!" Preston said proudly at his accomplishment.

Donaghy's face dropped and his mouth was left wide open. He didn't believe it, the young boy, who obviously had no magical talent, figured out their best riddle when no one had ever figured it out before.

"I'm impressed, young lad; I've given that riddle out to many people both wizard and other species and no one has come up with that answer. Everyone suspected it was a school of fish and that's what they said, but you thought better and discovered the truth. Well done, you have gained access to the city of Rill as well as gained our friendship and trust." Donaghy bowed his head low toward the water and then raised it with a grin.

"I thank you for your friendship," Preston said, trying to sound intimidating, "but I'm afraid that we really must be getting to the sorceress. Can you please open the gates and allow us to pass? Oh and please release my friends from your ropes."

Donaghy looked pleased with Preston and immediately the ropes were released from Zachi and Cane. One of the other warriors took his spear and pushed the back of the boat to get it a little closer to the gate, but just as his spear touched the boat a large slab of glass come out of the boat and encased all four of the travelers inside. The oars extended out to the rear and welded together and made what looked like a fin that you would see on a fish. The weight of the glass began sinking the boat. Preston didn't know what to do. He thought he had got the correct answer, but they were still going to drown them all, and it was his fault. He quickly shot a glance at Zachi and saw that he was just as relaxed as ever. His legs were crossed and his arms folded and he leaned back against the side of the glass as if it were some sort of ride.

"What are you doing? We have to get out of here! We are all going to die!" Preston cried.

"Peace, Sire, we are being granted access to the city of Rill. It's under the water, and our little boat has transformed into a mini-submarine so to take us there. The answers to the tests that they give are always the way you are granted access, and the answer to your riddle was a submarine," Zachi said. "Oh, and I too must also congratulate you on your answer, for I too suspected the answer to be a school of fish." Zachi smiled as he said this and then closed his eyes and seemed to drift off to sleep.

Cane looked at Preston and he too gave a smile and a nod of appreciation.

"Make yourself comfortable, it will be about an hour before we reach the city," he said, also closing his eyes.

Preston was surprised at their reactions but soon he forgot about his worries. The water started to encompass the boat and soon they were completely submerged. He could see the world like a fish, and it was even more interesting than he had ever suspected. He saw everything, including the Todswan and other types of fish and water creatures. Unable to keep his eyes open, he too closed them, and was quickly engulfed in a deep sleep.

9

The Master Puzzler

Jason slowly opened his eyes and started letting them wander around the room. He was so tired from their journey the previous day, he hadn't even removed his clothes. He sat up and peered around the room and saw beautiful oak dressers and armoires with large golden handles in the shape of swords, a large full-length mirror, and two large wooden doors. One he knew led into the hall outside, and the other he thought must be the bathroom. He swung his legs over the side of the bed and found a nice fluffy pair of slippers, so he slid his feet into them and stood up. After he gave himself a long stretch he journeyed across the soft rugs and stone floor until he reached the door. He pushed it open and found a large basin full of steaming water, which he assumed was for a bath; next to that was a bowl full of water and a white towel of some kind. He picked it up and found it to be very rough and not like the towels they had at home. There was another identical towel hanging on a hook on the wall, but this one was long and fluffy like his slippers. There was also a white bath robe made of what seemed to be some type of wool. In the corner of the room was a large block of wood. He supposed it to be around four feet high and three feet wide. On the very top of the wooden block was a hole, not just any hole, however; it was around a foot in diameter.

"Don't tell me that's the toilet!" he snorted. After a quick laugh at the sight of the bathroom he started slipping off his pants when there was a loud knock on the door.

"Come in!" Jason shouted from the confines of the bathroom and slipping his pants quickly back up to his waist.

The door opened and a young man entered wearing a long black robe, green pants and white satin shirt. Jason recognized him from the night before. The man was carrying a large silver tray full of a steaming breakfast. He quickly set it down on the bedside table as another man came in carrying a different set of clothes for Jason. They were identical to what he was already wearing, but were clean and smelled like lavender. Jason walked over to the two gentlemen and smiled.

"Will there be anything else, young master?" said the taller of the two men.

"No, I think that this is far too much as it is," Jason said, stunned at their manner of speech.

"Did you find your bath suitable, or would you like some more hot water?" said the second, shorter man.

"The bath is just fine, thank you. So what do they call you here?" Jason answered.

"Sir?" said the tall man.

"Your names, what do they call you?" Jason asked again.

"I'm called Aminon, and this is my protégé, Andres, sir," said Aminon confidently.

"That's a cool name, what does it mean?" Jason said.

"What do you mean 'cool,' sir? It's not cold," Aminon responded seriously.

Jason looked at him and then smiled; he realized that they didn't understand the slang that was used in Oklahoma.

"It means I like it, it a nice name," Jason said, trying not to laugh.

"Oh, I understand sir," Aminon stated. Jason knew that he still didn't understand, but he decided not to try and explain it again.

"Do you know the meaning of your name?" Jason asked.

"I know not the meaning of this name. All male servants are given names at birth by the current mistress of the castle. The males all have names that begin with the letter A. Most female names, however, start with different letters of the alphabet. For example, the cook is female and her name is Tabia, and your sister's attendant is Emelia. They all have certain meanings, I'm sure, but the knowledge is not of me," Aminon said. "If that is all, sir, we need to take trays to other parts of the castle."

"This is great. Again, thank you," Jason said. The two servants waited and Jason wasn't sure what to do next.

Do they want a tip? he wondered.

"May we be excused, sir?" Aminon asked.

"Of course," Jason said, "go."

173

"Thank you, sir," the two men said in unison and bowed their heads as they departed from the room, leaving Jason alone again.

I swear this gets weirder all the time, he thought.

Jason looked at his tray and found it full of meats and breads; a tin jug was full of white foamy milk, and there were fresh strawberries and blueberries. On a piece of china was a slab of creamy butter and next to it lay an odd-shaped butter knife. He slowly picked up the knife and began smearing the butter on a slice of bread. He found the butter a little bitter, but very desirable. The milk was also extremely thick and Jason thought it to be almost sour, but again he enjoyed it. He remembered his mother giving him milk just like this when he was little, but he hadn't had it since then. The different meats he thought were a little odd for breakfast. There was a large slab of steak and then also some duck that he recognized from the night previous. He wasn't in the mood for it so he left the meat untouched but quickly finished off the fresh fruit. After breakfast he meandered back to the bathroom and slipped into the basin. To his surprise it was still quite hot and he found it extremely relaxing. Soon he was dressed again and thought he had better head outside to find Chloe.

He opened the door to his room and stepped into the hall. It was a little bit cooler than his room but still comfortable. He pulled the door to his room shut and found a young lady just leaving Chloe's room.

"You are Emelia, right?" he asked. She quickly turned around and gave a slight bow.

"Yes sir," she answered without looking at him.

Jason thought this behavior strange, but wasn't sure what to say about it.

"Is my sister awake yet?" he questioned.

"Yes sir, she is in the courtyard with Master Avery. Would you like me to take you there?" she inquired.

Jason smiled at her and then gave an appreciative nod. He hadn't noticed earlier how beautiful Emelia was. She was the same age as Chloe with bright blonde hair, and sapphire-blue eyes. She seemed to be very well educated and proper. Jason found it extremely admirable. Emelia quickly turned to her right and led Jason back down the stairs they had come up the night before and then down a long corridor and out a large wooden door. As they stepped outside Jason had to squint to let his eyes adjust; he hadn't noticed how dark the castle actually was. They found Chloe and Avery sitting on a bench made entirely out of stone surrounded by sweet-smelling red, yellow, and pink roses.

"Good morning," he said. Avery and Chloe looked up at him and smiled.

"We didn't think you were ever going to get up," Chloe said, smiling. "We've been waiting for you for over an hour."

"Thank you, Emelia, you may go," Avery said, dismissing the young lady.

175

Jason sat next to Chloe and the smell of the roses empowered his senses. It was a beautiful day. The sun was shining bright and there wasn't a single cloud in the bright blue sky. It was warm with a gentle breeze that made the flowery garden smell even better.

"What kept you? We told you last night to meet us in the courtyard at eight o'clock; it's now a quarter past nine. I was told that you were awake and had your breakfast at seven-thirty."

Avery's voice seemed a little distant today, but Jason could tell that he was very upset at his late arrival.

"Sorry, Avery, I didn't remember our plans. I was taking a bath." As Jason spoke he saw that Avery's anger still hadn't softened.

"We must get going; you must reach the Barren Land quickly. Your provisions are ready as well as your horses. Aden is prepared and waiting at the castle gates. The guards of Loch will escort you out of the city."

Avery rushed his words and Jason and Chloe watched him in amazement.

"Aren't you coming with us?" Chloe pleaded. She didn't really know Aden; although he seemed nice, she wasn't sure how stable he was.

"Aden is a good man; he will take excellent care of you both. Before you go, Lady Cerella, the Duchess of Loch, requests your attendance in the Library. We will go to her, and then you shall be on your way," Avery said, standing.

Chloe and Jason quickly stood to their feet and Avery led the way back into the door that Emelia had led them all out before. Once inside they followed the passage to the grand stairway then proceeded to go left. They came to another corridor and followed it to another flight of narrow steps. They crept slowly upward and came to a stop in front of a small wooded door with an iron knocker. Avery approached the door. He gripped the knocker and rapped on the door with four distinct taps. The door was pushed open and a lady with gray hair and blue dress ushered them inside. They were led through yet another passageway and through two more doors before they first glimpsed the large room full of books. The shelves extended from the floor to the twenty-foot-high ceiling and it looked like the book shelves went about a hundred feet inside the room about five feet apart from one another. There were ladders that could be moved back and forth and some of the shelves had what seemed to be a little seat that could be folded in and out. There were lush leather armchairs, large wooden tables, gaslit lamps, and large picture windows with wooden shutters. The gray-haired lady led them to the very center of the room, curtseyed, and then left the way she came. Avery sat down in one of the armchairs and Chloe and Jason did likewise. Soon nothing could be heard except the chirping of the birds outside.

Moments later Chloe heard footsteps behind her and Avery and Jason both rose to their feet. Chloe mimicked them and she too also stood. Avery bowed low to the ground and Jason copied his gesture, Chloe did the best curtsey that she could, having never done it before.

"My lady, the times have made you even more beautiful," Avery said, walking over to the woman and kissing her hand.

He helped her sit in an armchair and then moved back to his own. Chloe and Jason sat down also and waited. Chloe thought that Lady Cerella was a very intriguing woman. She had long flowing red hair, green eyes, and wore a stunning green silk dress. Atop her head was a small crown with rubies and sapphires aligning the rim. She couldn't have been more than her early thirties because her skin was so radiant and full of color. Chloe noticed that the women here wore their makeup differently than they did back home. It was so natural that she wondered if they wore any at all.

"It's a pleasure to be in your company; I hope your stay here was to your liking." Cerella addressed both Chloe and Jason and waited patiently for an answer.

Jason wasn't sure what to say, so he shook his head in agreement. Chloe was the one who answered.

"Yes, my lady, your generosity is far more than anything we could have expected."

Chloe was flabbergasted at her speech. She didn't know that she could be so proper when she needed to be. She seemed to have said something grand because Lady Cerella smiled and blushed.

"Cerella, was there something that you needed to speak to us about? We really need to get Chloe and Jason on their way to the Barren Land," Avery said quietly.

"Yes, actually, I must warn you, that there is a new challenge that must be completed before you enter into the Barren Land. The Master Puzzler has set guard there and Master Jason could possibly have to duel with whatever puzzle he has when they reach the land. I've known only a few merchants and wizards who were able to succeed in his puzzles," she answered respectively.

"This Master Puzzler, is he a wizard himself?" Jason asked with curiosity.

Chloe thought this a strange meeting. *I've always been quite good at puzzles, but how do you duel with a puzzle?* she thought to herself. *And Jason doesn't even know how to fight.*

"As far as I know, he is not. However, they say he has a different kind of magic, one that plays many tricks on your mind and your body. Aden is aware of this venture and has prepared to train Master Jason in the ways of the sword and Mistress Chloe in the works of magic and how to defend herself against an attack on her mind," she said confidently.

"What have others had to attempt to do?" Jason asked, worry on his face.

"My sources tell me that some have had to go through mazes, others have had to fight off a series of invisible creatures. They say that he has the wind and weather on his side, and can call upon them to make your travels seem like you're climbing atop a mountain. I've also been informed that some have actually had to solve puzzles and mathematical equations. Since not many know of such an

179

education or trial, many fail." She answered him without taking her eyes from Avery's.

Chloe knew that it was not going to be the easy puzzles that she had done many times. Although she seemed to be quite good in mathematics and arithmetic, she wasn't sure if anything was the same in Mere. She could feel the tension in the room grow so thick that she was starting to worry that they would never make it home. Avery sat very quiet, thinking about what Lady Cerella had said, and soon he stood to his feet and ushered Chloe and Jason to do the same. Lady Cerella stood and looked at him, waiting for an explanation of his rude gesture.

"I apologize for not waiting for you to excuse us, Lady, but I really must get them on their way. I want to return to them before they reach this Master Puzzler, so I must also be on my way," Avery explained.

He reached down and grabbed Lady Cerella's hand and gently kissed it. Jason followed suit and Chloe quickly curtseyed.

"Do what you must, Avery, but keep them both safe, not matter the cost," she said quietly so Chloe and Jason couldn't understand.

Avery took one last bow and Jason and Chloe thanked Cerella for her kindness one last time and then followed Avery out the doors, down the stairs and passageways, and out the door they had entered through the previous night.

Aden was waiting for them there with the three beautiful horses from the day before all harnessed to a black carriage. It looked like one you might find in an old western movie. It had a large bench in front and a place to keep your items in the back. It was full to the extreme with pots, pans, blankets, and food for the horses. There were large metal canisters that were full of water and even larger crates full of food such as dried meats, fruits, potatoes, and some food Chloe didn't recognize. She knew that they were in for a long trip. Avery pulled Aden aside and talked out of hearing distance of Chloe and Jason and then returned back to them.

"Aden will be very good to you. I hope to return before your encounter with the Master Puzzler so to assist you in your task. Aden is a wizard, but his skills lie with the dirt. He knows enough other magic to keep you all safe, warm, and well fed, but I will need to be the one to take you through the Barren Land. You both must listen to Aden and do as he says. It's a long journey and you are going to be very tired by the time I return. Do you both understand?"

Chloe and Jason could both sense the urgency in his tone and they quickly nodded in agreement.

"Where do you have to go?" Chloe asked curiously.

"I must travel to Rill to find Zachi and Cane and then I will return," he answered.

Before Chloe and Jason had time to ask who Zachi and Cane were, Avery was already transforming back into the large red bird they both knew. Kamali had returned, almost as quickly as Avery formed back on the green grassy

181

plain. Kamali gave a loud squawk and pecked them kindly on the cheek.

"Be safe, young masters, for soon I will return." Kamali quickly took flight and was out of sight before either could respond.

"Well, what are we waiting for, everyone climb aboard. We are extremely late and must be on our way," Aden said.

He was dressed differently today; no longer was he wearing his long robe, but pants, a tunic, and a tinkling metal mail shirt. He had a large curved sword sheathed at his side and wore black leather boots that reached almost to the bottoms of his knees.

Chloe and Jason climbed up onto the seat of the carriage. Aden gave the reins a quick shake and soon they were riding out of the city gates. They turned east and followed a well-used road toward what Chloe suspected to be the Barren Land. Although she wouldn't see any sign of this desert plain for days, she already was dreading the heat they would soon endure.

The sun was high in the sky when the travelers stopped for lunch. Chloe was very hungry. She hadn't eaten much that morning at Loch because she was still a little nervous about this whole new place. She was getting extremely anxious that her parents were worried sick after they returned to the cabin to find it in pieces after the storm that had driven them to the cave in the first place. She knew that they would call for a search and rescue team from one of the nearby cities, but what would they do when they couldn't find them?

Avery and Jason had both explained the story of Mere and her appearance to her back on the hilltop, but she was still having a hard time believing that any of this was real. She believed that any moment her parents would come and wake her up and she would be in her own room with Megan at the cabin. For now, however, she sat down with Aden and Jason and ate her lunch. It was quite strange; she had some dried apricots with some bread that for some reason was warm and very soft. It was as if it just came from the oven. She knew that it was because of Aden's magic but it was still not normal for her to witness such a task. There was also some dried meat that reminded her of the beef jerky she used to get at the gas station just around the corner from their home in Oklahoma. She also was served a tin cup full of fresh cold water.

Their journey thus far was actually quite relaxing. She was really enjoying the scenery. She had seen many small cottages with smoke rising from the chimneys and fresh beds of flowers surrounding them. Cool rushing rivers and lush green plains. It was really some of the most fantastic sights she had ever seen. Compared to Oklahoma, it was heaven. Sure, Oklahoma was pretty in certain areas, but it was mostly a flat space with a few trees and farmland. The Kingdom of Mere, however, was a flourishing valley with green rolling hills, snow-capped mountains in the distance, and streams, rivers, and flowers.

183

The wildlife was also beautiful. There seemed to be abundant wild horses and deer all over the grassy plains, but there were also animals that seemed to just pop up out of the ground, disappear, and then come back up another fifty feet or so up the road. Aden had called them Mirales. He said they were something like a prairie dog, but more in the shape of a ferret with extreme power in their legs and jaws. They made burrows underground like worms and then dove in and out like dolphins do in water. Aden had warned her that if she ever got to close to a Mirale that she should not move or even breathe too deeply because, he said, *"they were extremely temperamental and wouldn't think twice before biting her and making her very sick."* Even after Aden explained this to her, it made Chloe smile when she saw them; they just seemed so innocent and sweet.

Jason too had an adventurous ride. Aden gave him a beautiful sword made entirely of silver with gold ribbons that wrapped around the two inlaid swords. There were also beautiful red and blue stones in the handle that was curved to fit almost perfectly in his hands. Jason had never held a sword before and was quite shocked to find it so heavy. He gave it a few quick movements and Aden laughed at his attempts.

"We shall make you a champion swordsman before we reach the Barren Land," Aden said smiling brightly.

Aden was instructing Jason the entire trip on how to fight with a sword. Aden couldn't believe that Jason didn't know how to use a sword.

"What did they use to fight up above?" he had asked Jason many times.

"Well they used guns, and little short knives, airplanes, and bombs and lots of other stuff. I'm not sure if too many people use swords or arrows anymore," Jason would answer.

Aden seemed very confused by what a gun was so Jason had to explain it to him over and over again.

"How fascinating. It's a long metal tube that explodes?" he would ask.

Jason tried to give him a better description, but came to the conclusion that it was almost impossible to explain such a thing to someone who didn't believe in such an object. Aden taught Jason all the moves he could do with his sword and all the different ways to kill an opponent. Jason found it mesmerizing at how serious and excited Aden was to explain the ways of the sword. It made him want to jump from the carriage and start fighting.

After they had finished their lunch Aden withdrew his sword and marched up to Jason and banged him upside the head with the flat end of the sword.

"You must always be prepared for a fight. That's lesson number one, and don't ever forget it." Aden laughed hysterically as Jason rubbed vigorously at the new bump on his head.

Jason rose to his feet and unsheathed his own new sword.

"Uh-uh, we are to use these to practice with," Aden said as he tossed Jason two swords made completely from wood. "This way we won't kill each other."

Jason resheathed his sword and grabbed the large clunky wooden one from Aden's hand.

"Now you must always remember what I've told you, your footwork can save your life, as well as your quick mind. I've seen how smart you are; now let's test your reflexes." Aden quickly lunged forward and Jason barely had time to lift his sword to block his attack.

Chloe watched them battle and winced every time her brother was hit with the sword. She thought that it was never going to end, but after at least twenty minutes of beating him with a wooden stick, Aden decided that Jason had enough for the time being. Jason, bruised and sore, dropped to the ground and rubbed his aching arms and legs.

"How do you expect me to learn anything? I never even touched you with that wood sword and you beat me almost to death. I didn't have a chance," Jason said, breathing hard from his recent attack.

"You must learn to let your mind take over; your body is nothing without it. However, your reflexes seemed to be working well. You blocked more shots than I expected," Aden said, now sitting next to Jason and putting his arm around his shoulder. "Don't worry, young master; you will be great when the time to fight comes along."

After the long break the two men had, they climbed back into the carriage and the horses lurched forward and their journey quickly began again.

"We will soon be leaving the safety of Loch and entering dangers beyond our borders," Aden said quietly. "There are more threats over that last hill than I dare to speak of. Have your sword ready, young master, for you will need it soon enough."

Jason's face dropped. How did Aden expect him to do any fighting? He had just been beaten half to death with a fake sword, there was no way he was going to survive a fight with a real sword.

It made him extremely nervous about this new challenge. He withdrew his sword from where it was sheathed and pushed Chloe between Aden and himself. He would do his best to protect his sister from any dangers that lay ahead, but knew that if anything happened to Aden, they were both doomed.

10

Held Captive

Kamali flew away from the group, knowing his destination. His plan was very simple. He could transform himself into any kind of animal or plant. He knew that Zachi and Cane were headed for the city of Rill and that would take time to find from the air, but he was certain that with the landmarks he remembered, he would be able to spot it.

He flew northwest toward the Rivers. It was going to be a long flight but he was looking forward to the beautiful scenery and the peace and quiet of the still plains he would cross. He caught a glimpse of the beautiful wildflowers that grew this time of year just outside the city of Kane. The city was extremely small and consisted of only farms and a few small merchants. It was here that he planned on staying for the evening. He wanted to hear of the news going around the kingdom, and the best place to hear anything was always at the Tavern Kane, located in the center of town. He wasn't sure how any of the city's residents found out the information, but he knew that they always knew everything. The city soon crept up in front of him.

Kamali flew onward and saw several wild horses and even a couple of farms. Shortly he would need to land and transform back into the man known as Avery. He watched a farmer herd his sheep across a small water way and over to a green grassy pasture on the other side. The farmer glanced up at the large red bird that cast its shadow over the land and he seemed to quicken the pace of his animals.

In the distance he could see the peaks of the rooftops and smoke rising to indicate it was nearing lunchtime in the small city. He spied a large bush of trees encased in numerous shadows near the River Rapine and decided that he would land and transform there, knowing it would block anyone from seeing his magical transformation. As he descended toward the ground he glanced around and found the silence of this bush rather edgy. He slowed his pace and peered into the darkness of the large trees.

Kamali thought he saw something move out of the corner of his eye. Suddenly, a large net flew blindly around him, engulfing him in a trap. He struggled to be let free, but to no avail. This material was made strong. He attempted to use magic to burn through the ropes tying it together, but the net was protected by magic, and his own magic seemed to be completely useless. He was trapped! He didn't have a plan to escape. He looked to the ground and tried to brace himself for the blow he was about to receive. The net was falling fast, and as the ground got closer he began to hold his breath.

Just before he smashed into the ground, a man dressed all in black came from a shadow and caught the net in his gloved hand. Two more men dressed the same, followed the first out of the shadows and laughed.

"Looks like we caught our dinner," the first man said, laughing as he spoke.

The other two men joined in the laughter and placed Kamali in a large black bag.

"Master will be thrilled!" squealed the other man.

There was no escape. The more he tried to wiggle out, the tighter the net became. He was in total darkness. He felt himself being flung over the back of what seemed to be a horse. He heard the men mount their steeds and then the unexpected happened. As the horses began to walk, it felt like the air in his net was diminishing. He could feel his lungs hardening and straining for air. He kicked and fought, but the net would not release its grip. He was going to suffocate. The seconds passed, but it felt like minutes to Kamali as he struggled to breathe. Just as he was about to pass out the air returned and he could feel himself taking large deep breaths. Whatever had happened was over. He wasn't sure what had happened, but he was glad that it was over.

"We got a large red bird for supper, Sire," Kamali heard one of the men say.

"Flew right into the net. I think that the charm placed on it works great," another said comically.

Kamali felt himself lifted off the horse and handed to someone else.

"I hope this pleases you, Sire," he heard the first man say again.

Kamali held his breath and released it. He couldn't transform now even if he wanted to. The magic in the net was too powerful. He waited for the men to speak again. The voice he heard, however, was a deep voice that sounded full of hatred.

"I'm pleased, we now know that the portals work and will bring back something from Mere without damaging anything, and we also now know that the invisible charm placed on the net will stay strong. This is good news. You may return to your previous posts."

The man's voice was overbearing. Kamali's head began to ache from the hatred this man carried. When the man stopped talking, Kamali's head stopped pounding and returned to normal. He was hoisted over the man's shoulder and Kamali could hear the tink of the other men's chain mail shirts as they ran off to maintain their positions.

"Abdal! Come take this bird to the cages. We will use it for our feast before the war."

Kamali was flipped into the air and caught roughly by another man. He was still unaware of his surroundings or where he was. He didn't recognize the smells or even the sounds of anyone's voice. Something the man said now caught his attention: *He said war, what war?* he thought quietly.

The man that now held him captive walked toward what sounded like metal clinking on metal. The captor stopped and Kamali heard him opening the bag. The air that came into the bag was thin and held the rancid smell of

191

burning iron. Black clouds of dust poured over the edge of the bag. He was lifted up, and for the first time, Kamali caught a glimpse of his prison. He was in the hands of the enemy. The men dressed in black were not men at all but Umbra. They were summoned from the depths of Myopia as a part of Jacan's army. Myopia was a dark and gloomy place that man could not travel to. It was full of betrayers from kingdoms all over the world. It was here that those not loyal to their kings went after death or after they chose to call upon the powers of darkness to give them a new life.

The Umbra were part of this place; they were the evil that lurked below the depths of the seas and through the blackness of a volcano. They dressed all in black to show loyalty to their mighty leader. The more black you wore, the higher your rank in the army. These men were foul creatures and ate anything and everything. They could pop out of portals made in shadows of trees, buildings, and other things. They almost resembled men as long as their hoods were up; however, they had many features that would scare even the mightiest of warriors.

Their faces were dark with long oddly shaped noses, with black distant eyes. Their teeth resembled the yellow of the sun, and they were completely hairless and made almost entirely of muscle. They had webbed toes and their fingers were long and scaled. Their women couldn't be distinguished by a normal man. To us, they all look the same. However, the worst of it was, they were almost entirely invisible when in shadows. You could see right through them, almost as if they

were a black mist. The only thing that gave them away was
their breath. They had been nicknamed the people of the
shadows by many sorcerers and sorceresses. Kamali knew
this meant trouble.

Abdal was just as ugly and hideous as the next, but
shorter. His muscles didn't develop like the others and for
this reason, he was made a slave and not a warrior. Through
the darkness of the chamber his features were faded and
nearly transparent. Kamali looked at his surroundings and
tried to find a place that he could escape. The only thing he
saw were large whirls of wind that resembled shadows. There
must have been dozens of these around the chamber he was
in.

Abdal removed the net from around Kamali and
grabbed him by his talons. He threw him headfirst into a
large cylinder-shaped cage. Kamali flew to escape his captor
and Abdal slammed the cage door closed. He bolted it with a
large chain and put a large metal rod through the middle and
rested it on the cage. Kamali knew it was meant to be a
perch, but he wasn't going to land just yet. The Umbra
servant retreated and came back moments later with a large
slab of raw meat and a bowl of dirty water. He placed it
inside with Kamali and turned with a smile and walked away.

Kamali flew down and perched on the metal rod and
watched the Umbra he could see around him. This chamber
was almost familiar to him, but he wasn't sure where this
was. He watched as many Umbra children came to stare at
him.

"Look at the color, he's huge! That's going to be a real treat!" a small child said to his friends.

A larger figure came up behind the children and slapped each on the back of the heads with a stick.

"Away to your duties!" boomed the voice.

It was the same voice Kamali had heard upon his arrival. The man, or beast, was dressed from head to toe in black. His face was covered with a veil of metal that was tinted black. The material he wore seemed rich and expensive, almost silky. He wore black rings on each finger with a black stone in the middle. The only color on this man was a necklace wrapped around his neck. It was gold with a ring dangling from the chain. The ring was also gold, but had the crest of Nebula imprinted in the stone.

Kamali gasped as he realized he was in the land of Jacan and was trapped above the well-guarded Mere in the confines of the castle atop the clouds that once held the King and Queen of Nebula.

The man withdrew his hood and revealed his ghostly features. He was almost entirely transparent, his face dark and wrinkled. His hair was now black as coal as were his teeth. He swished and moved quietly as his body blew from the breeze flowing through the chamber. Although he was ghostlike, he was entirely solid. Kamali knew he could not float through any walls, but his appearance was shocking.

Once, this man was trusted and sought after by all the women of Nebula. He had fair brown hair with dazzling green eyes. His smile was his key feature, full of beautiful pearly whites. He was courted several times by duchesses from other kingdoms around the world. He betrayed them all. The Duke called upon the Umbra and attacked all the cities of the kingdom.

He was sneaky and tried to trick the King and Queen by making them think he was not a part of any of it. When all his treachery upon the kingdom was complete, and all the people had retreated or joined his forces, the King and Queen knew they needed to depart secretly, and took shelter in the Kingdom of Mere.

Now Jacan looks like he is the ruler of all the Umbra, dirty and powerful, Kamali thought quietly as he watched his enemy closely.

"My friend, you shall make a fine meal for me before my attack on Mere. I was skeptical that my portals would work in the transfer, but now I see that they are nearly ready. You see, my large friend, I've finally penetrated the protective barrier that encompassed the Kingdom of Mere, and now in only three days, I shall enter with my warriors and overpower them with numbers. Their wizards won't even know I'm coming!" He growled with laughter and reached in to touch Kamali with his long pointy fingers.

Kamali snapped at him and nearly clipped his finger. Jacan pulled his fingers back quickly and smiled.

"Roasted bird! Sounds delicious!" He laughed a deep hateful tone and pulled his hood back over his face, hiding the ugliness that had overtaken the once handsome face of a duke.

195

Kamali knew now that he had to escape, but how seemed the larger question. He had to somehow do magic without any of the Umbra and Jacan noticing he was a wizard. He wasn't sure, but he didn't think that Jacan knew who he had caught or the welcome would have been a lot worse. He searched the chamber and watched and listened as Jacan's warriors did their chores. He saw them making several swords, quivers and arrows, shields, and daggers. Before the arrows were placed in their quivers, they were dipped in poison. Kamali had seen this poison only once before; it would kill immediately without any warning or signs that poison was used. He had read in several books about the poison and knew the only counter was a plant called the Lillias Holloack, a purple flower with black stems that provided a barrier to the poison. It only grew in the deep forest of Amorie. The clank of iron being pounded by the Umbra sent shivers down his back, and brought his attention back to the work being done by the warriors.

Every few hours Abdal would come and give Kamali large slabs of meat and to do this, he had to open the gate of his cage. Kamali knew that the meat was intended to fatten him for supper, so instead of actually eating it, he vanished it away piece by piece. Jacan walked by several times and had never said anything, only eyed him and showed his dark black teeth through the veil that protected his face. Kamali had discovered that Jacan held his meetings in a large room at the far left corner of the chamber away from all the noise of the hall. He would disappear through the black wooden door for only minutes at a time with a warrior or some other type of creature and return to walking around, keeping an eye on the progress of the blacksmiths and the poisoned arrows.

As he watched Jacan walk by for the fourth time, he let out an ear-shattering squawk. Jacan turned quickly and withdrew his sword, preparing for a fight. He looked over and laughed as he spied the bird trapped in the refines of his cage. He resheathed his sword and turned and walked without a word toward the meeting hall. He grabbed a large hooded Umbra and shoved the creature through the door.

A smile formed on Kamali's face. *I think now would be a good time to listen in on our little friend*, he thought to himself.

He thought about what needed to be done and cast a spell to let his ears be aware of the sounds in the room, and seconds later heard the deep dark voice of Jacan.

"The city of Loch and also the waters of Rill will be our first attack. I want all men ready to go tomorrow night. We will set up a perimeter around the cities and we will attack by midday. I want no prisoners, General Asen, and no survivors. As you know, I can't follow you until the full moon or the portals will be destroyed. That is also the night that their barrier will be destroyed completely and all forces can enter, not just your soldiers," Jacan's voice said coldly.

"Your orders will be done, Sire," Asen said quietly.

The meeting was over. Asen retreated from the room followed by Jacan. Kamali knew that he had no more time. He must escape tonight so he could warn Duchess Cerella

197

and send a messenger to Rill to inform them of the oncoming attack.

In the corner of the chamber, he could hear the calls of children having fencing lessons, and the thought to escape poured over him. He now knew exactly what to do to escape. Kamali knew that a major transformation to another creature would be far too suspicious, but knew that in a matter of minutes, Abdal would bring another large chunk of meat to the cage. Before this happened, he would put a spell on himself that would make him seem dead and the smell would be gruesome, as if he had been dead for days. He would shed several feathers and have blood dripping from the bottom of the cage so they would think he had been shot by a poison arrow. He would form the arrow entirely out of magic and lay it under him. It would start an all-out fight between the Umbra, and Abdal would retreat to find Jacan and inform him of the death and then his escape would be perfect.

Kamali performed the magic necessary and soon the arrow lay on the ground under his cage. He flew down and lay still on the bottom of the cage and gave the illusion of blood dripping from his breast. Seconds after the magic was complete, Abdal rounded the corner with his large chunk of meat. At the site of the bird lying on the bottom of the cage, dripping blood, with an arrow on the stone floor below the cage, the servant dropped the meat and raced toward the cage. He opened the large doors with a clank and touched Kamali.

"You pompous creeps, master will not like this."

At the sound of the servant's accusation, the fighting began. They began attacking and accusing those that had made the arrows. Abdal ran away, leaving the cage door wide open just as a large Umbra came running after him, weapon in hand. Kamali peeked out of the cage and took flight.

"Oy, it's alive!" came a shout from below him.

The fight halted and Kamali swooped wildly around the chamber. Arrows whizzed by his ears and all around him. A loud roar from above told Kamali of something large coming right at him. He looked up and saw three large dragons. Their scales were black, blue, and orange. From several books that he had read, he knew that this meant that the dragons were fire breathers. Kamali had not expected such a fleet; he had been educated that dragons remained neutral in wars and could not be convinced to join any force, good or evil. The large leathery wings on these creatures expanded a length that touched both sides of the large chamber walls. They were also draped in black fabric that had a dark embroidered dragon tail running the length of the middle of the fabric.

Kamali swooped to avoid a large spout of fire that was released by the smaller of the dragons and flew toward the portals. He didn't know where they would lead him, but he was sure that anywhere would be better than here. On the ground Kamali got a glance at Jacan.

"It's going to escape, you fools, block the portals!" he growled loudly at his warriors.

199

The Umbra raced Kamali to the entrance of the portals, but he reached one portal just before a rather large Umbra ripped him from the sky. The air around him tightened and his lungs felt like lead as he pushed through the portal. His eyes began to spin and he tried with no success to pull his wings in around his body. He saw a light forming on one side of the portal that looked like sunshine. He kicked and tried to fly harder and with the final kick, he was thrown out of the portal right into a river. He heard several Umbra jumping out of the portal so he quickly transformed himself unseen into a fish and swam deeper into the river and farther away from the portal.

After an hour of swimming he swam to the surface to see where he had escaped to. He peered out cautiously and searched the grounds and the shadows for any movement. He couldn't sense anything so he swam to the opposite edge of the river and transformed into a large white horse.

He took off galloping through the long brush toward a hill so he could get a better view of the surrounding area. He couldn't believe it; he had been thrown right back at the Hidden Cave where he started out with Chloe and Jason. The city of Loch was just beyond the Hill of Ivory. He ran as fast as he could toward the city. The clouds began to grow thick and Kamali knew that Jacan, with the help of his wizards, was searching for him. He quickened his pace and soon saw the gate to the city. It was late morning and the traffic into the city was extremely busy. He pushed through the crowd, knocking parcels and baskets out of the hands of several merchants. They yelled after him and shook their fists. He raced toward the castle and up a well-lit alleyway. As he rounded the corner, he transformed back into Avery.

He ran with his cape billowing behind him toward the castle gates. He knew that the Duchess would be convening with the people of Loch in the main gate at this time of day, so he flew as fast as his legs would carry him and pounded up the stairs and passed the two guards at the front gate. They yelled at him to stop, but he kept running. He pushed through the large crowd of people and they groaned at the hits by Avery and the guards now chasing him. He saw her standing with a child in her arms smiling over the crowd. He ran up to her and was completely surrounded by guards.

"Release him! That is Avery the High Wizard of Mere!" the Duchess called at her guards.

They retreated to their posts, and she looked at him and smiled.

"To what do we owe this pleasant surprise?" she spoke kindly.

"My apologies, mistress, but we have an emergency!" The tone in his voice was strong.

Cerella looked at him with lost eyes and ordered the room to be cleared. For the next few hours, Avery explained what was going to happen. Cerella gasped at each new bit of information.

"This is indeed terrible news, Master Avery. We must put the city on high alert and send a messenger to Mere and also to Rill at once, as well as other cities across the kingdom. I presume you will assist with this war?" she asked.

"I'm afraid, mistress, that I cannot stay to assist in the battle. I must fly on to inform Aden, Zachi, and the others of the attack and that they must be on their guard at all times. They should just be arriving at Gannon's Estate. I must leave immediately. However, before I depart I will put a spell across the city protecting it from arrows. Send riders to the Forest of Amorie to gather as much Lillias Holloack as they can, and have all your people eat one leaf of the plant. It will protect them from the poison. Shut your gates and I will also put a barrier around it as well. The dragons are not going to be joining this fight; they cannot enter until the full moon so that gives us nine days." Avery spoke with fierce authority.

Cerella agreed and sent out a guard to shut the gates and messengers out to warn the others. Avery spoke the magic after the city was locked down and bid farewell to the Lady Cerella.

"Use whatever you have to defeat the army of Jacan, my lady. I will return as soon as I can."

She acknowledged him, and Avery transformed back into Kamali and departed through the front doors of the castle. He lifted a small part of the barrier for him to escape through and then mended it as he flew to the north toward the city of Avis. He grew tired and hungry, but knew that he must continue or all would be lost.

11

The Black Riders

The long journey that had begun only a few days ago seemed to be endless. There was always so much to do and so much to see in this new land; however, they were never going to succeed in seeing anything but this dusty old wagon trail. The wagon trail seemed to go for miles and then there was a rather large hill at the top. You could just barely make out the green grass and then nothing more. The hill seemed to be coming up on them as slowly as a snail would cross a street, but the wagon ride was comfortable.

Aden and Jason kept discussing the correct way to disarm your opponent or how to correctly aim a bow and arrow to hit your target, and other warlike strategies. Chloe had become so bored with this discussion that she began drifting off to sleep. She was quickly awoken by Aden as he shoved a series of large books at her and told her that she needed to study and learn as quickly and as much as she could.

As she re-situated herself into a more comfortable position she grabbed the first book that she was given. *The Ways of Mere*, Chloe read. She opened the book and found large colorful pictures portraying Kings and Queens, Princes and Princesses, and many other fine and fancy things. It discussed the ways of curtsey, politics, and many other things Chloe found rather boring.

She continued to read a chapter titled "The Correct Way to Curtsey." *A lady always curtseys when introduced to someone, no matter their title. First grab both sides of your skirt, lower your head, and slowly lower yourself into the sitting position with one leg over the other and then return to your proper standing position.* Chloe thought that this was rather strange to give her a book on proper etiquette rituals.

How is this going to help me? Except when I'm introduced to the King and Queen of Mere. Maybe this would be something good to learn, she thought to herself.

She marked her page with the provided bookmark and shut the book. She grabbed the next book and read its title: *The Ancient Witches and Wizards.* She thought this one might be interesting so she set it down to read at a later time. The next two books were all about the Kingdom of Mere, its people and animals. She wasn't sure where to start with these books. She gave a soft sigh and put the books down at her side.

As she started to look up she spotted the final book that Aden had given her: *Beginner's Magic.* Chloe thought that she was going to jump from her seat with excitement.

He wants me to learn magic! she thought elatedly.

She quickly grabbed the book and opened to the first page. It was a very old book with yellowing pages and she could tell it was well used. It had been scribbled on, torn, and she could even see food stains on its pages. Like all the books Aden had given her, it was handwritten with hand-drawn illustrations. Some of the words were hard to make out due to the writer's handwriting or the smudges of ink, but Chloe didn't care. This was what she wanted to do, ever since she saw the first magic that Zach had done with Kamali in the cave.

She leaned back on the hard wagon bench and plunged into reading. She read about how to correctly pronounce certain words, how to summon water from the roots of a plant, even how to get your garden to grow without water. She was so fascinated and enthralled in her reading she forgot all about their journey. When she finally looked up from her book, the sun was starting to set and the hill that they were supposed to reach was still miles ahead of them. However, there were some lights ahead, just down a small hill. It was a town surrounded by a large wall of pure rock, with lookouts built upon every ten turrets or so. It gave Chloe the creeps and made her whole body shiver.

"That is the city of Avis; it is the final city before we enter what is called the Barren Land. We will be resting here for the evening at one of my dear friends' homes. He is expecting us," Aden said sleepily.

He gave a large yawn and then smacked his lips together. Chloe assumed that he was trying to keep himself awake.

"Jason, in the satchel on the right side of the wagon is a flag with the Mere emblem on it. Will you please grab it and hold it steadily in the air?" Aden asked politely.

Jason quickly turned around and rummaged through the satchel until he found the beautifully woven flag. It was the same colors as the ones in Loch and had gold sewn around the outer edges. He held it above his head and made both ends as taut as he could. Aden pulled the horses to a stop and then began waiting. After a few moments an arrow came whizzing down from one of the towers and hit the flag squarely in the middle of the two swords. Aden smiled widely and began laughing as Jason dropped the flag and both he and Chloe ducked their heads as low as they could for the attack that would soon befall them.

"My dear children, that was a sign of peace given by the Duke of Avis himself. It means we are clear to gain entrance into their city." Aden chuckled.

Jason and Chloe sat back up in their seats and both wiped the sweat from their brow. That was by far one of the scariest things that had ever happened to Chloe on this journey, scarier even than being chased down by a wild storm. She thought for sure they were being attacked and she was going to die.

Aden gave a wave of the reins and spoke kind words to the horses, which by now were sweating, hungry, and thirsty from their long journey. They gave a quick jerk and the wagon began traveling toward the gate of the city, which was being lowered for their entrance. As they got closer to the drawbridge, Chloe saw for the first time several archers in each lookout with their bows loaded and ready to fire at the oncoming visitors. Chloe pushed herself back into her seat as far as she could and Jason wrapped his arm around her shoulders. It made her feel much safer, but she was still a little nervous.

The horses dragged on and slowly crossed the drawbridge. Once they were over and had completely entered the city they heard a loud clanking noise and men shouting to pull as loud as they could. Jason and Chloe looked behind them and saw numerous large men turning a wheel and the drawbridge beginning to rise. They were trapped inside the walls of this strange city.

Chloe wasn't sure if they should be happy, or scared and ready to fight, but Aden gave no sign of fear. Instead, he was smiling and happy. He pulled the horses to a stop and a boy about the age of sixteen approached them and withdrew the reins from Aden's hands.

He gave a low bow before he spoke.

"My Lords and Lady, we welcome you to the city of Avis. My name is Kadeem. I'm the stable boy as well as house servant of Gannon, Duke of Avis."

Aden jumped down from the wagon and offered his hand to Chloe to assist her down as well. She accepted quickly, and as elegantly as she could, climbed down the wagon to the ground below.

"Thank you, dear boy, please take the horses to the stables and offer them the best of everything you have. They need a good meal, plenty of water, and a good brush down. Oh, and please make sure they get fresh straw in their stables.

Also, my dear boy, please have all our luggage taken to our rooms," Aden said.

Kadeem gave one last bow and glanced at Chloe and then turned and led the horses away.

"We are to travel to the house of Gannon, where we will be staying for the evening. My lady, it would be good to practice your curtsey as often as you can. You will need good manners when you meet the King and Queen of Mere." His voice was kind.

Chloe thought back to what she read in the book about a proper curtsey and then attempted to show Aden that she was capable of doing one correctly. She grabbed her gown that the Duchess of Loch had given her and bowed her head, but just as she tried to sit and cross her legs she stumbled and Jason caught her from an embarrassing fall.

Aden looked at her and smiled.

"You will get it, just be patient."

Chloe was humiliated. How could she not even do a curtsey? She felt her face grow warm and looked at her brother for support. Jason smiled and gave his sister a hug.

"Don't worry, soon we will be home and none of this will matter." Chloe gave a short smile and dropped her head.

As they started to walk further into the city Chloe got a glimpse at another city in this mysterious land that they entered into. Avis was slightly different from Loch. Instead of shops and farmers' markets, there were small little stone homes with wood and straw for the roof. Each home had its own garden with tomatoes, corn, broccoli, and many other vegetables. Some of the homes were surrounded by wood fences to hold their livestock. They had cows and goats, and one larger house with a white fence and a large garden with a cobblestone walk had a long-haired animal Chloe didn't recognize.

"What is that animal?" she asked without removing her stare.

Aden glanced in the direction that she was looking and then back at Chloe. She stopped and looked at him and awaited his answer.

"That animal is what is called a Cowala. It's what the people of Mere use to breed their champion cows," he finally answered.

"What makes their cows champions, and why is that Cowala used to breed them?" Chloe asked curiously.

"A champion cow is one that brings the best meat to market. The Cowala contains the best meat of any animal, and it's a privilege for any home to have one. It shows what type of home you are entering. For example, that home is a home of wealth in this city. The owner may work with the Duke himself, or own a nearby shop. Either way, he is a man to show extreme courtesy to," Aden answered.

Chloe wanted to know more about the family that lived in that home, but it seemed that Aden was finished with the conversation. He had started walking down the road toward an even larger home.

This home was made of a brick-type material, and was two stories high. It had many windows with no glass, just wooden shutters and a garden that took up the entire left side of the home. It also had cows, chickens, and goats as well as not one but three of the Cowala in the front yard. The fence was white as well, but instead of a white wooden gate, it had an iron gate with the symbol of Mere crafted within. The roof was not like the others; it was layer upon layer of square slices of wood. Chloe knew at once that this was the home of the Duke, and her nerves were starting to make her sick. She linked her arm into Jason's and he looked down into her eyes. With a quick smile and an affectionate nod he glanced back toward the house.

Aden approached the gate and stopped.

"What is it?" Jason asked inquiringly.

"It is not polite to barge onto someone's property. We must wait to be granted entrance," Aden responded.

Jason glanced back down at Chloe, but she was not looking at him; instead, she was staring straight ahead. Her face had grown pale and she looked as if she might throw up.

"Chloe, are you okay?" Jason asked softly. "You look like you are going to be sick."

Chloe turned her head and looked at him. Her eyes were full of tears and her bottom lip was starting to quiver.

"I…I'm not sure, I feel so scared." She cried softly.

Aden looked at her and a kind smile formed on his face. He knelt down on the ground and put his hands on her shoulders and glanced into her pretty green eyes.

"My dear Lady, there is no need to draw tears in the city of Avis. Gannon is a great man, and his wife and daughter are two of the kindest women I know. You will enjoy your stay here, I promise."

Chloe gave a half smile and wiped the tears from her cheeks.

Jason wrapped his arms around his sister and whispered, "I'll take care of you, don't worry."

Just as Jason released his grip, the door to the home opened and a little middle-aged woman about forty years of age stepped out onto the cobblestone path and gave a big smile. She reached the iron gate, unlatched it, and pulled it back. The woman gave the prettiest curtsey that Chloe had ever seen. Her form was perfect, from the bow of her head to the rise to proper posture.

Chloe's mouth dropped. "I'm never going to learn that," she said quietly to herself.

Jason gave a quick elbow to her side and she knew that it was her turn to curtsey. She reached for her gown, bowed her head, and tried very hard to keep her balance as she tucked her leg behind her and lowered her body in the sitting position. She then rose to standing position and smiled. She had done it. It wasn't pretty, but she managed to do it without falling over herself.

The woman smiled back at her and then began to speak.

"Welcome to the home of Duke Gannon of Avis, we have been expecting you."

Aden bowed his head in greeting at the woman and then began walking in the front courtyard. Jason nudged

Chloe's back and urged her to follow Aden. The wind began
to pick up a little and the gate began to sway. Just as Chloe
was about to take a step she felt her brother grab her arm. His
grip was so tight, she thought he was going to snap it off. She
looked behind her and saw three men dressed in all black
with their swords drawn and pointed directly at the back of
Jason's neck. The woman at the gate gasped and Aden spun
on his heel to see what was going on. When he saw the three
men sitting upon their horses he froze, speechless.

Chloe's mind began to race. *Who are these men? Why
are they threatening my brother?*

The little hairs on the back of Chloe's neck began to
rise and the fury built up within her body. She felt like she
could do anything she wanted. She raised her hand and
without warning, the three swords flew out of their grip. She
saw the look of terror shoot across the men's faces but that
didn't bother her. Soon Chloe felt the power of magic grow
within her and she was able to summon a serpent from below
the earth. At the sight of the snake, the three horses tore off
through the streets of Avis. The wind began blowing
furiously and the three men disappeared without a trace.

Jason stared at his sister. He was so flabbergasted at
what Chloe had done to rescue him that he was utterly
breathless. He tried to speak but nothing came from his
mouth. Chloe was also stunned at her recent discovery of
magic. She had no idea that she possessed such power to tear
the swords from their hands.

Aden ran to their side. "I'm so sorry, I couldn't move. One of them put a spell on me. They weren't expecting you to have the power of magic," he said apologetically.

Chloe looked at him, and tears began streaming down her face. The sound of horses' hooves and men shouting soon reached them and they found the entire Avis guard was coming to their rescue. The door of the house sprung open and a tall gentleman with black trousers, white shirt, and red vest, followed by two women, came running out toward them.

"Aden, what happened?" spoke the tall man.

Aden looked at the man who had just approached him.

"I'm sorry, Gannon, they have found us," he said quietly.

Jason and Chloe both stared at Aden and wondered whom he meant.

Gannon looked at Aden in disbelief.

"It can't be, weren't you careful?" he said.

"Of course, but I guess not careful enough. We stayed off the main roads and followed the trails of the traders instead of the merchants. I don't know how they found us, or how they entered the kingdom unnoticed."

Aden was looking away from Gannon as he spoke. He was still having problems with the spell that had been cast upon him only moments ago.

"Which way have they gone? They can't leave the city; all the gates were raised after you entered," Gannon said.

Aden looked at Chloe and Jason.

"Did you see where they went?" he asked.

Chloe couldn't speak; she was too scared by what had just happened as well as confused. When Jason realized she wasn't going to answer he spoke up.

"Their horses ran down the road and then disappeared," he answered with a trembling voice.

"You there, take ten of your men and search the entire city. When you find them, bring them to me!" Gannon shouted at what must have been a general in his army.

The man shouted out the names of the men he was going to take and ordered the rest to stand guard over the Duke's home.

"What has happened to Madam Eloise?" Gannon asked.

The group searched for her and found her lying on the ground unconscious. One of the ladies that had followed Gannon from the house ran to her and bent over her.

"She just passed out. Will you come help me carry her inside?" the lady said.

Jason quickly realized that she was referring to him and he ran to her side. As he bent down to help pick her up, he was taken aback by the beauty of the lady he was helping. She was the most beautiful woman he had ever laid eyes on. She had beautiful black hair with the most stunning hazel eyes he had ever seen. She was dressed in a red velvet gown with lace-up leather boots and had her hair curled in many ringlets and pulled behind her with a ribbon of lace.

"Are you going to help, or just sit there?" she asked quietly.

Jason quickly reached down and heaved Eloise from the ground and followed the girl down the cobblestone path and into the house.

Chloe looked around and found herself sitting on a stool in front of a fireplace wrapped in a warm fleece blanket. She had no idea how she arrived here, but she was grateful. She looked up and found her brother sitting next to her sipping a steaming cup of some sweet-smelling liquid. Aden was also sitting across from them, writing on a piece of paper. A large blue bird sat on the floor next to Aden and at the other side was the tall man Chloe remembered was called Gannon. A few moments later two of the most beautiful women Chloe had ever seen entered the room carrying a tray of snacks and more of the hot liquid.

"Where are we?" Chloe asked softly.

She must have caught everyone by surprise because as soon as she spoke her brother threw himself at her feet and placed both hands on her cheeks.

"You're okay!" he said, looking relieved. "You haven't said a word for hours."

He gave her a big hug and she returned it.

"What is going on? Where am I?" she asked after being released from her brother's grip.

215

"You don't remember what happened?" the older lady asked.

"The last thing I remember is entering the gate in Avis," she answered.

All eyes in the room were on her, except for Aden's.

"Aden, what is going on?" she said ever so quietly.

Aden stopped writing and caught her gaze.

"You used magic to save your brother from three men in black. I'm unsure of how they gained entrance to the kingdom, which makes our journey to Mere even more dangerous. You have been in somewhat of a coma for the last several hours because it took so much energy for you to beat their magic. I'm sending for Kamali for assistance in our journey. You are now in the home of the Duke of Avis, his lovely wife Calla, and their daughter Belle," Aden answered as he returned to writing on his parchment.

"I...I used magic? How, I don't know any magic," she asked.

"My lady, you were born with the gift of magic. I knew as soon as I met you. When you get trained a bit, you are going to be quite the little sorceress." Aden chuckled. "You lost a lot of energy this time because you aren't trained in such things. However, what you did was so great that I expect you to be even greater than Kamali soon."

Chloe didn't know what to say. She wasn't sure whether or not to believe Aden. How could she be a sorceress? She rose to her feet and faced Gannon and his family. Without hesitation, she gracefully curtseyed toward them.

"Thank you for allowing my brother and me to stay here." She knew it wasn't a perfect curtsey and that she even wobbled a few times, but she was as polite as she could be.

Jason reached for her hand and smiled at her.

"Can you please show us where we will be sleeping? I would like to get Chloe to bed as soon as possible," he said politely.

Chloe glanced at her brother. He had never been so polite to her in all his life. He turned from annoying little brother to protective, well-mannered big brother in only a few days. She wasn't sure how this was happening, but she was grateful for his help. Aden looked over at Gannon and sighed.

"We actually need to discuss a few things before you go to bed. What happened tonight wasn't a fluke. It was very dangerous and certain precautions need to be addressed." Gannon said. "I know you are tired and have had a long day, but please be patient and soon you will have the best night's rest of your life."

Chloe plopped herself back down in the large overstuffed armchair and gave a very rude sigh. She had never been so rude to anyone, but she needed to sleep. Jason stared at all of them and then impatiently joined Chloe and sat next to her in a wooden chair.

They were each given a fresh mug of the sweet drink and as Chloe took the first drink she felt it drain all the way from the top of her tongue to the very bottom of her stomach. She winced for fear that it may have burned her insides, but then she felt herself relax almost completely. All her fears and doubts were gone and the tiredness that she felt only seconds before had vanished. The cookies that were provided were also sweet to the taste with the best chocolate in the center that Chloe had ever had.

"I'm sorry, what do you call this drink and the cookies?" she asked, intrigued, as she took another large sip of her drink and mouthful of cookie.

"The drink is called brillion, which is translated to hot spiced apple lemonade, and the cookies are a chocolate drop with a hint of cinnamon," answered Gannon's wife.

Chloe nodded and then continued to drink her brillion. A few cookies later, everyone was satisfied of their hunger, and the unanswered questions lingered in the air. Jason looked at Aden, who had just finished his letter to Kamali and was now tying the little scroll around the leg of the big bird.

"Fly fast, my friend; we are in need of his guidance," Aden said quietly to the bird.

He rose from his chair and walked to the front door. As he opened it, the large bird took flight and disappeared outside into the dark night.

"Now, we must discuss the problems that have occurred this night. Jason, you must tell me exactly what they said to you, and Chloe, I need to know where you got the power for the magic that you used."

Jason and Chloe looked around the room. Jason
didn't know what he was supposed to say. He didn't hear
anything come from the men in the black capes. All he knew
was that they had held a cold sword to the back of his neck
and the next thing he knew Chloe had attacked them.

"Aden, they didn't say anything," Jason said.

He told them everything that he could remember and
Aden shook his head.

"You didn't hear anything, not a breeze or a hissing
sound?" he questioned. "Usually when attacked by a black
warrior, one says they have visions, or some say they have
been spoken to."

Aden sat edgily in his seat as he waited for Jason to
collect his words. Jason pondered for a moment and tried to
think back to what happened. Chloe sat staring at her brother
as did Belle, Gannon, and Calla. The only thing he could
remember was the wind. He explained how quickly the wind
had come and how he had felt when the breeze had hit his
face.

"The wind sort of got stronger and that's when I felt
the sword, and when their horses ran, the wind picked up
again and they were gone. I don't know if that's anything
important, but that's all that happened."

Aden sat very still and pondered. He wasn't sure what
had happened and how Jason couldn't have heard them
speak. He was sure that he heard someone call to him and try
and get his attention, but wasn't sure who it was. Maybe it
was just his imagination or maybe it was Chloe sending a

signal for help through his mind. He needed Kamali here to help him. Why would the King and Queen think he, an earth-shifter, could bring these two people to them safely by himself? He looked around the room and saw everyone staring at him.

"Gannon," he said almost at a whisper, "we need extra protection until Kamali gets here. Can you spare some of your guards?"

Gannon looked at him and smiled.

"Did you expect me not to do anything?" He chuckled. "Of course, you and your friends can have as many guards that you see fit. I know that this is not easy, but you know just as well as I do the importance of getting them to Mere as soon as possible. I don't know how those men got into the gates of the kingdom unnoticed, but I have some of the finest men I know watching the house as well as every gate to the city. You should have no problems getting a good night's sleep."

Aden stood and shook Gannon's hand and walked toward Chloe. He bent down on one knee and stared right into her eyes.

"You must learn to control your magic. We start heavy lessons tomorrow so get a good night's rest, you'll need it. Also you will accompany Belle for lessons in etiquette."

Chloe nodded her head and gave a big yawn.

"And you," he said now to Jason, "will get a sparring partner that will teach you how to defend yourself, as well as those around you."

Jason didn't like the sound of a sparring partner—he had no idea what that meant—but he was sure it wasn't going to be fun. He too nodded his head.

"Now Calla will show you to your rooms so you can sleep."

Aden rose from the ground and held his hand out to Chloe. She took it and he assisted her up from where she was seated. He looked at her and she knew that she was expected to curtsey for Gannon to show her gratitude. She did so, and she felt like she was getting better at it.

Jason wrapped his arm around his sister and they followed Calla out of the living room into a long hall. They were led to two doors at the far end of the house and she announced their quarters for the evening.

"There are fresh linens and towels, as well as a bell if you need anything. Don't worry, our house is well protected, you can sleep peacefully tonight."

She surprised Chloe by giving her a hug and kiss on the cheek.

"Sleep well," she said as she turned to go back down the hall.

Jason gave Chloe a quick hug and opened her door.

"Thanks for saving me," he whispered.

He turned around and opened his own door and stepped inside and shut it again. Chloe stood in the doorway

for a moment and stared at her brother's door. What had
happened to him? He had never been so worried about her as
long as she could remember. She closed her door tightly
behind her and found her room to be quite cozy. There was a
small fire and a plush bed with lavender-colored linens. She
didn't even bother to take off her clothes before she lay
down. She closed her eyes and her mind began to wander.
She remembered waking up in the Kingdom of Mere, she
remembered the horseback ride to the city of Loch, and their
journey to Avis. She quickly fell asleep and began to dream.

She heard a faint tapping on her door, and she rose
from her bed to answer it. As she pulled it open a man
dressed in all black was standing there with his sword drawn.
Chloe recognized him; it was the man that was standing out
the window at their cabin by the lake. The man that her father
and Megan's dad searched for all night had found her.

The man reached for her and grabbed her by the arm
and began to drag her out the door. She screamed and felt
herself getting angry again. She felt the magic draw up inside
her body, but it wouldn't move. She wiggled to escape and
hit and punched him with her free hand.

Why isn't anyone trying to help me? she screamed in
her mind.

She closed her eyes and began crying and then felt
herself being shaken. She opened her eyes and found
Gannon, Jason, Aden, and two guards in her room. Jason was
holding her arms and his nose was bleeding. Aden had a rag
and was cleaning a scratch down his cheek and Gannon also

had many cuts and scrapes down his arms and face.

"What happened, where is he?" Chloe cried. "Did you catch him?"

Jason stared at his sister and then looked around at Gannon and Aden. Aden walked over to her and put his hand to her forehead.

"There's no fever, but she's going to need some company tonight," he said, still wiping blood from his face.

"Chloe, you were dreaming. You attacked all of us and were screaming at the top of your lungs. You had a complete fit every time someone touched you. We had to pin you down and try and wake you up. If the guards wouldn't have been fully armed, you probably would have given them both serious injuries," Jason said.

"What do you mean I was dreaming? The man that was outside our cabin by the lake, he was here. He tried to drag me down the hall. He attacked me, Jason. Where is he?" Chloe bawled.

Aden shot Gannon a look of concern at the story Chloe had portrayed happening.

"No, Chloe, we heard you scream and we ran in to see what happened and you were flipping around on your bed. Your arms were flying everywhere and you were crying. I ran over to you and touched your hand and you punched me right in the face. That's when Aden, Gannon, and the guards showed up. We were all trying to wake you up and keep you from getting hurt, but we ended up getting beat to death by you." Jason spoke quietly but with seriousness in his voice.

Chloe looked around the room again and now saw Belle and Calla standing at the door along with two other women she hadn't seen before. One of the women brought in a tray with a steaming cup of water and laid it on the bed next to her.

"Drink this, it will help soothe your mind," Gannon said with a somber look.

Chloe took a drink of the hot water. It burned her tongue as soon as it touched it, but she didn't care.

"Mable, I want you to stay here with Chloe tonight, she will need looking after," Gannon said now waving everyone out of her bedroom.

Chloe looked at her brother and her eyes sank. She had dreamed of being hurt by a man she didn't know. What was happening to her?

"Jason, I'm sorry," she whispered.

Jason gave her a hug and kissed her cheek.

"You get some sleep, I'm right here. I promise I won't let anything happen to you."

Chloe returned his hug and lay back down on her pillow. Before Jason left, she was already sound asleep. Mable, a maid in the home, sat close by and dabbed her head with a warm cloth. Jason shut the door quietly and turned around. Aden and Gannon were standing there waiting for him.

"Who was she talking about? What man did you see at the cabin?" Aden asked sharply.

"Chloe saw a man standing outside in the woods at the cabin one night. My father and Mr. Pearson went out searching for him almost all night and didn't find a thing, not even a footprint. We all thought Chloe was seeing things," Jason answered.

Gannon looked at Aden and a frown formed on his face.

"They have entered the kingdom with them. We have a traitor amongst our group and it's getting more and more dangerous. We have to start the preparations for war. I will send a message to Mere letting them know of the situation and start the preparations immediately." Gannon ran down the hall and entered a room and was gone.

"Aden, what is he talking about?" Jason asked.

"The Kingdom of Nebula was overrun by the Duke of Calidity, as I'm told you know, and a special protection was put upon our kingdom to keep them out. However, when we let you enter into the kingdom, they must have known when the gate was going to be open and are now here. If we don't get you and your sister to Mere as soon as we can, then our entire kingdom might be overtaken as well. I don't know how to explain any more of this right now, and I must go and see if I've received a letter from Kamali. I want you to get some rest, you are still going to have lessons tomorrow." Aden left just as quickly as Gannon had, leaving Jason alone in the darkened hall.

Jason went to his room, grabbed a blanket and pillow along with his sword. Returning to the hall, he lay down in

225

front of Chloe's room. He knew he wasn't going to be able to sleep tonight so he might as well be on guard if anything did happen. He wasn't sure what was going on, but he knew that it was serious.

12

Aurora

Preston's eyes shot open. He had been dreaming
about three men dressed in black and they were chasing him.
He looked around and they were still traveling deeper into
the water. He wasn't sure how long he had been sleeping, but
he was sure they had to be getting close.

"Where are we?" he asked Cane. Cane glanced at him
suspiciously.

"My young Prince, you've only just closed your eyes.
We have just left the guardians at the gate. Are you feeling
all right?"

Preston eyed the man and then looked again at his
surroundings. He looked up and sure enough he could see the
wall and the gate not too far above him.

"I guess I was daydreaming, that's all," Preston
answered quietly.

Cane stared at him for a moment and then turned and
watched as they drifted further and further down. Preston
knew that he wasn't going to sleep now. He looked out of the
tiny little submarine and frowned as he saw a faint reflection
of Megan in the glass. He had almost forgotten that she was
ill. He turned and looked at her and slowly stroked her hair.
He had never really noticed how shiny her hair was. Now

227

that he paid attention, she looked almost exactly like his
mother.

"It's going to be okay, Meg, we'll make you better,"
he whispered quietly as he continued to stroke her hair.

He looked over at Zachi and found he was watching
him.

"Do you think she's going to be okay?" Preston asked
him.

Zachi gave a quick nod and then shut his eyes again.

Preston looked back out the glass dome and watched
as the numerous fish swam by. He caught many glimpses of
different types of turtles and seaweed; he even thought he
saw coral, but he was sure it was a mistake seeing as how this
wasn't salt water. As Preston watched he saw something out
of the corner of his left eye. He quickly spun around, and
looking him straight in the face was a merman. He had pale
skin and long silvery hair. At his waist began his large fin.
He was holding what looked like a pitchfork and his eyes
seemed distant.

"Uh, Cane, what am I supposed to do?"

Cane smiled and gave him a slap on the back.

"You greet him, you know, say hello."

Preston looked at Cane. "You mean, it can talk?"

Cane shot him an angry look. "What have you done?
You have just offended one of the most powerful mermen in
all of Rill. It is not an 'IT.' They are people just like you and
I. Of course they speak, and it's the same language you and I
are speaking right now."

Preston turned and saw that the merman had left.

He looked back at Cane, stunned. He didn't understand what he had done to offend the creature or merman. He had never seen one in his entire life, only heard of them in stories from his father.

"They speak English?" he asked.

"Preston, have you forgotten so quickly, I've explained this already. You aren't speaking English anymore; you are speaking in the tongue of Mere," Zachi said harshly. "You have a lot of manners to learn; now we will be lucky if we are allowed presence into Rill. People recognize you as the Prince now because of the sword which you hold. It has inscribed on the blade as well as the hilt the symbol of Mere. Two swords joined together with a gold band. It stands for unity and it means 'Combined Strength Will Conquer All.' Only royalty are allowed to have this inscribed on their swords."

Preston withdrew his sword from where it was sheathed and glanced at it. Sure enough, there was the inscription.

"I think I remember my father telling me about the symbol. It was made when Nebulans took refuge in Mere, with the people of the lake, when their kingdom was taken. It meant that they were going to fight to save their kingdom together."

"It's about time you remember something. Cane, we are going to have to fix this situation," Zachi said, annoyed.

229

Cane gave a quick nod and Zachi turned to Preston once again.

"Cane and I have to step outside for a moment to fix what you just started. You must stay here and keep and eye on Megan. Don't touch the glass, it will be weak until we return, which hopefully won't be long."

Before Preston could say a word both Cane and Zachi stood up and jumped through the glass. However, it didn't shatter as Preston expected, it just melted away from them. Preston saw that both of the men now had part of the glass around their heads. It looked like they had put their heads in a fish bowl.

Zachi and Cane disappeared underneath of the boat and Preston was left alone with Megan in the middle of the water surrounded by fish and merpeople.

Preston wasn't sure what he really had done to offend the merman. He was actually quite surprised to see something living down here besides fish. He looked at his sister and moved closer to her. He felt her head and it was still burning hot. She had sweat beads on her nose and running down her face. Her hair was wet from how hot she actually was. He had to admit to himself that he was very afraid for her.

What will happen if she doesn't make it? Will Chloe ever forgive him for letting her best friend die in his arms?

As he spoke Chloe's name in his head, a new fear began to form. He had almost completely forgotten this girl that he had drifted madly in love with. Of course he really had only known her a couple of days, but from the moment he laid eyes on her, it was like he would never be able to breathe again without her by his side. He began to picture her in his mind and a smile formed on his face. How absolutely beautiful she was. He had to find her. He needed to be with her and protect her. He was snapped back to reality when he heard a loud shluup. He realized that his eyes were closed and opened them quickly. He saw Cane and Zachi back from their journey into the water. Neither of them were the slightest bit wet. It was as if they hadn't gone anywhere at all. Preston wasn't sure how they had managed to stay dry, but assumed it was all part of the magic he still needed to adjust to.

"Is everything okay?" Preston asked cautiously.

He had learned the hard way that ever since he woke up Zachi had been in quite a bad mood. His temper seemed to always be on the edge.

"We have fixed what you have done; however, they wish for an apology from the Prince himself before we go any further." Zachi spoke quickly and with sharp tones.

"Well then, what do I need to do?" Preston asked.

Zachi looked at him in surprise and then glanced back a Cane.

"You need to enter the water the same way we did and swim to the bottom of the river. There you will find fifteen mermen awaiting your apology," Zachi said.

231

"How do I enter the water? Is there some special word that I have to say to get the bubble over my head?" he asked again.

"No, all you have to do is push your head through the glass. It is already bewitched so it will automatically form around your head." This time Zachi actually sounded kind and full of patience. "You must speak as royal as you can. I know you haven't had any training on this subject, but I know your father has read you stories and used his own royal voice to do so. Speak as your father spoke."

Preston smiled at the thought of his father reading him stories and using that commanding voice he used many times when he read the lines of a King or Prince in a book. He nodded his head in acceptance and pushed his head through the glass. Before he got through the glass, he came back into the boat and reached down and stroked Megan's head.

"Zachi, I need you to watch her as carefully as if she were still your sister. You know she's still your friend and you still care for her deeply." He smiled and then pushed through the boat before Zachi had time to answer.

Once outside in the water, Preston expected to feel the cold wetness engulf him, but instead he felt complete warmth. He found it quite easy to swim and the bubble never shifted from around him. He kicked his legs hard and started to swim to the bottom of the river bed. The darkness started to form around him and he could feel his heart beating wildly. The adrenaline in his body started to rise and he found himself being sucked down further and further. He tried to free himself of the grip the current had on him, but it was no use. Soon he could see nothing, not even his own hand. Preston had never been in such darkness before. He stopped struggling against the current and tried to make himself calm down.

Breathe, he kept telling himself, *just breathe. It will all be over soon.*

He kept blinking, hopeful that the light would return. Just as he began to think that he was never going to reach the bottom, he saw a light. It was very bright and was shining up from what he suspected to be the ground below. He felt himself pass through some sort of opening, like entering a cave and he beheld a beautiful city. It was made completely of white stone with several glass spheres surrounding many different turrets on buildings. He was no longer being sucked down by the current but could swim freely. He looked around and spotted the mermen that Zachi had told him about. He kicked hard and found himself surrounded within seconds by fifteen mermen all armed with spears or three-pronged pitchforks.

Preston raised his hand and smiled. "My deepest apology for any pain that I may have caused to come upon you. It was a deep error on my part to not address one so wise. Please accept my apology, the apology of Paden, the Prince of Nebula."

He only hoped that he spoke "royally" enough. He had tried to use the voice that he remembered his father use during battle scenes in his books. His worst fears were over when one of the mermen embraced him warmly in a deep hug.

"My brother, how is it that thou does speak so well to me. It is I that should be apologizing. I did not know I was in the presence of the son of Adara." Though the merman spoke clearly, Preston wasn't sure what he meant.

"I ask you, who is Adara?" Preston asked kindly.

The merman shot him a look of bewilderment.

"My Prince, she is your mother, the Queen of Nebula." He bowed as he spoke.

"You must be mistaken; my mother's name is Jennifer, Jennifer Minnow." Preston felt his curiosity growing as he waited for the merman to answer.

"There is no mistake, you have the mark of a mermaid's son behind your right ear. The mark of the star Aurora. Your mother married the King of Nebula to secure peace between Rill and Nebula. After Nebula was taken captive by Jacan, they fled with you and your sister to the land above. We feared we would never again see her or any of her family, but here you are apologizing to me, a simple merman." He laughed as he spoke as if this were all some sort of game that Preston was playing.

Preston reached up and felt behind his ear, sure enough, he had a bump there that felt to be in the shape of a star.

"Your mark only shows up in water and only shines white when in Rill," the merman said as he watched Preston feel his new star shaped birthmark.

"My name is Nirvelli, I am a guard of the Sorceress Aurora. I understand that your sister is ill and you need an audience with her immediately. Zachi has informed us all of the situation at hand, that was the reasoning of the strong current, we couldn't risk your sister getting any worse," Nirvelli said.

Preston looked at him and then turned around. There was the boat, Zachi, Cane, and Megan not ten feet from where he was swimming. Preston felt the anger swell inside him.

"Zachi knew that my mother was a mermaid, and instead of telling me, he sent me down here to apologize and had me believe that they were to wait above for me to return?" Preston's anger was well known as he yelled at Nirvelli.

His face grew red, and he swam quickly over to Zachi and tried to enter the boat, but wasn't able to get in. Nirvelli put a hand on his shoulder and immediately he felt himself starting to relax.

"My Lord, you must relax for a spell to work, but I feel I must tell you that Zachi had no knowledge of this. He believed your mother to be a mere Sorceress that your father married. We told him that we needed to see you alone so he sent you. As soon as you left the boat, it was attached to you and you pulled it into the current. Zachi and Cane are not to blame, but the ones to thank. For they won't let even us into the boat to try and save your sister," Nirvelli said calmly.

Preston looked up from Nirvelli's face and saw that Zachi and Cane had their weapons raised and were fighting off anyone trying to touch Megan.

"Zachi, it's okay, they are going to take her to Aurora." Preston shouted. "Lower your weapons."

Zachi and Cane lowered the weapons and two mermaids came from out of the rocks and entered the boat and came out moments later with Megan wrapped in seaweed and a bubble over her head.

"We must follow them, Sire, if you wish to speak with Aurora," Nirvelli said quietly.

Preston turned and swam after them. He was followed by twelve mermen; Zachi and Cane were escorted by the other three into the city. After only a few short moments of swimming they entered a large white stone arch that stood about fifteen feet high and around twelve feet wide. It was the entrance to the most beautiful city in the world, the city of Rill. As soon as they entered, they were surrounded by large stone buildings that sparkled each time they swam by. It was an amazing sight. Preston couldn't help but wonder what the stone actually was. It seemed to be almost coral, but it was far too thick and strong. It was almost as if the building had been carved right into large boulders. There were merpeople in every direction. Not only were merpeople in the city, but Preston saw numerous fish, crab, and snails the size of a flounder fish, Todswan with long spears, and every now and then he might spot a human shopping with a bubble engulfing their head. Preston was amazed at the awesome beauty of the city. Not long after swimming down the pebble-stone paths, all the different creatures stopped what they were doing and stared at the newcomer. Some made a scene and bowed low to the ground at Preston and others just turned and swam away. It was hard to tell if people were enthused about him being there.

They entered another large gateway and found themselves completely encircled by a pure white castle. It wasn't a very big castle, but it definitely had the turrets, the arrow slits, the arched windows. It even had a moat, but it wasn't filled with water; it was a maze of seaweed and other plant life. Preston felt as they drew closer to the maze of plants that it had some sort of pressure that started to pull him down. He found he couldn't swim in any direction, but just let the plants suck him down. He landed feet first on a large stone bridge that led into the castle.

If that bridge wouldn't have been let down for us, it would have sucked us right into all of those plants. It was definitely a better strategy than a river, Preston thought to himself.

As they began to cross the bridge, Preston noticed that at the bottom of the plants were what looked like cages. Nirvelli must have noticed his curiosity, because his thoughts were answered.

"That is what we call a tomb. It draws in anything that gets within two hundred yards slowly downward. If you aren't in the right spot and the bridge hasn't been let down, you will get sucked right into one of the cages at the bottom

237

and will have to wait there until either a castle worker lets you out, or Aurora lets you out. It's really a great thing, being able to swim right over the walls. Aurora had to develop a technique that would get trespassers that swam over the walls. There is also a spell put over the entire castle as well. If you are an unwelcomed visitor, the castle isn't visible. It just seems to disappear. It's interesting to see humans come down and try to see the castle and some try and touch it, but to no avail. You have to have an invitation to be here."

"How, then, are we able to enter and see the castle, since we haven't received an invitation to see Aurora?"

"That's simple. You are the son of a mermaid, you are the Prince of Nebula, and you also have received an invitation from Aurora many years ago. She told you that you were always welcome in Rill and to come back as soon as you could."

Preston couldn't believe it; he had already seen Aurora when he was just a little boy, but it was so long ago that he had no memory of it all.

How could my mother be a mermaid? Wouldn't she have to live in water all the time? he wondered.

He had so many questions that he wanted answers to, but he wasn't sure whom to ask. He had only known Zachi for a few days, Nirvelli only a matter of minutes, Cane about a day, and Megan couldn't answer anything at all. He was stuck with no one to confide in, and no one to trust. He hoped that Aurora would be able to answer his questions, if she would actually see them.

They arrived at the main doors to the castle and
Nirvelli grabbed a large seashell off of a hook on the stone
wall. He inhaled and blew hard into it. A loud sound like a
trumpet bellowed throughout the castle walls and he did it
once more. It was so loud, Preston and the other humans tried
to plug their ears, but couldn't due to the glass bubble
surrounding their heads. However, the merpeople just waited
patiently. Preston looked around at their large group.

He saw Megan just behind him now being carried by
the two mermaids. Zachi and Cane were still being escorted
by the three large mermen, and he noticed that their weapons
had been confiscated and were being held by a small
Merchild that seemed no older than eight or nine. Of course
he wasn't sure about the ages of any of the people or
merpeople around him, but was sure that it was only a child.
Then there he was, being escorted by twelve beautifully
groomed mermen, each with their spears angled on their left
shoulders. He still couldn't quite get over the way they
looked. Half the body of a man, and half a large fish tail. It
was really quite a sight, but they were stunning, to say the
least.

Each merman had a different color of hair; some had
silver and others had a light blond, while others had an
almost perfect white. The two mermaids were also very
beautiful. They had very long hair that reached well past their
waist and they both had different colors of hair as well. One
had red, and the other had a sort of turquoise green. They
each wore the same color of clothing as their hair to cover

their chest. Around their neck were necklaces made of elegant stones, maybe even gems. They also had small seashells on the right side of their head. Preston imagined that they were used to hold back the hair from their eyes.

He returned his gaze back at the large doors and soon they were opened. Nirvelli entered and urged Preston and the others to follow suit. After everyone was inside, Preston heard the large door close with a soft thud. The room that they had entered was the most well-designed room he had ever seen. Of course he had only seen the two cabins by the lake, but this was stunning. It was made entirely of glass. Some of the glass was colored and others kept clear. There were spirals and chairs, benches, statues, and chandeliers that were lit by a soft glow of light. He wasn't sure what the light was made of, but his curiosity only grew. They were led by another mermaid—this one with purple hair—down a glass corridor and into an even larger room. She urged Preston to sit down on a glass sofa and then Megan was laid on a soft bed of seaweed right next to him. Zachi and Cane were also led to two glass chairs and the others moved back away from them. No sooner had Nirvelli moved, than a large air bubble started to surround the travelers and soon they were breathing fresh air and their protective bubbles had been removed. Preston turned his head to look around and found that the merpeople and the rest of the room were still immersed in water and their air pocket was a large round ball.

The room was suddenly lit with a brilliant light. It was almost as though the sun had been let into the room. The light was so bright that Preston, Zachi, and Cane all had to cover their eyes to prevent themselves from blindness. When the light died down to a soft glow and the bubble that they were in grew warm, Preston slowly opened his eyes. He looked around, his eyes still burning from the bright flash of light, and spotted a very beautiful mermaid with fair skin, long golden hair and piercing yellow eyes. She had a long rainbow-colored cape wrapped around her neck and it flowed elegantly toward the floor, but never quite touched it. He couldn't decide what material the cloak was made of, but its beauty only increased the mermaid's own beauty. She was also surrounded by a faint light that made her seem even more mysterious.

Preston felt his mouth fall open, but he was too awestruck to bring it back to its normal position. He sat quietly and just stared at the newcomer. Zachi and Cane both had stood from their chairs and bowed slightly, but Preston couldn't seem to move. No matter how hard he tried, he couldn't bring himself from that glass sofa. Zachi shot him an evil stare, but Preston only shook his head.

"My young Prince, why do you not rise to greet me?" the mermaid said quietly with a voice so calm and melodic that Preston would have described it as a lullaby.

Preston stared at her and tried to speak, but no words left between his lips.

"Preston, you need to speak. This is Aurora!" Zachi urged with strong but quiet words.

Preston tried to speak to her again, but still nothing. He was trying with all his might to speak and to bow to her, but something was holding him down in his chair, and he couldn't move.

"Young Prince, you can not move because you do not believe. You must let yourself believe in what you are seeing in order to move and speak. I am as real as your mother or father, even just as real as your sister, who desperately needs my assistance," she said nonchalantly.

At the thought of Megan still unconscious on the floor, he felt himself relax. He rose, put his feet close together, and bowed so graciously and beautifully he even surprised himself. He had never before bowed in this way that he could remember, but here he was doing it like he had been doing it his whole life. He glanced over at Zachi and Cane and they were both focusing all their attention on the mermaid in front of them.

"Aurora, we have come from afar to seek your assistance with my sister. She is not well. Her fever is extremely dangerous and she is slowly slipping away. I've been told you are the only one that can save her. So for this reason, I seek your aid." Preston spoke brilliantly and he knew it. He wasn't sure where this was coming from or how he knew what to say, but it felt all very natural.

"Paden, do you not know who I am?" she asked quizzically.

Preston was shocked at her question. Nirvelli had explained that he had been here before, but he couldn't remember this mermaid for anything.

"Of course, my lady, you are Aurora, Sorceress and Leader of the city of Rill," Preston answered.

She looked at him with aching eyes.

"Yes, young one, that is correct. There is more to me, however. Your mother, Adara, is my daughter. I am your grandmother."

Preston's mouth dropped again. How was any of this possible? He fell backwards into the glass sofa and stared down at the floor. He wasn't sure how this mermaid, a sorceress, a leader of Rill, and one so young, could be his grandmother.

"You must all be confusing me with someone else. My mother's name in Jennifer Minnow. She is a human and lives in a cabin by the lake. If she is a mermaid, then that would make me a merman," he said bluntly.

"Paden, when your mother was a young girl about the same age as Hanna, she was to be married to the Prince of Nebula to seal a peace treaty between our kingdoms. In order for her to live out of water, she had to become human. Kamali and myself transformed her into what you know her as today, a beautiful human and the Queen of Nebula." Aurora spoke quietly and seemed sad. "Since your father was human already, we were unsure how the children would be born, merperson or human. Before I had the chance to find out, the city Nebula was ambushed and my darling daughter and her family were sent to live in the world above. New identities meant that they could have no communication with their families elsewhere, and vise versa. It has been difficult not to see my grandchildren, but I knew that when you were the right age, you would return and see me."

Preston's whole body grew cold. He was so tired of these stories and of not understanding what everyone else knew. He wanted to know everything he didn't already know, from the time his parents were born, to the second they entered this castle. All he had to go by were stories that his father told him and what these other people told him. In all his life, his father never once mentioned that his grandmother was a mermaid. He could feel the anger swelling within his chest and his mind. He was tired of all of this; he just wanted to be alone to think about this new information. He stood to his feet again and faced his grandmother.

"Can you help Megan? She is getting worse." Preston didn't try to hide the anger in his voice and knew that he had just been very rude and hurtful, but he didn't care.

"Of course. Millie, please take Han—I mean Megan to her quarters and I will be up in a moment." Aurora spoke to her servant now, the one with light purple hair. The water that surrounded the travelers started to grow smaller and Megan was soon swept through the water and was being carried away up a spiral staircase.

"Gentlemen, I wish to be left alone with the Prince. Please escort Master Zachi and Sir Cane to their quarters and provide them with anything they desire."

At her words, fourteen of the mermen that had escorted them all to the castle urged Zachi and Cane to leave their bubble of air and enter the water again. Without hesitation Zachi and Cane departed through the wall of air and entered the water with an air pocket surrounding their heads and followed the mermen up the stairs and out of sight. The only ones that remained were Aurora, Preston, and, surprisingly, Nirvelli.

"Paden, please follow me, I have something I wish to show you," Aurora said calmly.

Preston stood in place and stared at his new grandmother. After looking at her for a moment, he felt his whole body begin to ease itself from the bitterness that he had felt moments before. He gave a half-hearted smile and walked to the edge of the air bubble. He didn't like the feeling of leaving this place of air, but pushed himself through the wall of water. Immediately he felt himself lurch forward and his air supply was gone. He couldn't breathe. The air pocket that he thought would surround his head never came and he felt himself sucking in water. He was drowning. His head started to spin wildly and he caught a glimpse of Aurora with a broad smile on her face. This was it; she wanted him dead. She was going to let him drown. He felt himself slipping out of consciousness. Seconds later his eyes closed and the blackness engulfed him.

13

Standing Guard

Zachi and Cane were taken to two small rooms just large enough for them and their belongings. The beds were made of glass, but had extremely soft plushy fabric draped over them to make them look even more extravagant. There was no need for the air bubbles in this room; it was completely free of any water. Zachi looked around and placed his small pack that he brought with him on the wooden dresser near the small circular window. A knock sounded at the far corner of the room. Zachi hastily walked over and opened the door.

"Our rooms are connected; do you wish to leave it shut or open?" Cane asked sarcastically.

Zachi glared at him.

"This is no time to play around. We have to leave immediately and roam the city for any information on Mere. The short time we have been here could very easily be enough time for war there."

Cane's smile quickly receded as Zachi spoke.

"Yes sir," he answered quietly.

Zachi shut the door and opened a drawer of the wooden chest that was placed near a small window. Inside he found numerous weapons. He suited himself with a water-friendly sword and hilt, as well as several arrows and a bow. He didn't know what was going to happen while they were here, but he wanted to be as prepared as he could be. He sat down on the plushy bed and laid his head back on the pillow.

I hope that she's okay. I don't know what they are going to do to her, he thought to himself.

Another knock on the door brought him back to reality and he walked over and opened it.

"Ready?" Cane asked.

Zachi took one last look at his small quarters and turned and left the room. They swam back down the spiraling staircase and out the front doors. The guards nodded as they passed, and a couple even gave them a small wave. It had been a while since Zachi had been to Rill, and he wasn't sure what new things to expect once he entered the city. Cane was just as quiet as he was. He had never been here, and Zachi could tell that the merpeople made him a little nervous.

The city was extremely busy this time of day. It was almost dinner time, and everyone was swimming around trying to get the freshest ingredients for their seaweed pies and such. Zachi pulled Cane away from one shop that was selling large pieces of conch shell. They sold for quite a bit on land and people would always try and get their hands on them in Rill, as that was the only place you could buy them.

"We are here to listen, not to buy," Zachi explained to Cane.

The small children that were playing around the city stopped and watched the two humans try to swim around the busy streets. Cane smiled at a few small boys that were playing some type of game that involved an extremely light piece of stone; each boy carried carved hoops. He watched them play for a few moments. After the smallest boy finally caught the ball in his hoop, the two men swam on. They heard nothing out of the ordinary from the merpeople, they only cared about the task at hand. Soon they turned a corner and found a small café that was run by a human, and were able to release their bubbles and enjoy the fresh air. They were brought small glasses of ice tea by a large man in white clothes.

"I don't think I've seen you all in here before. Are you from around here, or are you from above?"

Zachi smiled at the owner.

"Yes, we are guests of Aurora, we are from Mere," he answered.

"Well, then, my name is Theodore Bates, I'm the owner of the café, as well as the Duke of Rill. It is I that all humans here listen to." He held out his hand in greeting. "Aurora had made sure that anyone that survived the attack on Nebula was welcome here in Rill as long as they always had a leader that listened to her."

Zachi shook his hand willingly and Cane followed suit.

"I'm Zachi, and this is Cane. Tell me, Master Bates, have you heard any news from Mere as of late?" he asked politely.

Theodore looked at them both.

"Afraid not. I haven't been on land for a month, and last time I was there it was fine."

Zachi smiled. "Well, not much has changed then. If you hear anything, let me know right away."

"I'll do that. You boys have a great day."

He refilled their tea and walked away.

"Do you think that we will get a message from Avery?" Cane asked.

Zachi shrugged his shoulders and looked around the small building. There were several other humans in here, but Zachi was unsure if any of them would be carrying a message. He quickly finished his tea and stood up.

"We need to ask around. Why don't you go over there and ask them if they have been up on land lately."

Cane guzzled his own tea and walked over in the direction of three men enjoying their own cups of tea.

"Hey, fellas, name's Cane," he said loudly.

The men acknowledged him with a polite nod.

"My friend and I are traveling north and were wondering if anyone had heard any news of Mere?"

The larger of the men stood and shook Cane's hand.

"I was there a week ago with my brothers, and heard talk of a war, but saw nothing that would point toward one starting. It was strange, though, people were walking on the edge and would startle if a noise was too loud. Why do you ask?" he answered.

"No reason, we just don't want to be caught off guard when we go back on land," Cane answered.

The man looked heavily at him. "Name's Icion, these are my brothers, Ivian and Ivore. We moved here shortly after the attack on Nebula. A few of those black riders destroyed our blacksmith shop. When the King and Queen gave sign of their retreat, we did the same. I've heard talk of those black creatures back on land in Mere. Do you know anything about it?"

Cane searched the man's expressions. His talent as a wizard was always something he thought strange, but he could always tell when someone was lying, or if they were friends of the crown. After he decided they were no threat to the crown and Icion was telling the truth, he confirmed their story.

"There have been rumors, but I have not seen them personally."

Icion and his brothers sighed.

"Why do you ask?" Cane questioned the three large men.

Icion sat back down in his chair and stared blankly at the wall.

"They took our families away from us. We searched and searched, but never found any trace of them." Ivian spoke quietly.

Cane knew at that moment it was time for his retreat back to Zachi.

"I appreciate your information, gentlemen. If I hear of anything, Master Bates will be informed. Enjoy your drinks."

The men gave him a half-hearted smile and he threw a large coin down on the table and the three men shook his hand in thanks.

"Nothing new since yesterday," Cane told Zachi when he returned from the table of blacksmiths he was talking to.

"Yeah, maybe we should head back to the castle. I want to know if Megan is any better."

Cane looked awkwardly at Zachi.

"She's not your sister, you know. They will take good care of her."

Zachi paid him no attention. They pushed themselves back out the door through the wall of water and the bubble returned around their heads.

As they traveled back toward the castle, they noticed a bright light coming from one of the east windows.

"Come on, we need to check it out!" Zachi hollered over the bustle in the streets.

They swam quickly toward the castle and reached the bridge. As they swiftly swam across, they could feel the pull of the tomb trying to suck them down into the cages below, but made it across safely.

"Ah, you are back. Nirvelli wishes to see you in the east wing," the guard at the gate told him.

"Thank you, we shall go see him at once," Cane answered.

They entered the castle doors and swam quickly toward the east wing. They found a mermaid there with a letter.

"Zachi, Nirvelli asked me to give this to you," she said with a sweet smile.

"Thank you," Zachi answered.

He opened the letter and read quietly.

"We need to go to Megan's room. He says we need to see her."

The mermaid pointed them in the direction that they should go, and they swam up the stairs and toward the small room.

14

New Beginning

"Paden...Paden, wake up! You need to open your
eyes! Come on, boy, wake up!"

The shouts could be heard throughout the entire
castle. Preston felt someone slap him hard across the face. He
opened his eyes and put a hand to his cheek. The pain was
throbbing and he was sure there was going to be a red mark
where the person had just slapped him. When he had gained
the focus back in his eyes, he noticed Aurora standing over
him wide-eyed and Nirvelli holding him under the head with
his hand raised.

"Why did you just hit me?" Preston asked, scowling.
"I could hear you just fine."

Nirvelli smiled and so did Aurora.

"We thought maybe you were lost, young master. It
was all I could do to help you. Sorry about that." Nirvelli
chuckled slightly as he spoke and his long hair waved in the
movement of the water.

"How do you feel, my Prince? Can you breathe all
right?" Aurora asked.

Before Preston could answer she reached down and
grabbed him by the arm and hoisted him up from the glass
sofa where he was lying and embraced him in a warm hug.

"I'm fine, except for a slight headache and a sour stomach. What happened?" he asked, a little nervous to return the embrace from the sorceress.

She pulled back and looked him deep into the eyes. She smiled and Preston saw the beauty of his newfound grandmother. Her eyes were so full of radiance, beauty, and kindness.

"Paden, haven't you noticed anything different about yourself?" she asked with a short tone but still polite.

Preston really hadn't noticed anything different. The last thing he remembered was Megan being carried away up some stairs. He felt his face and nothing felt any different. He saw a mirror on a wall and went to walk over there, but he couldn't move his legs. He looked down to see what was going on, and his legs and feet were gone. In their place was a fin! He was a merman!

"How did this happen?" He somehow felt both anger and enthusiasm in his tone.

"Do you not remember?" Aurora asked quietly.

"I don't remember anything after Megan being carried away. What happened?"

"Paden, after Hanna was taken up the stairs and your friends Zachi and Cane led to their quarters, I asked you to follow me. You stepped through the wall of water and passed out. But the reason you passed out is because in my presence, your true form appeared. You are a merman, but not entirely. Since you are male, you take most of your father's genes, which means that you are only a merman temporarily. As

254

soon as you leave my presence and the city of Rill, you will
again be human. However, once you are a merman,
something always stays with you. You will always be able to
breathe under water from this day forward, but your fin is
only temporary, as well as your new hair."

Preston ran his finger up and down his fin. It felt so
different and yet it also felt natural to him. He wasn't sure if
he should be grateful or upset at his new transformation. He
then raised his hands and felt the long hair he had now grown
in a matter of minutes. He grabbed some and pulled it in
front of his face and saw that he now had not only long hair,
but hair the color of a blue sapphire. It was an amazing
transformation. He felt like a completely different person
now that he knew what was going on. He gave a little smile
and looked at his grandmother.

"Grandma, is there any way to make the change
permanent? I mean, well, I really like the way that Nirvelli
and the other mermen look. They are so…sure of themselves.
They seem to have the confidence they need." It felt strange
calling Aurora Grandma, but he didn't really care.

Aurora smiled at him and gave him another hug. "I've
missed you, Paden. I'm sorry I couldn't be there for you
before. I promise I'll do my best to always be there for you
now. But we really must go and visit Hanna; she really was
in a poor state when she left us."

Preston usually hated when people avoided his
question, but this time he didn't mind all that much. He just
returned his grandmother's warm hug and gave a kick with

his new fin. He shot through the water at top speed and would have run right into the wall if Nirvelli didn't stop him.

"Whoa, you need to take it easy with your new fin. Remember, they aren't legs and the harder you kick the faster and stronger you'll go." He laughed loudly and released Preston.

Aurora laughed slightly and gave a little kick and started on her way up the glass stairs. Preston did likewise, and found himself really having a hard time controlling where he was swimming. He wasn't sure how to make himself turn or even how to stop but Nirvelli was there with him the entire time guiding him this way and that and helping him follow his grandmother up the stairs and into a large glass hallway. Each hallway was lit with little lanterns and inside the lanterns were small glow-fish. Preston had never heard of such a thing, but here they were shining for the whole castle. Each chandelier and every lantern had as few as one or as many as one hundred.

Soon they turned down another hallway and entered a door made of the white rock with engravings all over it. The engravings were of mermaids, and mermen and also fish of many different types. On the top of the door the letters H-A-N-N-A were engraved. This was definitely a room designed especially for Megan.

As they entered, the room was full of sea flowers of every color and more glow-fish inside a glass chandelier. Everything in the room was made either from the white rock or carved from glass. Megan was lying on a bed made of glass and surrounded by a large air pocket. Aurora drew herself closer to her unconscious granddaughter and every time she moved, the water followed, making Megan's pocket of air smaller and smaller. Nirvelli moved over to the other side of the bed and both put their hands out of the water and touched Megan on the side of her head. They held hands and the water rushed over Megan and completely encased her in water.

Megan took a big breath and her eyes shot open. She tried to scream but the water rushed down her throat and she threw her hands up in protest. Preston watched as his sister scrambled and tossed her head, trying to get air. She soon closed her eyes and her breathing became slow and steady. A bright light flashed from around her body and lifted her in the air. Her legs disappeared and now became a golden fin. To Preston it seemed like it was made purely from gold, it was so beautiful. Her hair grew to the length of about four feet and then the color began to fade from red to silver and back to red. It stopped and Megan was laid back on the glass bed. Nirvelli and Aurora let go of her.

He reached over and gently slapped her face and she slowly opened her eyes. She sat up and felt her hair. It was no longer the red that Preston remembered; it was now a bright red with silver streaks that glittered and shined. She looked almost like a drawing in a book. Her eyes changed from piercing green to lightly colored amber. Aurora smiled and Nirvelli grinned broadly. Preston thought she was pretty before, but now she was breathtaking.

257

Megan looked around at everyone in the room and her eyes and face dropped in terror. She looked for something she could grab to protect herself from these strange things that were surrounding her. Preston swam toward her.

"Megan, calm down!" he yelled.

But she didn't know who he was. She screamed and this time, there was nothing to hold it back. It was so loud that the glow-fish swam away and the chandelier came crashing down and shattered on the floor. Everyone quickly covered their ears and soon the screaming stopped. Megan looked around and saw the door. She tried to get up from the bed, but instead she fell flat on the floor. Aurora swam down and rested her hand on Megan's arm.

"You need to calm down, sweetheart, and let us explain. If you keep screaming I'm afraid you will damage the entire castle."

Megan looked at Aurora in absolute terror. She then looked down at her legs and saw the large golden fin. Her eyes rolled into the back of her head and she fainted. Nirvelli swam down and swooped her up in his arms and laid her softly down on the bed. Another mermaid swam past Preston and handed a small glass bottle to Aurora. She tilted Megan's head back and poured a silvery substance into her mouth. Megan swallowed and then her eyes opened again, but this time she looked peaceful.

"What happened? What was that stuff?" Preston asked.

"It's a medicine to help calm her down. She's still extremely frightened, but now she will listen. The medicine is from the root of a Gala weed. It gives the patient trust and helps soothe any harmful thoughts," Nirvelli said, not taking his eyes off Megan.

"Megan, are you all right?" Preston asked.

Megan looked up at him and stared wide-eyed.

"Who are you, and how do you know my name?"

Preston explained to her who he was and who she was. He told her how they came to Rill and explained how she was now a mermaid. Megan listened to what Preston had to say and never once interrupted him. She waited patiently until he was finished and then turned her head and stared across the bed at her fin.

"So my name isn't Megan, it's Hanna, and I'm a princess of a kingdom called Nebula. What about Zach, where is he?"

She was extremely confused, but she spoke as calmly as she could. At that very moment, the door opened and Zachi and Cane were escorted in by several mermen. Zachi swam as quickly as he could toward Megan and saw that she was now a mermaid. He looked at her and his smile turned into a frown.

"Are you all right, Megan?" he asked with a quiet voice.

He still had the bubble around his head as did Cane, so it was very difficult to understand what he was saying.

259

"Zach?" Megan asked. "But I don't understand, what happened to you?"

Zachi looked at her and frowned.

"My lady, Preston is and always has been your true brother. I was only a guardian placed with you for your own protection. When we had to move your family from Nebula, we couldn't keep you and Preston together because Jacan would know who you were. He had seen you and your brother many times, so we had to split you up and put you with two other guardians and myself. I'm truly sorry, but that is what had to be done," Zachi said even more quietly.

He realized for the first time how hard this was going to be. He had become so attached to Megan over the years and she truly felt like a sister to him. He sat down as well as he could next to her and gave her a hug. Before he pulled away, he whispered in her ear something that no one else could hear and then pushed off the ground and swam out the door with Cane at his side.

A frown formed on Megan's face and she closed her eyes. Tears began to flow freely down her cheeks. Aurora sat on the bed next to her granddaughter and stroked her long red silvery hair.

"I know this is hard for you to understand, and I'll do my best to help you in any way I can."

Megan looked up at her with teary bloodshot eyes.

"I don't even know you. How can you help me?" she said abruptly.

Preston looked at his grandmother, who smiled. He hadn't told Megan that Aurora was her grandmother. He was still not used to the idea so he really didn't feel comfortable explaining that part.

"My dear Hanna, I'm your grandmother," she said.

She then explained all about her daughter and the marriage treaty between the two kingdoms. Megan was a true mermaid, and not just any mermaid—she was the heir to the throne of Rill. When her mother married she sealed her firstborn daughter as the heir of Rill, so that meant that Megan was going to have to learn to be a sorceress.

After Aurora finished explaining to Megan the details of her newfound talent, Megan began crying once again. Nirvelli approached Megan and handed her a piece of soft green material. Megan took it gratefully and wiped the tears from her face. But the tears weren't the tears she was used to. They weren't wet tears at all, but tears of air. She had almost forgotten that she was immersed in water.

"Can I be left alone please?" she asked, still not looking up from the green cloth.

"Of course, my dear, I'll have Maida bring you your dinner in about an hour. If you need anything or anyone before or after that time, just speak into the seashell near your bed. It will alert the person you desire and they will be at your service." With a small hug and a brief kiss on the cheek, Aurora stood to leave.

Megan looked up at her and gave a sigh. "Thank you," she said.

261

Aurora, Nirvelli, and Maida turned and walked toward the door.

Preston swam over to his sister and sat on the bed.

"I'm sorry about this, I know what you're going through. I've never had a sister, so I'm not sure if I'll be a good brother, but I promise I'll do my best." He leaned down and kissed her softly on the cheek.

"Preston, will you stay with me? I really need someone to explain this more to me."

Preston smiled at her and swam over to their grandmother.

"I'm going to stay with Megan. Please send my dinner up as well." He didn't mean for his voice to sound so demanding.

Without even a grimace at his tone of voice, she nodded and kissed him on the cheek as well.

"Tomorrow we start lessons, so I suggest you both get some sleep," she said.

Preston didn't know what lessons that they were going to have, but didn't want to worry about them. Megan was awake and had just gone through the same thing he did and he was anxious to talk to her. The threesome left the room and Preston closed the door with a thump. He swam slowly back over to where Megan was and pulled a chair from her vanity and sat next to her bed.

"Preston, you left out some stuff from your story. Where are the others? Chloe and Jason must be somewhere in this place if we are," Megan said. "Are they merpeople too?"

"I don't know where they are. Zachi said they were with Kamali and that everything was okay. I tried to force him to take me to them, but he refused. He said that we would meet them in the city of Mere. Shortly after that, we entered the water and now here we are."

She looked up at him and he watched as the air filled tears began spilling down her cheeks again.

"Look at it this way, we get to experience life underwater for a while."

She shot him a piercing look.

"Weren't you listening?! I'm the heir to the throne here. I have to learn magic and how to be proper. I was happy where I was. Why would Zach bring me here? He knew I was happy! I had my first real boyfriend, I was a straight-A student, and I was starting driver's ed after we got home. It was perfect, and now it's ruined. We can never go back, ever!" She threw herself face first into her pillow and continued to cry.

Preston had no idea what to do. When his mother cried, his father was always there to comfort her and he never really had to do anything. He reached out to her and pulled her up from the bed. It was quite easy, for she seemed as light as a feather under water. He wrapped his arms around her and gave her a hug. She sat and cried on his shoulder for the next ten minutes and then pulled herself away and stared at him. She was quiet for a long time and then smiled.

"I hope I'm a better swimmer than you with this thing." She laughed as she pointed to her golden fin.

Preston joined her mirth and told her how he almost hit a wall. This put her in an uproar of laughter and soon they were talking like they were best friends.

An hour later a ring sounded from the seashell near Megan's bed.

They looked at it strangely. "Yes?" Megan answered the call.

"I have dinner for you and Master Paden. May I bring them to your room?" Maida said.

"Um, sure, I guess," Megan responded.

She looked at Preston and smiled again.

"Do you like your new name?" she asked.

He grimaced at the thought of being called Paden but it seemed like it was proper for this place.

"I'm getting more used to it than before. When Zachi first told me that was my name, I thought it was hideous for a prince, but now that I've been 'him' for a day, it's kind of starting to stick to me. How about you, do you like Hanna?"

She frowned again, "My mom, or I guess Misty, actually called me Hanna sometimes. I guess it slipped, especially when we were playing when I was younger. I thought it was so cute, I named my doll Hanna. I guess I'm going to have to learn to like it for myself."

There was a brief thump on the door and Maida entered with two trays, one in each arm, and sat them on the bed stand next to them. They had two plates, each filled with

264

exactly the same items, some sort of plant thing with more plant things. It was colorful to say the least, but it definitely wasn't a meal that either of them was expecting.

"What is that?" Megan blurted. "Where's the rest?"

Maida looked at her strangely.

"I'm sorry, mistress, I'm afraid I don't know what you mean."

"I mean where's the meat. You don't expect me to eat weeds do you?"

Maida looked shocked.

"All merpeople here in Rill are vegetarians, miss, we don't eat meat. I was told that this would be your favorite."

Preston and Megan looked at each other with disgust on their faces.

"Um, can you have my grandmother come here, please?" Preston said as politely as he could.

Maida left immediately and the two eyed their plates.

"Yuck, I hope they really don't expect me to survive on this stuff. I was hoping for a hot dog or maybe some beef stew," Megan uttered.

"Oh, Mom's beef stew is the best! I wish you could have tried it. I know you would have liked it," Preston told her.

There was another brief tap at the door and Aurora came in followed by Nirvelli.

"Is there something wrong? Maida said you were dissatisfied with your meal," she said.

"What is this stuff? It looks disgusting," Megan said, unable to keep the rudeness out of her voice.

"This is the finest meal in the city. The Anacaris is the green leaf plant on the left. The red plant is called Hivin, it tastes like a cinnamon cake, it's like a dessert. And the plant with the yellow flower is called Millis. It is the plant that provides the protein you need to survive in the water. They only grow near the edge of the city and people rarely travel there because of the high dangers, but when they do, they get several plants and bring them to the castle as sort of an offering to our table. Try it, you'll like it." She reached down and placed the platters on their laps.

Megan looked at it and smirked. Preston felt his stomach growl and couldn't remember the last time he had eaten. He looked at his grandmother suspiciously and then back at the plate of plants in his lap.

"Try it, I assure you that your taste buds have changed along with your physical appearances." She smiled this time, almost as if it were all some sort of joke.

Preston picked up the red plant and took a small bite. Aurora was right, it did taste similar to a cinnamon cake. He took another bite and then another. Megan watched him and then followed suit. She too quickly ate the Hivin plant. Preston tried the green Anacaris next and found it to be quite salty, but it was also enjoyable. The yellow Millis was the last that he tried, and he enjoyed it the most. It tasted like a hot steaming bowl of soup running down his throat. Soon the food was gone and his stomach was full. There was no need for anything to drink; he assumed merpeople didn't need to drink because of all the water. Megan was the same; she had finished her meal and now the two leaned back and sighed.

"You see, things may be different, but never judge a book by its cover." Aurora laughed and gave each a kiss on the cheek. "I'll see you both in the morning. I've some business to take care of in town and won't return until quite late. If you are in need of anything, call for Maida, she will assist you."

She and Nirvelli quickly turned and left. Preston and Megan heard them laugh as they shut the door and then it was quiet again.

Neither Preston nor Megan said anything; they were both too full to speak. The food turned out to be delicious and now they found themselves ready for a nice long nap.

"I think I'm going to have Maida take me to my room. I would like to snoop around a bit before I go to bed," Preston said, reaching for the seashell.

"Not without me you're not!" Megan shouted.

She grabbed the shell and looked at it.

"Um, Maida, are you there?" she said shyly.

"Yes, mistress, what can I do for you?" came the reply.

"Preston, I mean Paden and I would like you to show us his room please?" Megan said again.

"I'll be right up, miss," Maida said.

Sure enough only seconds later a tap was sounded at the door.

267

"Come in!" Megan called.

The door opened and Maida came in followed by a merman. Maida was a pretty mermaid with fair skin, yellow hair, and black eyes, and the merman swimming next to her, holding a spear, had white hair, rippling muscles, and blue eyes. He looked intimidating. Preston wanted to know if the hair color on a merman meant anything, but he wasn't about to ask this one.

"This is Eri, your royal guard," Maida said to Preston. "He is to be with you any time you leave your room. Follow me please."

Megan hadn't had a real chance to try out her swimming ability with her fin yet, but she seemed to be better at it than Preston. As she pushed herself off of her bed, she glided, a little wobbly, toward Maida, unlike Preston, who veered off to the right and left as he tried to follow her.

Megan laughed hysterically. "Well, that's something I'm better at than you, I guess."

They laughed as they left the room and followed their guides out the door.

15

Battling Lessons

Chloe slept soundly through the night. She woke up
the next morning feeling stiff and weak. A maid was asleep
in an overstuffed armchair with a small blanket made of wool
wrapped around her shoulders. The fire that had been lit the
night before was out now and the room was quiet. She slowly
pushed back the covers and slid to the edge of the large
queen-sized bed. On the floor near the bed were a pair of soft
white slippers and hanging over a chair near the vanity was a
matching bathrobe. She quietly slipped out of bed and into
the robe and slippers and crept to the door. She turned the
handle and pulled it open. It was extremely heavy and
squeaked loudly, as if it were in agony at being asked to open
so early. Lying on the floor wrapped in blankets and fast
asleep was Jason. He was still wearing the same clothing as
the day before and had his sword gripped tightly in his hand.
Chloe smiled at the thought of him trying to protect her.

She stepped gently over him and tiptoed down the
hall to where she thought the kitchen was. Her stomach
growled impatiently and she felt herself quicken her pace.
She pushed open another large heavy door and found
Mistress Calla sitting at the table with Gannon eating toast
smeared in what looked like grape jelly and drinking what

she assumed was some sort of hot tea.

"Good morning, my dear, did you sleep well?" Calla asked.

Gannon got to his feet and pulled a chair away from the table and waited for Chloe to sit down. She smiled at him and remembering her manners, curtseyed before sitting as gracefully as she could in the plush chair.

"Yes, thank you for asking," Chloe answered.

"Would you care for some breakfast, my lady?"

Chloe looked around for the voice that had asked her the question and found a very short stout woman near Calla that she hadn't seen before. Her stomach growled again at the thought of food.

"Yes, please, may I have some toast with jelly and some hot chocolate?" she blurted.

"Of course, my lady. What kind of jelly would you like? We have strawberry, peach, marmalade, grape, and of course my famous huckleberry." The little lady smiled brightly.

"Oh, I would love to taste the huckleberry, I've never had that," Chloe said quickly.

The little lady curtseyed and quickly left the room.

"You will be accompanying my daughter Belle today for some quick lessons in manners, and Jason will be accompanying Aden and me to learn more swordsmanship. It will be short, however, and immediately after lunch you will be continuing your journey toward the city of Mere," Gannon said.

"I thought we were going to stay here a couple of days and continue lessons before going on," Chloe remarked.

"I'm afraid some things have come up and you must get going. I wish your stay could have been longer with us; however, times are changing and we have to move quickly,"

Chloe wasn't sure what to say but before she had any time to answer, Gannon rose from the table and kissed his wife on the cheek. She gave him a wan smile as he left the house.

The little lady arrived around the same time and placed a large platter in front of her with four slices of hot homemade bread lightly toasted and smeared in huckleberry jam. Then she placed a large mug of steaming hot chocolate next to the platter.

"Anything else for you, miss?" she asked.

"No, thank you very much, it looks fantastic." The lady's smile extended clear across her face and she scooted herself away from the table, beaming.

Just as Chloe took a bite, Jason came pouring out of the hallway in a rage, his sword drawn and ready to strike anyone in his path. The little lady screamed and ran behind Calla.

"What is going on?" Calla said calmly.

"Chloe is…" His voice trailed off as he spotted her sitting at the table staring at him.

He raced over to her and threw his arms around her neck.

271

"I thought someone had taken you. When I woke up and you weren't there, I panicked."

He gave her another hug and then glared at her.

"Don't ever sneak away from me, you don't know what's out there! You should have woken me!" he howled.

Chloe smiled at him and touched his face.

"I'm fine. You looked so peaceful I couldn't wake you. I knew that you had only just fallen asleep, I could tell by how soundly you were sleeping."

She gave him a hug and motioned for him to sheath his sword and sit down. Jason took a big breath and did as he was told.

The little lady came out from hiding and cautiously walked toward him, eyeing his every movement.

"I'm sorry, this is Mignon, she's our cook," Calla said.

Mignon stopped in front of Jason and smiled. She asked what he would like for breakfast. He answered her by pointing toward Chloe's plate and mug and then let his face drop onto the table. Mignon quickly disappeared behind the kitchen doors and returned moments later with a platter full of toast and a full mug of hot chocolate.

"Thank you, it looks delicious," Jason said.

Chloe watched him carefully as he slowly ate his toast. She didn't waste any time. She was almost entirely finished with all her toast, and her hot chocolate was gone long ago. She nibbled the last bit of her toast and sat back in her chair and sighed.

Jason was still eating when Belle came through the door. She was dressed in a beautiful long blue dress and her hair was pulled back in a bun and held in place by a small silver crown. She wore a pearl necklace that changed color when she walked. She looked absolutely stunning.

"Good morning, Mother, Chloe, Jason. How did you sleep?" she asked just as quietly as her mother.

"Just fine. You look beautiful!" Chloe answered.

"Thank you. A lady never comes to breakfast in her nightgown." Belle looked at Chloe and urged her to go and put on something more suitable.

Chloe glared at her, but stood up from her chair and left the room.

"Jason, get the chair for her," Calla said sternly.

Without hesitation Jason stood and pulled her chair out from the table. Belle curtseyed and sat down gracefully. He smiled at her and sat back in his own chair to finish what was left of his breakfast. When he was finished, he rose from the table and excused himself. He found it rather nerve-racking to be in the same room with Calla and Belle, even though they were both very kind. He opened the door to the hallway and slowly walked toward his sister's room. He knocked and found it quickly opened by Chloe.

"What took you so long? I've been waiting for like ten minutes," She said, scowling.

"Waiting for what?" he asked.

"I don't know what to wear. She looked beautiful and all I have is the dress I received from Cerella in Loch."

273

Jason smiled at her and walked over to where the dress was hanging.

"Gannon told me that there was a new dress in the closet that you were to wear today. Also, you are to call your attendant and they will assist you in getting ready," he said jokingly.

She ran toward the armoire and opened it. There, hanging up, was a beautiful emerald green velvet gown with a shear fabric making the long split sleeves.

"Look at this dress, it looks like something from one of those old movies. Isn't it gorgeous!"

Jason laughed at her. "I'll go and ask Eloise to come help you."

He smiled as he left the room. Chloe took the dress from where it was hanging and put it up to her body. She walked over to the large mirror and spun herself around. It really was a beautiful dress. A few moments later there was a small knock on the door and Eloise came in with two other servants.

Soon Chloe looked like she was ready for a ball. The gown fit her perfectly. She wasn't used to the corset, however, and found it very hard to breathe. She had asked Eloise if it were really necessary for her to wear it, but Eloise just laughed at her. Her hair had been left down, but had ribbons placed strategically throughout. A pearl necklace was placed around her neck and black riding boots were laced on her feet. She had tried to do everything herself, but was glared at by the other two servants who were assisting Eloise.

Chloe walked elegantly toward the mirror and found herself looking like a princess and not just a guest in the Duke's home. Eloise and the other servants curtseyed toward her and left the room without a word. Jason came in moments later, followed by Belle and Calla.

"Wow, don't you look different," Jason said.

Chloe stared at herself in the mirror for a long time and then turned around. She curtseyed toward the ladies of the house and smiled. The dress made her feel so graceful, almost as if she were a different person. Jason had also had a change of wardrobe. He was now wearing black pants that were tucked into knee-length riding boots and a white long-sleeved shirt that hung loosely at his waist. The shirt had the two swords with the golden sash engraved right in the middle and his sword was now sheathed in all black leather. His hair still needed to be combed, but he looked like a man and no longer felt to Chloe like her little annoying brother.

"Shall we?" Belle asked politely.

"Where are we going today?" Chloe asked.

"Jason shall be accompanying my father and Aden around the town having lessons from many different people; you shall stay with me and my mother for lessons in etiquette. I'm only sorry it will be short lived."

Chloe thought about what Belle had said and realized that she meant that she needed a lot of work. She already could tell by the tone in Belle's voice that today was not going to be an easy day. She said goodbye to Jason and followed Belle and Calla down the hall into a large room

275

filled with books. It wasn't nearly as large as the one in Loch, but it had hundreds upon hundreds of books. In the middle of the room was a small table surrounded by plush chairs and atop the table sat a tea set with biscuits of some sort. Chloe wasn't really hungry, but she decided she would do her best not to upset her teachers. Calla sat first and Chloe was awed at how gracefully she had accomplished it. Belle followed and both women stared at Chloe and waited for her to sit. She moved slowly toward the chair and lifted her dress slightly from the floor as she backed up until her legs touched the chair and let herself slip quietly and gracefully down onto the soft cushion.

"Impressive. Have you been taught before?" Calla asked her nicely.

"The only training I have received has been from the books I've read on our journey," she answered.

The morning continued in this manner and on some things Chloe was just as good as Belle and Calla, and others took a lot more work. It was excruciating taking advice from two women she had only just met and on such a topic that she didn't seem to think was all that important. Her mind wandered constantly to how Jason's training was going. However, just as she was settling in to this new lifestyle, it was time for them to continue their journey toward Mere. They departed the library and met the others in the dining room.

Jason was full of welts, bruises, and cuts. Dirt completely covered the new clothes he was wearing, and blood dripped down his dirt-stained face.

"What happened?" Chloe screamed as she ran toward him and held his face near the flickering candlelight.

"We were attacked only moments ago by the same three that came last night," Gannon said breathlessly.

Chloe now noticed that Gannon looked the same as Jason and so did Aden and two other men she didn't recognize.

"Jason fought like no man I've ever known. He is better with the sword than some of my finest captains. If he hadn't been there with us today, we may have been defeated," Gannon said.

Chloe looked at Jason with pure shock written all over her face. He looked up at her and a smile widened across his dirty face.

"It was like a dream. I knew exactly which way they were going to strike and I knew exactly how to defend myself and the others. It was like someone was guiding my sword and my mind to ensure our victory," he said.

Chloe took the rag from the housekeeper and began wiping the dirt and blood from his face. He had a large cut down his left cheek and another smaller one near his right shoulder, but other than that he was fine. Calla and Belle were standing next to Gannon and each wiped the blood, sweat, and dirt from his face as well. Chloe noticed that outside the house were nearly twenty or so soldiers armed and ready to fight. She felt her heart ache at the thought of Jason having to fight again. She didn't know how much longer luck would be on his side.

"Jason, are you sure that you are okay?" she asked sadly. "You are bleeding pretty badly from your face and even more from your shoulder."

Jason felt his face with the tips of his fingers, and as he withdrew them, he saw for the first time the blood from the battle he had won. His stomach had lurched at the thought of blood before, but now it was a sign of strength.

He wiped the blood away from his face with a towel and smiled.

"I'm fine, sis, nothing a little love can't cure."

Chloe had never heard her brother so sure of himself. It seemed like his confidence had risen and he was now capable of being a great soldier.

"Time is not with us. We must continue our journey toward Mere right away," Aden said sharply, bringing everyone back to the reality of war. "Sire, I believe that you must evacuate the city of Avis and journey with us. It won't be as easy to hide the entire city, but I believe that it's necessary for the safety of your people." He spoke forcefully toward Gannon with some fear rising in his voice. "We don't know who has betrayed us, but we mustn't wait around to find out."

Gannon watched his friend and dropped his head in pain. He knew what Aden was saying was right, but it would take hours, if not days, to prepare a city as large as Avis for evacuation. There were the animals and the mothers that had recently had children, the sick and the old. It was not going to be easy. Gannon had never dreamt that it would come to this.

"I believe you are right, my friend." He spoke quietly and full of remorse.

"Reider, you need to inform everyone in the village that we will be departing the city and heading toward the city of Mere in one hour. Tell them only to bring what they need and the rest to be left behind. There will be no one left behind!" he said sharply.

Reider jumped up from being doctored by the cook and ran toward the door. As he opened the door a big bright red bird swooped down over his head and landed with a thud on the floor in front of Aden. It was Kamali!

"Avery! Are you okay?" Aden blurted as he reached down and lifted the big bird from the floor and laid it on a chair near the fire.

Kamali transformed back into Avery, the man that Chloe remembered meeting on the hill when they arrived in the Kingdom of Mere. Only this time he wasn't as clean and well kept. His hair had turned from brown to almost completely gray and his clothes were torn and tattered. They were covered in blood and sweat and his face was unshaven. He looked as though he had been lost for years and only now found his way home.

"Need water…" he sputtered.

The cook ran into the kitchen and brought Avery a large cup full of clean clear water. He guzzled it and then took a deep breath.

"What has happened to you? Were you attacked?" Gannon asked.

Avery sat and stared for a long time at the fire flickering in front of him.

"They have reached the gates; no one is safe anymore. They have an army that outnumbers ours ten to one. They are large and have weapons I've never known. It is the people of Umbra. We must all move quickly and get out of here. They know where we are and they are coming." Avery's eyes never moved as he spoke.

Seconds after his last word, he fell into a deep sleep and couldn't be woken. Aden and Gannon picked him up and carried him to a rug near the fire and laid him down. Mignon covered him with a large blanket and then retreated to the kitchen.

"Reider, get everyone ready immediately. We have no time to waste," Gannon yelled.

Reider burst out the front door. Ten of the guards followed him down the streets, yelling at everyone they saw to pack their bags and meet at Gannon's home.

Within an hour, people were lined outside Gannon's home with wagons full of provisions, horses, cows, goats and their precious Cowala right in front. Chloe and Jason had both learned that the Cowala were sacred here and were treated like royalty. Gannon, Calla, and Belle were in the front of the procession and Aden, Jason, Chloe, and now an unconscious Avery right behind them in their own wagon with their beautiful horses they had gained help from a few days before.

They left the city and the gates were closed behind them. Hundreds of people walked or rode behind their leader and followed him faithfully. They had managed to obtain everyone in the entire city, including all livestock and enough provisions to last the entire convoy two weeks. It amazed Chloe at how quickly they were able to get it all done.

Gannon led them off the main road and down a less-traveled one heading for the last hill of the safe valley. Chloe had been told that over the hill lay the most dangerous land in the entire kingdom, the Barren Land. She wasn't given exact details of what lay before them, but she didn't think it could be any worse than what or who was chasing them.

"Aden, how are we all going to make it through the Barren Land? We have nearly three hundred people, not including the livestock, and only about a hundred or so men with swords and arrows," Chloe said.

Jason reached down and gripped his sword to make sure it was still there.

"I've put a spell over the entire procession. We will be safe as long as no one gives away our location. If you remember, I have the ability to make the earth change. I can grow flowers, trees, even provide a stream, so what I've done is made us the same color as the ground we walk on. It is an extremely difficult thing to do with this many people, so I'm using extra energy from Avery and also from you," he said.

Chloe gasped. "You can do that?" she blurted.

Aden laughed. "Of course, and so can you. We have to continue with your lessons on our journey, so I've brought a book I would like you to start reading. I'm told by Lady Calla that your etiquette skills are far more advanced than she imagined, so I'm hoping that your magic is the same." Aden spoke with humor in his voice this time.

It made Chloe feel more relaxed. She dug through the knapsack that Aden had pointed to and found the book he was talking about. *The Magic of Magic*, she read to herself. She opened the book and felt a warm breeze blow across her face. She wasn't sure if it came from the book or from the trees blowing around them, but all the same the effect it had was calming. She started reading and as she read, she felt the magic brew within her. It was almost as if her mind already knew what she was reading, and it was feeding on every word that she read and learning all over again. One page stuck out in her mind as she closed the book to ponder on what she had read. It talked about solving the impossible puzzle. She wasn't sure what it meant, but she couldn't get it out of her mind. It had told her that the only way to solve an impossible puzzle was with the help of someone you love. In the past few days, the only person she had in the whole world was Jason, so she knew exactly who would help her if she ever came across an impossible puzzle.

As they came over the last hill they came upon a large hedge overgrown with thorns and many sharp needles from plants. Gannon ordered them to stop and rest a little while before entering the Barren Land. Chloe tried to imagine what lay behind that hedge, but fear was the only thing on her mind. Jason still gripped his sword tightly and Chloe could tell he wasn't ready to fight again. He had proven himself a great fighter earlier that day, but she still wished that none of it had ever happened.

"Where are we?"

The sound came as a startle to her and also to Jason and Aden. Both men drew their swords, ready to attack.

"What happened?" Avery lay very still in the back of the wagon, but he was awake.

Aden resheathed his sword and jumped back to where his friend lay.

"We are almost to enter the Barren Land; we have stopped to rest a little," Aden said, feeling Avery's head and also checking his pulse.

"Where is Gannon, I must speak with him at once." Avery's voice was very hoarse but he still spoke with such force that Chloe backed away.

Jason jumped from the wagon and ran to get Gannon. Avery rubbed the back of his neck and slowly propped himself against the sideboards. Chloe gave him a flask of cool water, which he willingly took and drank.

"You have grown," he finally said to Chloe.

Chloe looked at him in surprise. It had only been a few days.

"I don't think so, it's only been a few days," she said aloud.

283

"I didn't mean physically, I meant mentally. I can feel the magic within your soul. You have grown," he said weakly.

"You can feel my magic? But I don't understand, I've only used magic once and that was last night. How have I grown?" she asked.

He smiled at her. "My lady, you have been teaching yourself through the reading of Aden's knowledge. I'm sure he has told you that he is the author of all the books you are studying."

This was the first time that Chloe had heard this. She was not aware that Aden was so well educated in the manner of all things.

"No, he didn't mention that," she said.

Avery looked shocked and cocked a head at his friend.

"I'm surprised, he usually babbles that piece of information every time he gets the chance. You see, Aden is very good at what he does and most of the books in Mere are here because he either wrote them himself, or assisted in the writing or research of them. He is very educated and extremely smart when it comes to magic and manners." Avery said this with enthusiasm and Aden chuckled.

"Oh yeah, you are just fine. Same old Avery, always too modest to admit that he is High Wizard of all Mere for a reason."

Chloe wasn't sure what that meant, but the two friends exchanged looks of enthusiasm and Gannon shortly arrived with three of his captains.

"I'm glad that you are awake, we have a problem," Gannon said seriously. "I'm afraid this hedge is a game of the Master Puzzler."

Avery stood quickly and wobbled a moment and then his face fell with panic.

"Is he here?" he asked quickly.

"He speaks through the hedge, but says he will only speak with the dreamer. I don't know about you, but I have no idea who he is talking about," Gannon said.

Avery's anger was well shown. He stared so hard at the hedge that it started to burn. Just as quickly as the flames started, they were extinguished with an ear-piercing laugh.

"Only the dreamer may pass and lower the hedge to allow passage, but in order to do so, she must have help from far below." The voice was so loud and overbearing that Chloe and Jason both covered their ears.

Several babies began to cry and their mothers tried to hush them to no avail. Avery slammed his fist into the side of the wagon, splitting one of the boards in half. He looked around the camp and saw for the first time how many people were actually there.

His face finally fell. "I'm afraid I don't know the answer to that question, but he will let us know in his own way. We must make camp and stay the night here. We have no other option."

Gannon looked at Avery and motioned for the captains to prepare the area for camp. Gannon began to leave, but Avery grabbed his arm.

"We must talk. I'm afraid I have even worse news than this meddling Puzzler."

16

The Magical Dream

Gannon, Chloe, Jason, and several others clambered around the old wizard. He was still a sight for sore eyes and his clothes looked even worse than when he showed up at Gannon's house. Chloe watched the wizard pace back and forth and thoughts started creeping into her mind. A faint laughter, the sound of popping bubbles in water, the roar of a waterfall. She looked around to see the cause of the sounds, but saw nothing except for the multitude of people setting up camp. Avery still paced and not a word was spoken from the old man. Jason was also searching the camp for something. Chloe recognized the look of curiosity running along his face.

"Do you hear it?" she whispered.

Jason jumped slightly at the sound of her voice, as though he were not expecting anyone to be near him. She glanced quizzically at him and he frowned.

"I hear water and laughing, but I also hear screams and fighting." His voice trailed off as he spoke even more quietly.

Chloe noticed that Avery had finally found a seat. He stroked the beard that had formed over the last couple of days.

Gannon looked at Avery. "Tell us the news of your trip, Avery. We all are anxious to hear why you are so glum."

Avery looked at the tall broad leader of the expedition with a blank face.

"I'm trying to decide where to start, and how to explain without everyone getting nervous." Avery let his head fall to his chest and Chloe elbowed her brother.

"I hear it too, but I only hear the water and laughter. Do you think we should tell the others?" she whispered.

Jason looked at her, his face still distant, but from the look on his face, she knew that he didn't know.

"I was captured by the people of Umbra," Avery began.

He told the story of his capture, the hideous face of Jacan, the warriors he had trained, and the dragons that chased him out of the chamber. He explained the aid that he sent to the city of Loch, and the messengers that he sent to the city of Rill and other cities across the kingdom.

"It was then that the flight back to you began. I left Loch and Cerella to come to your aid and inform you of the attacks. During my flight, however, I was being followed. I tried to land and escape the shadow of darkness that kept trying to engulf me. I was finally able to land in a river not to far from Loch. I transformed into a large black fish so I could camouflage myself against the darkness of the water."

"The shadow kept searching and I hid for hours among the depths of the river. When the sun shined brightly down upon the water and the clouds in the sky disappeared, the shadow was gone. I knew then that Jacan somehow had discovered a way to move his portals to any part of the country as long as it was shadowed by the clouds and the sun didn't disrupt his searching." The crowd listened intently as Avery spoke, none daring to say a word.

"I knew that it wouldn't be safe to continue my quest as Kamali, so I swam upstream for a couple of hours and then transformed into a Mirale. As I jumped and dug the earth among the other Mirale, I discovered that many of them were spies for Jacan. They have been following your party, Aden, for some time. They talked of a battle between you and our young warrior as well as a beautiful lady that watched as they danced through the many holes of the earth." Avery watched his fellow comrades with worry, but he continued on.

"As soon as I heard their plans, I surfaced from beneath the ground and searched everywhere for any shadow that may be lurking. I discovered one that was surrounded by several Mirale who were indulging themselves in the fresh meat that was being served to them by dark-covered hands. I knew that the Umbra had bribed the Mirale and that our safety was in danger. I transformed back into Kamali and heard the yells of the two men below me that they had found the wizard. I put a shield of light around me and flew hard toward the city of Avis. The sun would be rising and I knew that soon I would have no more energy to work my magic. It had been least two days since my last meal, a drink of fresh water, or even a wink of sleep. Every time I used my magic, I was losing energy, and also time.

"I knew that the city of Avis would be well guarded, but not against the shadows that lurked there, so I kept speed. My shield was almost out when I saw the wall of the city in the distance. I had been flying for several hours and had no more energy to keep my shield. Just as I flew over the city, the shield vanished and the door to Gannon's home opened. I remember flying in and saying something, but that's all. Using all my energy took its toll on my appearance, and I was lucky to even be able to transform back into myself. Caution is needed, as well as lights around the entire campsite all night. We are most vulnerable in the darkness against our enemy."

Gannon, Aden, and the others looked at Avery and each had a look of fear spilling across their faces. The sun was already beginning its descent upon the mass of people and with no sun to block the shadows, they were all in danger.

Chloe's thoughts turned back toward the sounds she and Jason had heard previously.

"Avery, Jason and I both heard something just before you started your story," she said nervously.

She wasn't sure how this sounded to the rest of the group, but she was sure that they needed to know. All eyes focused on Jason and her.

"What did you hear?" Aden asked abruptly.

Chloe looked at Jason and he nodded in agreement that they needed to tell them everything.

"At first I thought it was nothing, but then I heard laughter and water splashing. I also heard the sound of popping bubbles, you know, the sound a bubble makes as it surfaces the water. Anyway, the laughing stopped and then I noticed Jason had heard it also. When I asked him about it, he said he too heard the laughter and bubbles, but he also heard screaming and a battle. I hadn't heard that, but the look on Jason's face told me it was true."

Chloe relayed the story to the wizards and Gannon and as soon as she stopped talking Avery shot out of his seat and ran to get a pail of water. When he returned, he placed it in front of Chloe and told her to look inside. Chloe did as she was told and soon the picture was ever so clear. She saw mermaids, and mermen, small children and fish, some type of creature she didn't know, and several small dark splotches circling around the scene. She could hear the laughter of all the creatures and the splashing of water. She saw a waterfall in the background and watched it fall from the steep cliff above her. It was like she was there enjoying the party that the merpeople were having. She heard music and saw a beautiful red-haired mermaid playing a small instrument, somewhat like a piccolo. The song was so beautiful and made her feel so comfortable. The dark shadows were drawing closer toward the crowd of creatures and the instrument stopped playing. The picture faded and she could see or hear no more.

"What was that?" she asked quietly still calm from the music of the mermaid.

"What did you see?" Aden asked her impatiently.

Chloe recounted the scene to the others and relaxed on her small blanket when she was finished. The song still made her feel so safe and comfortable, she just wanted to sit and fall into a deep sleep.

"You just witnessed the celebration of a new life. The merpeople celebrate with other animals from above the water when someone lost returns. It's a wonderful festivity to be a part of. What you saw is happening right now, or will soon be happening."

Avery was looking west toward the mountain range as he spoke.

"However, what Jason heard is a cry for assistance from those that you have just seen. They are in danger!"

Chloe jumped up from her small blanket, the song completely forgotten. The merpeople she just saw were being attacked by the Umbra that Avery had spoke of only moments before.

"You mean that was real? I was really there? And now they are being attacked by those nasty lifeless ghosts called the Umbra?"

Chloe was devastated. Why had this happened to her?

"I don't believe it has happened yet, my lady. I believe that it was something that you saw happen in the near future," Gannon quickly added. "Indeed, you were witnessing a terrible crime that will shortly be happening to our friends below the surface of the water. You were not there, however, only using magic to see the sounds you heard

292

and therefore it seemed real and believable."

Avery watched the sun retreat behind a tall mountain peek and a bright light washed over the campsite. Chloe felt a surge of energy push through her and she felt her energy slowly retreating.

"I've had to use a good deal of your energy to keep the camp lit. I'm afraid that we will have to keep you hydrated and well fed," Avery said quietly to Chloe. "I still haven't received enough energy to perform such magic and you seem to have more magical ability in you than I thought. You must eat and get some sleep. When you do, it will help the camp stay lit until Aden takes over."

Chloe was still awestruck over what she had just witnessed in the small pail of water. *Why wasn't anyone worried about those poor people?* she wondered. *What if what I saw already happened?*

She walked over to Calla, who immediately dished her up a large bowl of soup, a slice of warmed wheat bread, and a mug of brillion. Chloe retreated and sat down on her blanket and indulged herself in her food. It was an excellent feast. The soup was creamy potato with mashed carrots and small shredded bits of meat. She didn't think it was the Cowala meat, but the meat was still delicious. The brillion was cold and soothed the aches in her muscles from their ever-increasing journey toward a place Chloe had never known. She felt her energy perk up only to be drained by the exertion that the magical lights were causing. Jason walked over and sat beside her. She laid her head in his lap and he stroked her hair gently.

"Do you think those people are okay?" she asked between yawns.

Jason looked at her and without smiling gave a nod.

"Avery says they have sent a messenger to the city of Rill to inform them of the oncoming attack. It will arrive there before sunset. Why don't you close your eyes and sleep, I'll watch over you,"

His eyes drooped, and Chloe could tell that her brother was exhausted. She knew that the early morning fight had taken its toll on him. She could still see the dried blood from some small cuts on his face and arms.

The night grew chilly and Chloe tossed restlessly around in her blanket. She could hear the song of the mermaid and a faint scream that grew louder and louder. She flipped her arms wildly.

"You won't get them!" she screamed.

A hand reached out of the dark clouds and vanished. The light appeared around the small group of creatures on the bank and the song grew louder.

"Thank you for warning us." Chloe didn't recognize the voice. It was the voice of a man.

She searched her surroundings but saw nothing. She only heard the faint song of the mermaid.

"We saw you through the waterfall earlier today and hoped that you would come back and join us. When you disappeared, we could still hear the voices around you, but couldn't understand what was being said. Then the dark clouds appeared and we heard you scream to run away. We dove back into the water and now you are here safe with us. Thank you for letting us know the danger that was surrounding us."

Chloe still didn't know who was speaking.

"Who are you?" she asked, still searching her surroundings.

"I'm a friend of the merpeople. It was I who invited you to our celebration."

"CHLOE!" Jason grabbed his sister and she opened her eyes. "Are you okay?" he asked.

Chloe noticed that she was surrounded by several people with their swords drawn and their faces all turned toward her.

"Where am I?" she asked sleepily.

"We are just outside of the Barren Land. You fell asleep and then screamed and started flailing around on your blanket.

"Where is he?" she asked as Jason pulled her up.

"Who?" Avery asked her.

"The man that invited me to the celebration of the merpeople," she answered.

Avery looked at her and a smile formed across his face.

"Gannon, we have found the dreamer that the Puzzler seeks." He sat down beside her and she recounted her story of the incident.

"Are you aware that you were using magic in your sleep?" he asked her when she was finished with her story.

"What kind of magic?" she asked, now full of energy and curiosity.

"When you were asleep, we all heard you scream that they weren't going to get them, and then the sun shot up into the sky and lit up the entire valley. Then all at once you threw a spark of fire that hit our wagon and lit it on fire. You were fighting the Umbra while you were sleeping. I must admit, that kind of magic is very advanced and takes our training to a new level." Avery smiled as he spoke. "I'm extremely surprised at your talent, my lady."

She looked toward the wagon and saw that it was completely burnt. She looked at Avery and saw him smiling.

"I did that?" she asked, blushing.

"Indeed! I've never seen such a thing from someone who was asleep." He patted her on the back.

"Avery, if she is the one that the Puzzler wants, then she is going to have to go through that hedge alone," Gannon said, surprised.

"We don't even know what lies on the other side," Aden sputtered.

Avery looked up at the two tall men.

"No, she will go in with Jason. She is the only one that can enter; however, she is allowed help from one other person and that is her brother."

Jason's face dropped. He was still in shock at finding his sister throwing flames in her sleep.

"It's settled then. As soon as Chloe gets the sun to retreat its current position and resume its sleep through the night we will present them at the hedge."

Chloe glanced up and saw the sun shining brightly right in the middle of the sky. The entire valley was engulfed in sunlight, but it was only two o'clock in the morning. She wasn't sure how she was supposed to get the sun to go down, but she pictured what she wanted in her mind, flicked her wrist, and the sun started its retreat and disappeared behind the mountain. The faint light of magic, and the small campfires were all that remained.

"Good, we shall proceed!" Avery stood up and pulled Chloe to her feet.

Jason followed, but he didn't speak. They followed Avery toward the hedge. Avery put his hand on the hedge and urged Chloe and Jason to do the same. As soon as Chloe touched the hedge, a doorway appeared.

"You have chosen correctly. The lady is to enter with only a single guard. They will be protected in the hedge from any outside intrusion; however, what lies within the hedge must be defeated before it will clear and passage will be made for the rest of your party. I know from what you run, and I promise that inside they cannot enter."

The voice was deep, but friendly. Chloe didn't know very much about the Master Puzzler, only that he liked games. She wasn't sure if trust was something she could count on with him.

"Listen, you must be prepared for anything. This is going to challenge you both with magic and sword, and also possibly with manners or etiquette. I know the Puzzler quite well, he won't leave anything out. Usually his puzzles steer toward things you may have already learned or should know. He has obviously chosen you for a reason. We have packed you both provisions for two days, but we don't have that much time. You must go quickly!" Avery was very confident as he spoke.

Jason put the pack on his back and stared at his sister. She nodded her head in agreement. The doorway opened and revealed a land full of steep terrain and snow-capped mountains, and beautiful butterflies fluttering around a small blue stream. There were sand dunes in the distance and the sun was in the middle of the sky. They could feel the immense heat radiating through the doorway. Jason grabbed her arm and they both walked into the doorway.

"Remember, you must hurry, we can't stay here for long," Avery yelled.

The doorway shut and Jason and Chloe were alone.

17

The Warning

Zachi couldn't get over the thought of Megan now a mermaid. The golden fin and long silvery red hair stayed in his mind as he ate the meal brought up for him. Cane had retreated to his own quarters to eat his meal, leaving Zachi alone to think. The meal was quite delicious—mashed potatoes and gravy with a slice of meat. They also had hot homemade bread with cold goat's milk to drink. It was really rather pleasing to him. After he finished his meal, he laid his sword and other weapons out on the bed and began cleaning them with a rag. He hadn't yet used them, but while being trained as a warrior, he was taught to always clean his swords at the end of every day. He really wasn't sure the real reason, but he found it somewhat relaxing.

Cane knocked on his door and walked in slowly with two large pieces of chocolate cake.

"I convinced a young mermaid that we needed chocolate cake, so she brought some to us. I could really get used to this place." He sat a piece down on the bedside table and began quickly eating his own large slice.

"What did you think of Megan?" Zachi finally asked after a few moments of silence.

Cane looked up from his cake and a mischievous grin formed on his face.

"She's gorgeous! I mean she was beautiful before, but she's a knockout now."

He chuckled and Zachi shot him a vicious stare.

"Calm down, she looked great. You are going to have to realize sometime soon that she's not your sister. You are her protector, and nothing more," Cane said shortly.

Zachi glared at his friend.

"I thank you for the large piece of chocolate cake, but I think it's time for us to get some sleep."

Cane stopped mid-bite and placed the fork back on his plate.

"Sure, I'll be next door if you need me." Cane rose from his chair and walked out the door to his own room.

Zachi threw himself on the bed with a thud before remembering how hard the beds actually were. He rubbed his backside and then laid his head on the soft fluffy pillow. Thoughts of Megan kept running through his mind. He closed his eyes and within moments drifted off to sleep.

TAP...TAP...TAP. At first Zachi only thought it was himself dreaming, *TAP...TAP...TAP.* This time he knew it wasn't a dream. He opened his eyes and searched his dark room. The lamps had all been put out, and his cake had been moved to the dresser and a glass lid put over it to keep it fresh. He grabbed his sword that he had laid under his pillow and pulled it quietly from the sheath. *Light,* he whispered. A small faint light appeared over his head. It slowly got

300

brighter and soon the room was lit brightly. Zachi, sword raised in the fighting position, began searching the room. There was nothing around. He lowered his sword and knocked on Cane's door. He turned the knob and Cane slowly rose from his bed, rubbing his eyes.

"What's going on?" he asked with a yawn.

"Something isn't right. We need to check on Preston and Megan," Zachi answered.

Cane slowly rose from his bed and asked for light and soon his room was also lit brightly. He quickly got dressed and put his own sword around his waist. They went back into Zachi's room, where he grabbed his arrows and bow and put them on his back.

TAP...TAP...TAP. Zachi and Cane spun around, both drawing their sword, and faced the door that led to the hallway.

"Master Zachi!" came a hushed whisper from outside the door.

Zachi cautiously opened the door. A young mermaid floated there.

He lowered his sword. "Yes?" he asked.

"There is a large blue fish asking for you at the gate," she answered. "He says a Master Avery has sent him."

Zachi quickly put his sword in its sheath and Cane did the same.

"Avery?" Zachi asked her.

"That's what he said," she answered.

"Please, take us to him at once!"

Zachi and Cane pushed through the wall of water at the doorway and the bubble of air formed over their heads. The small mermaid swam quickly in front of them and led them to the front gate. Two large armed mermen stood watching the blue fish at the front of the gate. They nodded at Zachi and Cane and let them pass. They swam toward the large blue fish and stopped in front of him, their hands both gripping the hilt of their swords.

"My Lords," the fish bowed, "Avery has sent me to inform you of danger on land. The black riders have made their presence and he has seen Jacan himself. The danger is high. He instructs me to inform you to get the prince and princess out of Rill immediately, as the attack is already in play. Mistress Chloe has had visions of an attack on Rill."

Zachi stared at the blue fish.

"How do I know to trust you?"

The fish turned slightly and showed the sign of Mere imprinted on his fin.

"I am a messenger for the King, that is all I can guarantee you." The fish bowed slightly again.

"Is there any news of the others?" Zachi asked the fish.

"Only that they are alive and currently trying to fight the Puzzler, My Lord."

Zachi frowned. He had heard of the Puzzler before, a nasty fellow, but would keep them safe. "Thank you friend, would you return a message to him for us?"

The fish agreed.

"Tell him that we are leaving Rill quite soon, we only arrived a day ago. The Princess Hanna is now a mermaid, as well as Prince Paden. We have run into no trouble as of yet, but will be on our guard."

The fish bowed and Zachi returned the bow.

"Be gone, friend, and swim quickly," Cane urged him.

The fish turned and disappeared in the darkness of the water.

Zachi and Cane retreated to the castle.

"Is there danger, my lords?" the large guard asked.

"Indeed, we need audience with Aurora at once."

The small mermaid bowed low and retreated toward the Queen's quarters. Zachi and Cane moved into the small sitting room and waited for Aurora to arrive. After only a few moments, Aurora appeared with Nirvelli at her side.

"What is it?" Aurora asked without hesitation.

Cane and Zachi bowed at her presence and she lifted the water around them and let them have fresh air. Zachi explained the messenger's words and then again bowed.

"Is this the only news he has brought?" she asked.

Zachi nodded.

"Yes, ma'am. I think it's time we moved on toward Mere. We must leave immediately," Zachi answered.

Aurora looked at them briefly and then spoke quietly to Nirvelli.

"Zachi, I wish to introduce Hanna and Paden to the kingdom in the morning. Also I would like to give Hanna a few lessons in Sorcery before you depart. You shall leave tomorrow afternoon, and I shall send with you some of our finest guards," Aurora informed them.

"Your Majesty, I think it would be better if we left immediately," Zachi responded.

"Nonsense, they cannot leave without training, they'll never survive. Now I must get back to sleep, Nirvelli will inform the guards of the chance of attack and the city will be on guard. Please excuse me."

Aurora retreated from the room and Zachi gave a loud sigh.

"Nirvelli, please try and change Aurora's mind. I think danger is nearby. I can feel it," Zachi said as the water now resumed its normal position and the air bubbles fashioned themselves back over their heads.

"She has made up her mind. You best get some sleep. It's going to be a long day tomorrow." Nirvelli retreated, leaving Zachi and Cane alone in the sitting room.

"What now?" Cane asked.

"Nothing, we go back to our rooms and hope we leave in time," Zachi answered quietly.

They followed the mermaid back to their rooms and she left them with a faint smile. Zachi instantly sat down at his writing desk.

"I better plan a quick escape, just in case," Zachi told Cane.

The two men sat together the remainder of the evening and worked on a quick route to their next destination, the city of Alchemy.

18

Fighting Shadows

The room prepared for Preston was far more masculine than Megan's room. There were no large fancy mirrors, elegant chandeliers, or an all stone armoire full of different tops and glittery hair things. Instead, his room had a smaller chandelier with a stone dresser that had not clothes, but weapons. The merman here wore no clothing, but always had some sort of weapon. Their hair was always left alone and there wasn't even a brush to be found. His bed was just as large as Megan's but it was covered in a colorful seaweed blanket that had been neatly woven to make pictures of the stone castle. He had three windows, two with clear glass that overlooked the entire city. He felt he could see for miles. The city was busy at every time of day with shoppers and merchants swimming around and guarding their items. Each window stood approximately fifteen feet from one another. In the very center was a larger domed-shaped window with stained glass that held a detailed map of the city. Preston began studying the map before he quietly fell asleep.

He slept well all night, and as his stomach gurgled with hunger, he looked forward to a large breakfast. Eri knocked briefly on the door and entered.

"Her Majesty wishes that you prepare yourself for the day's events," he said, bowing low toward the ground.

"With what?" Preston asked, pointing around his empty room.

Eri swam over and opened his dresser.

"Choose your weapon, Sire," he answered quietly.

Eri had his own long spear in his right hand and also a sword sheathed at his side. Preston hadn't expected to be carrying a weapon while he was here, it seemed so peaceful and quiet, but he searched through the drawers and found it full of spears, bows and arrows neatly tucked into a quiver, swords, shields, a large pitchfork-type thing, and then, in the very last drawer, he saw his weapon of choice. It was a large sword that looked as though it had been made entirely of titanium metal. It was a darker metal but as he picked it up, he found it light and easy to handle. As his fingers wrapped around the handle it quickly adjusted to his own hand size. He looked at Eri and saw the fascination on his own face as it magically formed to his grip. He returned his gaze back to the magical sword and noticed that it was double-edged with a ridge running down the middle and perfectly balanced. He eyed the hilt of the sword and saw that it was also made of the same metal, only this time a bit lighter color, and was wrapped in some type of soft waterproof leather. The blue sapphire stones, green emeralds, and diamonds were laid neatly in a row along the hilt.

"It's called a broadsword blade, common among your people. I, however, carry a knuckle bow sword. It has special metal to protect my hand," Eri explained as he unsheathed his own sword to show the young prince.

Preston smiled and continued his gaze upon his own sword. He noticed a part on the sword that wasn't sharpened.

"That is called the ricasso. It's the part of the blade where the maker will engrave his sign of workmanship so you know who made it," he said, noticing Preston eyeing that part of the sword.

Preston noticed the engraving was of two swords crisscrossing one another and encircled by a ribbon of gold.

"What is this?" he asked Eri. He held it up for him to see.

"That is the crest of Mere, it stands for unity. I haven't seen it for ages. You can only find that type of engraving on the sword of royalty. It fits you perfectly, Sire, an excellent choice."

Preston brought the sword back toward himself. He looked back into the drawer and pulled out a long hallowed piece of stone with a seaweed belt.

"That is your sheath; it was made by our own blacksmith for that sword. It's made of a type of pumice and is very comfortable and lightweight. That particular type of stone will also keep your blade sharp. The seaweed belt adjusts well to your torso, but does take time to get used to." Eri spoke with knowledge.

Preston thought he seemed like he was all too excited to share any information he could with Prince Paden. He wasn't sure how often Eri knew more than a royal Prince, so he stayed quiet and let him continue with his explanation of the sword he had chosen.

"That sword was brought here by two men. They were very anxious to get rid of it, actually. I don't think they liked being so far under water with only a small bubble to protect them." Eri laughed and shook his head.

Preston smiled and remembered how he had felt at the thought of having a bubble around his head. He didn't blame the two men for being anxious to get out of here.

"Do you think that this will be enough for today's lessons?" Preston asked Eri as he sheathed his sword and strapped it around his waist.

"If it were me, Sire, I would also pack the quiver full of arrows and a very strong bow. Everything here is made of coral, or some other type of stone, so you can imagine the damage one arrow can do."

Preston pulled out the quiver and threw it over his shoulder. Eri helped him place it correctly on his back so he would have no trouble reaching for the bow and arrow if the need came up.

Preston sloshed his new fin back and forth, trying to lunge himself toward the door. He still hadn't quite got the hang of just having a fin instead of two legs. Eri smiled and laughed every time he tried to change direction or even swim straight.

"Sire, may I make a suggestion?" Eri finally asked after Preston hit the wall for the third time.

"Please!" Preston said breathlessly.

Eri straightened up and held his spear at ready, not expecting the harsh tone from the Prince.

"I'm sorry, Eri, any help would be excellent."

Eri pushed his own fin in a downward motion and came to a halt at Preston's side.

"You are trying too hard. You need to just swim. Let your body do the work, not your mind. With every motion you make with your fin, another must be made. For example, if you push your fin down gently, you are going to move slowly forward. If you push hard, your body is going to jolt forward quickly. To turn, you move slightly in the direction you want to go." Eri made each movement so Preston could see and then it was his turn.

He stared at the wall ahead of him in his room and gently pushed his fin in a downward motion. His body lunged slowly forward and then his fin came up and balanced him out. After a few minutes of practicing with Eri, he had it down slightly better and wasn't staggering quite so much. Eri opened the door to his chambers and they both slowly inched out into the hall of the large castle.

Eri led him down a flight of stairs and then turned left down one glass corridor to Megan's room. The letters shone brightly above her door welcoming any guest to her room. It looked as if it had been recently polished. Preston gave a quick knock and then opened the door.

"Preston! You must wait until you are called on to enter a girl's room," Megan shouted. "Please wait outside, I'm not dressed."

Preston quickly backed out of the doorway as best he could and slammed it shut. Eri was laughing hysterically at Preston. Preston gave him a side smile and looked around for somewhere to wait. The hall wasn't very large and having a large guard laughing at you made it feel even smaller.

"You can come in now!" Megan yelled through the doorway.

Preston swam over to the door and slowly pushed it open.

"Are you sure?" he asked shyly.

"Of course I'm sure," came the short reply. Eri waited outside, still laughing slightly as Preston swished his fin and entered his sister's room.

The chandelier that had been shattered the day before had been replaced by a new one and was shining bright light throughout the room. The temperature in this underwater stone castle didn't ever seem to change, but Preston felt his own temperature rise at the sight of how beautiful Megan looked. Her long red and silver flowing hair was pinned up halfway by a mother-of-pearl tiara. The white pearl necklace wrapped around her neck and the large pearls in her ears complemented her radiant skin and smooth golden fin. She wore a tightly fitted short-sleeved top made from what seemed to be the inside of a conch shell. It bubbled and moved well with her body. The material was slick and smooth while still remaining soft. The vibrant colors and hues that shimmered around the ribbed shirt made her features stand out even more. Her amber eyes popped with

311

each graceful movement. Preston's jaw dropped and she smiled.

"It's beautiful, isn't it?" she asked, still smiling. "It's made from Lilivious petals. Maida said that it's a type of plant that grows around the castle just so they can make clothes for all the mermaids."

Preston looked at her and finally shut his mouth.

"You look beautiful. I wouldn't have recognized you if your name wasn't on your door," he teased.

She swam elegantly toward him and did a spin in midair.

"I feel so different, like I'm royal or something." She couldn't hold back the sarcasm in her voice. "I can't believe I'm a princess, and not just any princess, I'm a powerful sorceress." She squealed.

She wrapped her arms around him and gave him a warm hug. Preston cleared his throat.

"Eri is waiting just outside to take us to breakfast. We are going to be spending the day with Aurora, I mean our grandmother. How did you get so good at swimming?" he asked with a tinge of jealousy.

She smiled and zipped quickly around him.

"It wasn't that hard. I've been snorkeling and scuba diving since I can remember, so I just had to adjust to having the one fin instead of the two artificial ones on my feet." She grabbed his arm and they swam around in a circle together.

"Do you think that our grandmother will let us go to the city?" she asked as they approached the door.

"I hope so, I've been watching out my window all morning. It seems so great," he answered.

He opened the door and found Eri waiting with Maida. Eri had the same shocked expression on his face as Preston had. Preston swam over and pushed shut the jaw of his royal guard. Eri straightened up and cleared his throat, embarrassed by his poor manners. Megan giggled quietly at the attention.

Maida led the way back through the maze of walls and stairways and finally they arrived at a large dining room hall. The glass table was neatly set with plates made from some type of shell, the silverware was made of smooth stone, and the cups were fluted glass with different hues of colors. There were more servants swimming around the edge of the room placing different types of sea flowers and plants to bring more color to the room. However, to Preston it seemed all you had to do was have a couple merpeople in the room and there was more color than anywhere in the world. Their different hair colors, skin colors, shirts, and weapons made the room look like one large rainbow. Aurora was seated at the head of the table with a cup full of some type of thick gooey purple liquid.

"Ah, I see you have finally decided to grace us all with your presence," she said mockingly.

Megan smiled and swam to greet her grandmother. She had obviously taken to this mermaid idea a lot better than Preston thought she would. She had adjusted like it was never any different.

"Hello, Grandmother! How did you sleep?" she said as she kissed her softly on the cheek and swam to her right to sit in the nearest chair.

A tall merman with orange hair quickly glided over and pulled the chair out for her to sit on. Preston couldn't help but notice that the man inhaled as she carefully placed her fin on the glass chair.

"Good morning, my dears. I slept quite well, and how about yourselves?" Aurora asked as she sipped her purple goop.

"Oh, quite well, thank you," Megan said sweetly. Preston watched as Megan spoke with their grandmother. Her tone was perfect and her manners excellent. She was definitely born for this.

"Are you going to sit down, Paden, or would you prefer to eat while swimming around."

Preston started at the sound of his grandmother's voice.

"Yes, ma'am, I'm sorry," he said, embarrassed.

He swam over to the chair opposite Megan and it too was pulled quickly out by the same tall merman. He wasn't sure how to properly sit, so he just sort of glided down and gently put the back of his fin on the chair.

Another servant brought in large platters of food and a jug of the purple goop and placed it softly on the table. It was full of more plants. Some were the same as last night, like the Millis. However there were other colorful plants as well.

314

"Um, what exactly are we eating?" Preston asked, still staring at his plate full of weeds.

Aurora laughed and smiled at her grandchildren.

"These are our breakfast plants. The green one is known as Mican, it gives you energy. The purple drink is called Plauso, it's almost like the tea that you drink on land, except it's made entirely out of a type of sea weed. The orange plant is called Hectrum, it keeps you alert and revives your spirit. The others are nutrient plants that give your body the vitamins it needs to live. They are all very tasty; however, the Mican is a little bitter." She smiled at them and urged them on with a wave of her hand.

Preston eyed Megan and could tell that she was thinking the same thing. Instead of complaining, however, she picked up the Plauso and took a sip.

"This is excellent. Thank you." She spoke so politely.

Preston picked up the orange Hectrum and took a small bite. Its taste was a little sour, but it was pretty good.

"This really is good," he said with a full mouth.

Megan shook her head and turned back to her grandma.

"What are we going to do today? I was hoping maybe we would be allowed in the city. It looks so beautiful," Megan said, looking hopeful.

"Of course. I would like to announce you both to the entire city in an hour. Nirvelli is preparing all the details as we speak. But first, Hanna, I would like you to turn this glass to stone." She handed Megan one of the fluted cups on the

315

table. Megan took it cautiously.

"How would I do that?" she asked timidly.

Preston could tell she was a little nervous, but was trying not to show her emotions.

"It's quite easy, I want you to picture the goblet in your mind, but not just the goblet, I also want you to picture a piece of stone."

Megan nodded her head to acknowledge that she had completed this task.

"Now, I want you to put the stone through the glass in your mind and think they are one."

Megan did as she was told and the glass shattered and the bits of glass floated around the room. The servants quickly gathered the small pieces and returned to their posts. Megan's face went white. What had she done? Aurora sighed and stared at the spot where the glass had been only moments ago.

"You will need to practice your skills. I have a room where I would like you to practice as soon as we return from the city."

Megan looked down at the table and Preston noticed her smile turn into a frown.

"You'll get it, Meg, you just have to keep trying." Preston rose from his chair and swam over next to his sister.

She looked up and gave him a half smile.

"Thanks, Preston, I've never actually failed at anything before. I was a straight-A student at school and never settled for anything less then a ninety-five percent on

any test or paper. If the teacher gave me anything less I
argued and fought until he realized his mistake. Chloe always
told me I was crazy for trying so hard. Maybe she was right."

Preston heart ached at the sound of Chloe's name. Of
course he had thought about her and also of Jason, but didn't
know where they were or even if they were safe.

"You'll get it!" was all Preston could say.

His thoughts were now turned toward Chloe. He
couldn't believe that he had fallen so deeply for that girl. He
had never felt that way about anyone.

"It's time to go," Aurora said, swimming away from
the table. "We are going to go out onto the top balcony and
announce your arrival. I've been told it may not be the wisest
thing to do, but I feel it important to let the city and its
inhabitants know their future leader is here."

Megan's face went white.

"Grandmother, are you sure that I'm supposed to be
your heir? I mean you saw what I did to that cup," she
protested.

"Enough nonsense, of course you did that to the cup,
you haven't ever had a lick of real sorcery training. In a
week's time, you'll be almost as good as me. I can tell these
things. You have real talent, and by your mannerisms, I can
tell you have always been extremely proper." She smiled at
Megan and the doors were opened.

They all swam up through the stairwells, corridors,
and darkened hallways. Soon they reached a large door made
entirely from seashells. A large guard was there waiting for

them. Zachi and Cane were there as well. Megan swam quickly over to Zachi and gave him a hug.

"I've really missed you. Are you OK?" she asked quietly.

The bubble around Zachi's head was really awkward, and Preston tried to hold back a laugh.

"Did you have some breakfast?" Aurora asked.

"Yes, my lady, we were able to get some underwater fruits from a small shop in town. May I again inform you of the dangers that this announcement may bring upon your city. We have reason to believe that the war has already begun." Zachi tried to hold his voice down at the last few words, but Preston and Megan heard every word.

Aurora shot him an irritated glance and nodded at the guard at the door.

Nirvelli was already on the balcony.

"I'm pleased to introduce her majesty, Lady Aurora!" he boomed.

Aurora pushed her two grandchildren out onto the balcony and waved her arms gracefully at the large crowd swimming just outside the castle's protection barrier. Preston saw hundreds of mermaids, mermen, dolphins, Todswan, and even several humans with little bubbles over their heads to breathe.

"My people, it is with great pleasure that I introduce to you someone who is to lead you after I have gone. She has been away from us for many years, only recently returned. I give you Hanna, Princess of Illusion and Heir to the city of

Rill!" Aurora's voice was extremely loud.

Megan swam cautiously over to her grandmother and waved shyly at the crowd. The crowd cheered loudly. Preston even heard several merman whistle. Aurora hushed the crowd and then again raised her arms and smiled.

"I also want to introduce her brother and future King of Mere, Paden, Prince of Power!"

Preston's face dropped. He didn't know that he was to be the King of Mere. He crept slowly forward and gave a brief wave and then backed away from the balcony edge. As he backed up he noticed a large, dark shadow forming over the city. The voices surrounding the cheers of the crowds were quickly hushed and people stared at the dark shadows forming over them.

Nirvelli quickly grabbed Aurora's and Megan's arms and pushed them back through the doorway. Zachi, Cane, and several other mermen came barging up to the edge of the balcony and swam out over the crowds. Merpeople were going in every direction. Mothers were pushing their small children through the doors of their homes. The mermen grabbed their weapons and stood guard outside their homes. Nirvelli swam over to Preston.

"Grab your sword, it's time for your lesson. The city is under attack!" he boomed.

Preston reached down and pulled his sword from the rock sheath. He held it up and Nirvelli looked at him strangely.

"Have you never fought before?" he asked.

319

"Not with a sword, only my fists, and only against a pillow that my dad was training me with," Preston stated.

The terror in his voice must have shown through because Nirvelli put two of his best guards with him.

"Teach him the proper way to hold his sword!" he yelled as he swam toward the city.

Preston was given a brief lesson on how to battle with his new sword and how to correctly fire an arrow and then they all swam toward the commotion now coming from the city.

Preston felt the adrenaline rushing through his body. He swam as fast as he could, pushing his fin downward quickly, closely following his guards. When they arrived at the street that was usually filled with merpeople and shoppers, they found a battle. The mermen were fighting something in the shadows. Preston really couldn't make out what it was, but as they drew closer to a dark shadow, he saw the ugliest, meanest fish he had ever seen. It was dark green with pointed teeth protruding out of its mouth. It had not the three fins you would see on a regular fish, but it had six on each side and two large fins in the back. It was about eight feet in length and almost entirely camouflaged in the darkness of the shadow.

"What is it?" he yelled, trying to be heard over the sounds of war.

"I don't know, Sire. I've never seen one before!" the guard in front yelled back.

"I've been watching how they are killed, and it looks like you have to protrude your sword or arrow into its heart, which seems to be located underneath the left front fins," he yelled again.

Preston readied his sword and with all the courage that he had, swam right toward one of the green beasts. He flung his sword and as it came down he saw several sparks from his blade disintegrate into the water. The creature had sharp little swords on each fin and its tail, now that he was close enough to get a good look, was made entirely out of sharp pieces of flesh. They looked as though they could slice his sword into pieces. He took another slash with his sword. This time he connected with the animal and a fin fell to the ground and disappeared. The battle continued and with each slash Preston made with his sword, the creature made one in return. The sword vibrated violently through his fingers. With each movement, the creature seemed to be one step ahead of him.

"You aren't going to get the best of me, you foul creature!" he screamed.

He grabbed the hilt of his sword tighter and thrust it forward. The creature hissed and Preston noticed a green mist coming from his mouth. He had done it. His sword had struck the creature right in the heart under the left front fin. The creature didn't fall to the ground, however, but disappeared in a dark green mist.

Preston looked around and saw that the battle was still going on, but he noticed someone else swimming slowly up the street from toward the castle. He swam quickly over to where his guard was fighting a large creature and withdrew his bow and arrow from his quiver. He loaded the arrow and pulled back hard. He concentrated hard on his target and released the arrow. It whizzed by the creature, not even touching it. He grabbed another arrow and pulled it back on the thick string and released it again. This time, it connected with beast right in the face. The creature howled with fury and reached up with one of his back fins and snapped the arrow away. He turned and stared at Preston. His guard took this as his chance and slayed the creature. It hissed and disappeared in the same dark mist.

"There's someone coming from the castle!" Preston yelled.

His guard looked toward the castle and sure enough, there wasn't just one but two mermaids. Preston recognized them immediately. It was Megan and Aurora. He didn't recognize them the first time because of the green mist but now it was like watching the sun rise over a mountain. They were both absolutely beautiful. Their brightly colored fins and hair shined brightly through the green that was surrounding the entire kingdom. Preston swam quickly toward them as well as three other strong merman.

"Move away, Hanna has to train with these animals," Aurora boomed.

The sound of her voice shocked Preston. It wasn't the sweet sound that he had heard the last few hours, but it was commanding and purposeful. The mermen moved away from the sorceress, but Preston held his ground.

"They are dangerous, Grandma, I don't want her hurt," he yelled back over the sound of the battle behind him.

"My dear boy, do as you are told! Or I will move you myself!" she commanded.

Preston still didn't move. He held his sword high and blocked their way. Aurora sighed and raised her hand. She gave one swift movement and Preston was shot ten feet to the left and sat down with great force in a chair near a small shop. No matter how much he wiggled and fought, he couldn't budge. A chair was not a very comfortable place for a man with a fin, but he was stuck there.

He watched as Megan inched closer to the battle. As she reached a spot five feet from a rather large monster, she looked at it deeply, raised both hands in the air, and brought them down hard to her side. As she did this she yelled as loud as she could. Her screams caught the attention of every creature that had invaded their city and they all watched her and stopped their attack on the merpeople. She raised her arms again and this time a large red shark appeared over her head. It was probably twice the size of a regular shark with large protruding teeth that stuck out in every direction of its mouth. The muscles of this shark were so large that they could be seen from any direction. It swam around Megan and Aurora and you could hear it grumble as it protected them. The green creatures eyed the new threat and growled with furious snares. They glided around and came to rest surrounding Aurora, Megan, and her creature. The other

323

mermen swam back to allow their queen to do as she wished. Aurora watched as her granddaughter made her illusion become real. With every swish of her arms, the creature became larger and more threatening. The green beasts came closer and closer. Preston tried again to move, but was still held tightly to his chair. The other mermen watched as the red shark circled around overhead.

The larger of green beasts decided he had had enough, and shot out of the crowd toward Megan and Aurora. The red shark gave a flick of its tail and without any effort the creature disappeared into the green mist. The other monsters watched and were now outraged at the attack on their leader. This time, each creature decided to attack, but neither Megan or Aurora were the target anymore. It was the shark that Megan had made appear from thin air. The battle between the creatures was short. The shark had only to touch these creatures, and they would be gone. Preston wasn't sure how that was, but they were soon gone. The shark became smaller and smaller as Megan lowered her arms and without a trace it disappeared. Megan dropped to the soft ground below and breathed heavily.

"I'm proud of you, my dear. The shark was a great illusion." Aurora beamed happily.

Nirvelli raced over and swooped Megan into his arms. Preston finally felt the force lift and he too swam over to join them.

"What was that thing?" he asked once he realized that Megan was okay.

Zachi and Cane both were there already, and Zachi's face was dumbfounded. Megan looked at them wearily and smiled. She didn't say anything but closed her eyes and took deep breaths. After a few moments Nirvelli started swimming with Megan in his arms back toward the castle.

"Zachi, Cane, you need to prepare to leave immediately. We must get a message at once to the city of Alchemy," Aurora commanded.

Zachi gave one more glance at his once sister and departed. Megan opened her eyes and looked at Preston. He took this as a sign that she was ready to answer his questions.

"How did you do that?" he asked as they all swam back toward the castle.

"After we went back into the castle, Grandma told me that I could make an illusion real just by using my imagination and I needed to try it. She took me to her little room where there were all sorts of weird things. She told me to figure out a way to make light stay inside of a glow-fish while at the same time making it larger. She handed me a glow-fish and told me to concentrate and think hard about what I needed to do. She said that light would be the only way to destroy all those nasty creatures. So I began to think hard about what I wanted done and in only a matter of seconds, I made a glow-fish brighter and larger and soon it was so large that it had no more room to grow. So I made it very small and had it stay in my palm and then Grandma told me it was time to use my newfound talent. As soon as she said this, my mind went into a trance and all I could think

325

about was that glow-fish. We swam quickly out of the front gate, and I brought the glow-fish out of the castle and when I felt the danger of those creatures, I turned him into a shark, but gave him so much light, that it was like the light of the sun." She opened her closed hand and a glow-fish swam out and swam around their heads.

"You see, Paden, your sister is a sorceress. She realized that she could do something to help and that's exactly what she did. Once she realizes that she can do something, she must act quickly. Her mind is not yet trained to hold the knowledge that she learns until it's put to a test. The glow-fish was a perfect defense against a shade-fish. They have to have darkness to live, such as shade. They were summoned here by Jacan. I've been warned that he is ready for war and will be using any means necessary to take control of Rill. This is a powerful city, and we have access to every city in Mere through the rivers and streams. It would be the perfect place for his creatures to hide," Aurora explained.

"Jacan? You mean the guy that betrayed our family and over took Nebula?" he asked.

"The very same," Nirvelli answered. "Jacan has become very powerful over the years that you have been away. He now has access to many creatures and their powers. He has always wanted Mere. Nebula was a small task for him to control, but the beginnings of his powers. He has taken over many other small kingdoms and by doing so has gained control of all of their creatures. They fear him, and will do what he asks."

Preston absorbed the new information. He had heard so many stories over the years. Jacan was always the guy he had nightmares about as a small child and the thought of him being alive and not just a character in a story made him shiver.

"How does he plan to take control of Mere? If I understand correctly there are more spells and guards around this kingdom, that to even gain access is impossible," he asked.

He looked at his sister, who was now sound asleep in Nirvelli's arms. She looked so peaceful.

"We have seen today that he has found a way to enter his creatures. However, the spells prevent him from being able to gain access to the kingdom himself until the night of the full moon of this year; which is only eight days away," Nirvelli answered.

They had reached the castle and entered through the large gateway into the foyer. Preston still couldn't get over the beauty of the glass and rock that it was made from. The glow-fish swam quickly over to a lantern and joined his friends, relieved to be home.

"So war is the only way to stop him?" Preston asked finally after a long pause.

Nirvelli glanced down at Megan asleep in his arms and then over at Aurora.

She nodded. "Take her to sleep, I'll explain the rest."

He excused himself and took Megan to her room.

Aurora led Preston to a large room full of sea plants and several books that were made to last under water. There were several long glass sofas sitting around the room with glow-fish–filled lanterns near each one.

This must be the library, he thought to himself.

They swam over to a sofa and each lay, down gently resting their fins on the smooth surface. She rang a bell and then looked carefully at Preston.

"This might take a while, better get some Plauso." She smiled and they waited patiently for her ring to be answered by one of the many servants within the castle walls.

19

The Message

As the servants brought in the small glasses of the purple Plauso, Aurora began to feel anxious about explaining everything to her precious grandson. She was afraid that it might scare him and he might then be afraid to take his place on the throne. Preston eyed his grandmother as she took the glass from the servant. After they had everything they needed, the small-figured maid bowed low toward the floor of the library and swam away. Aurora took a small drink of the Plauso and then watched Preston as he did the same.

"Paden, what do you know of Jacan?" Aurora asked.

Preston thought for a moment.

"Not much, I know only what my father has informed me. I know that his powers increase with each creature that he gains control over," Preston answered. "My father used to tell me the story of Nebula's attack. He told me that Jacan's strength was with the people of Umbra. He used their powers against the kingdom and they were so powerful that none of the wizards were able to control their strength. His exact words were, '*The black riders of Umbra came from the dark corners of earth appearing from thin air with no apparent trace of where they were from and no noticeable way of destruction. The people of Nebula were at a loss of how to*

protect their lands, or even their families.' I used to have
nightmares about him and the Umbra. I dreamt that they were
attacking our home and we had to run through several
different types of tunnels and sometimes I dreamt that we
flew to get away. I was always so shook up by the end of the
dream I had to sleep with my mom and dad in their bed. My
mom always told my dad not to tell me those stories, but my
dad always said I would thank him one day. I thought he was
just trying to make me tough or something. I didn't think that
I would actually be part of the story," Preston explained.

Aurora watched her grandson closely and understood
when he finished that her son-in-law had done everything he
could do to protect her grandson.

"Your father told you correctly. Jacan surprised
everyone with his Umbra warriors. They too use shadows
and darkness to attack their victims, just as the shade fish.
The wizards of Mere found a way to block them from
coming through the many shadows of Mere and also Rill.
There are several other kingdoms that use the same
protection as well. It seems, however, that Jacan has become
so powerful that he has found a way past that spell. I fear that
everything becomes weaker here the closer we come to the
full moon." Aurora took another drink of her purple goop.

"Paden, did your father ever tell you that you are to
be married to the King's daughter? I believe her name is
Lillie," Aurora said.

She knew that this would be a touchy subject for a
young boy to take in, but he wasn't young anymore. He was

a man of twenty-two years. Preston looked at her sharply and his eyes grew narrow.

"She's the Princess of Mere?" Preston gasped. "My father said that it was family tradition, he didn't mention that she was the Princess of Mere."

Aurora wasn't shocked by his response; she actually expected it to be worse.

"He didn't tell you because you wouldn't have believed him. Think about it Paden. Would you have believed him?"

"No, you are probably right, I wouldn't have believed him. Why do I have to marry her?" Preston asked.

"By marrying Princess Lillie, you will be sealing a protection over the kingdoms of Mere and Rill. It is, and always has been the plan. That's what happens when you are royalty, you don't get to choose who you marry, it's usually all politics."

Preston twisted and turned on his small glass sofa. He was really uncomfortable with the thought of being married.

"Do you not wish to be married?" Aurora's question was still fresh on his mind when a knock came on the wall of the library. They both glanced up and found a man with a bubble surrounding his head for air.

"My lady, I have news from Mere," the man spoke.

Aurora glided up from where she was laying and the man kneeled down at her feet and handed her a letter that was also surrounded by a bubble of air.

"How have you come by this letter, Master Bates?" she asked.

"I was given the letter by a member of your Todswan guards, my lady. They say it's an urgent message from Avery."

"Thank you for bringing the message. How are your people getting along here in Rill?" she asked.

"Oh, quite well, thank you for asking, mistress. We appreciate you allowing us to seek refuge in your mighty kingdom for a while."

He smiled and she returned his smile.

"Thank you again, you may go," she said with a note of authority. Master Bates bowed low and retreated from the room.

Aurora quickly swam over and rang the bell near the sofa. Seconds later the small maid was there to service her queen.

"Yes, mistress, what can I get for you?" she asked quietly.

"Find Nirvelli and have him meet us here at once. It's very urgent!" Aurora commanded.

The maid quickly swam away, leaving the two of them alone again in the library.

"Preston, do you remember me telling you that you would only have your fin as long as you were in my kingdom?"

Preston nodded.

"Well, I fear that you and your sister will soon be leaving and continuing your journey toward the city of Mere," she said. "It is very difficult to explain right now, but I will explain as soon as Nirvelli arrives."

Preston didn't know what to say. He thought that they would be here far longer then two days. It had been very difficult for him to accept that he was part of this magical world. He could have easily passed it up as a dream, but he was starting to feel more and more like a prince every day. He couldn't quite understand what could be so urgent that they would have to leave immediately.

Nirvelli arrived within minutes. He swam right up next to the Queen and bowed.

"Yes, Your Majesty, what is it?" he asked.

Preston noticed that he had his hand tightly gripped around his strong spear. His knuckles were white and he was out of breath.

"We've received a message from Avery," Aurora answered.

The shock that overtook Nirvelli was not very well hidden.

"How?" he asked, stunned.

"It was left with Donaghy at the gate and was brought to me by Master Bates. I feel it's time," she answered firmly.

"What does the message say?" Preston asked, confused at what had just taken place.

"Mere is under attack. Jacan has sent his army through the shadows and they are currently taking their place to attack the city of Loch."

Nirvelli's face dropped into a sullen stare. Preston knew that this was very significant.

"Is this a powerful city?" he asked after a few minutes.

"It's the third largest in the kingdom. It is also where the armory is. Avery has put a spell of protection around the entire city, as well as ordered the Duchess there to close all the gates and let no one in or out. He would be sending an army to assist them in fighting the Umbra," Aurora explained.

Preston understood now how dangerous this could be for the Kingdom of Mere.

"I thought that they would want Rill first," he said. "Isn't that what you said? They would have access to every city in Mere that way."

"Yes, he is attacking both at the same time," she answered. "Nirvelli, I need you to go and seek the wizards of Rill, Zachi, and also Cane at once. Have them all meet me here in twenty minutes. Also, Princess Hanna must be awakened for her protection."

Nirvelli hadn't said too much since he had arrived, but he straightened up, drew his spear in fighting position, and departed the library.

"Grandmother, what can I do to help?" Preston asked quietly.

334

"Go to your sister and bring her back to me. You are to leave with Cane and Zachi at once. Pack all your belongings, as well as several other backup weapons. You will be traveling to the hidden Kingdom of Alchemy to seek shelter among the rest of the wizards of the world. Only Zachi and Cane can take you there. From there, several wizards will escort you to your wedding in Mere."

Preston looked at his grandmother in shock.

"You mean I'm getting married now? As in, a few days from today?" he choked.

"You must marry before the full moon meets the center sky in eight days. Actually, it's less then eight now," she teased.

Preston watched his grandmother, hoping for a just kidding, but it never came. His face fell into a trance. He had no choice.

"It's not going to be so bad. From what I'm told, Lillie is among the fairest ladies in the world." Aurora swam over and gave her grandson a hug. "Now go, gather your things and your sister and come back here."

Preston gently pushed down with his fin and swam out of the library.

The questions about this place were still fresh on his mind. He hadn't had the chance to have everything explained to him before the message from that Avery person showed up. As he thought about the name, he started to feel like he had heard it before. He swam along the stairs and approached Megan's large door. He knocked three times, but there was

335

no answer. He slowly pushed the door to her room open and peeked inside. The glow-fish had dimmed their lights and he saw Megan lying very still on her large glass bed, fast asleep.

That spell must have really worn her out, he thought to himself.

He swam quietly over to her and placed himself gently on the chair next to her bed.

"Megan, it's time to go," he whispered.

She slowly opened her eyes and yawned. "What time is it?" she asked groggily.

"It's around noon, I believe," he answered. "Come on, we have to pack our things. Aurora says we must leave with Zachi and Cane at once."

Megan pushed herself up and steadied herself with her elbow.

"I have to tell you about this dream that I just had. It was amazing."

Preston repositioned himself to be a little bit more comfortable.

"We have to hurry; Aurora wants us back in the library soon all packed and ready to go," he answered.

Megan sat up on her golden fin and looked at him.

"You and I were on a beach surrounded by many different animals and creatures. I was playing an instrument that the merpeople call a Pinoa. I was playing a traditional folk song that I had heard as a baby. We were laughing and telling jokes and all of the sudden a beautiful girl showed up, but it was only a picture of her through the waterfall. She was smiling and I could see several other people surrounding her, and watching her. It started to get dark and her face disappeared, but it returned and she started screaming for us to get away from the darkness. Well, we all immediately jumped back into the water and were surrounded by those nasty shade-fish. She raised her hand and threw a ball of fire the size of a small boulder toward the trees and the sun jumped back into the sky. The shade-fish disappeared and Zachi came up and thanked the girl for warning us and told her she was safe. Then she disappeared and you woke me up. Isn't that an amazing dream?" Megan's excitement showed through on her face. Her eyes were lit up and sparkling and her smile grew from ear to ear.

"It sounds like you had an exciting sleep." Preston chuckled.

She reached over and slugged him on the arm.

"Ow, what was that for?" He laughed.

"For teasing me! Now tell me why we are leaving," she giggled.

Preston spent the next couple of minutes explaining what had happened in the library. He told her of their father's stories and all about what he had learned about Jacan. She watched him intently explain everything he had learned and when he had finished, she inhaled and took a deep breath.

"I thought this all might be a dream, and when I woke up I would be lying on the beach next to Chloe and listening to her go on about how much she liked you." She frowned.

Preston again was caught off guard by her remark of Chloe. He so wanted to just see her again and maybe then everything would be okay.

"We better get packed," Megan said, bringing his attention back to reality.

They spent the next several minutes packing the things they wanted to take. Megan packed several shirts, hair accessories, her mother-of-pearl tiara, and several other things that she thought she might need. Preston was shocked to see how much she was taking. They had been given two seaweed-type bags to load all their possessions into and she could have easily taken several more. Preston had only packed weapons. He took several more bundles of arrows, an extra bow, he had carefully chosen a spear and two other swords both wrapped in a linen type material. He also decided to pack the pitchfork weapon. His two bags still had plenty of room for more items. Megan called for Maida and Eri to come and help, and soon they were making their way back down toward the library.

When they arrived, they found the room full of merpeople, both male and female. Zachi and Cane were both there talking to Aurora. They swam over and Megan gave Zachi a hug.

"We've received another message. This time it came by a small black fish. Avery has told us that the Umbra plan on attacking Rill very soon. We must put a protection spell over the kingdom at once. However, we can't accomplish this until you are both out of the boundaries of Rill. It also

338

states that several of our people may have already been attacked while celebrating near a waterfall."

Megan gasped. "A waterfall?" she asked.

"Yes, why?" Zachi asked. Megan explained the dream that she had moments ago and that they were the ones celebrating.

Aurora eyed her granddaughter. "My dear, you have the power of vision. Is this your first dream like this?" she asked.

"Yes, I mean I've had dreams before, but nothing like this."

"We must get you out of here immediately. Zachi, Cane, prepare to leave," Aurora boomed.

Zachi and Cane both swam as quickly as they could toward the large doors and several merman joined them.

"Hanna, you have the ability to maintain your brother's fin. You must keep him as a merman for as long as you can. It's not difficult. All you need to do is visualize him as he is right now, and then touch his arm or face and he will maintain his look. If he loses the fin, your trip will be slowed immensely. I've given Zachi and Cane a chariot pulled by octopi, but it only holds the two of them and your provisions. You must all swim quickly and remove yourselves from Rill at once." She wrapped her arms around Megan and then Preston. "Take care of her, she needs to return to me once this is all over. After all, she is the heir to the throne of Rill."

Preston smiled as she kissed him on the cheek. "Thank you for everything. I hope to come back again soon."

Aurora took Megan by the arm and led her to a small out-cove near the far wall.

"Hanna, you must keep practicing your spells. When the time comes, you will have to transform your fin into human legs, and that spell is very difficult. I've prepared this book for you to read on your journey so you always have me with you. Be careful and come back to me when you can."

Megan took the book from her grandmother and smiled. She wrapped her arms around Aurora and gave her one last hug and then swam through the doorway after Preston.

Eri and Maida had both joined their questing party, as well as the three guards that Nirvelli had sent with Preston to fight the shade-fish. Zachi and Cane looked extremely ridiculous being towed along in a larger than life seashell by two large brown octopi. Their journey through the city was quiet. As they passed under the large stone archway that led to the city, a large flash of light beamed around the castle and the homes placed ever so softly on the sea bed. The long journey that lay before them had started and all Preston could think about was his soon-to-be marriage to a princess he had never met.

20

Battle of Loch

Cerella watched out her window in hopes of anyone coming to their aid. Loch had been in total darkness for several hours. Shortly after Avery's magical spell and his departure, the city turned dark. The patrons of the city were hiding in their homes and armed with several weapons, many only a small sword or a few arrows. Cerella had sent the guards of the castle to their homes to collect their families and bring them back to the castle. All the rooms were full and the servants were busy making up beds for either their own families or the other people that came to seek refuge here. The sounds of Loch's powerful battle bells were ringing outside the castle, only to be returned from escaping from the powerful spell.

Nothing shall leave or enter the city, Avery had said before leaving.

As the darkness continued, Cerella could see the armies of Jacan taking their place outside the city walls. There must have been hundreds of them, if not thousands. It was the people of Umbra. She had heard of them only briefly from her father who passed away when she was young. He had been a survivor of the attack on Nebula. The King and Queen of Mere gave him the city of Loch and built him a castle. It was now up to her to take her father's throne and keep the city safe. She was always told that the Wizards of Alchemy would always be her aid in times of need, and when the time came, a duke would be her companion to fight against any evil that comes through the gates of Mere.

Where are they all now? she kept asking herself.

They were all alone. The one wizard that did come to her aid flew away without offering her any assistance to her army, but gave her a protection spell.

"How long is this going to stay?" several servants asked her. "Are we going to have to fight?"

She didn't know how to answer the question. She would just smile and tell them the aid would come.

The sounds of drums caught her attention. She ran over to the window on the far side of her room and saw several Umbra playing battle drums, while others were trying fiercely to gain access through the gates, only to be thrown backward and given a nasty shock.

It's going to hold, we are going to be safe after all, she thought quietly to herself.

BOOM! The sound shook the castle walls and the echo vibrated every person throughout the city. Cerella was knocked back onto the floor. She pushed herself up and ran to the window. Large cannonballs were being used to try and break the spell around the walls, but were not the normal cannonballs she had seen before. These were glowing green and each time they shot one at the wall, it would turn that portion of the protection spell green.

342

"My lady, what is that?" Aminon pleaded.

"I don't know, but we must prepare ourselves for war. I don't think that the protection spell is of any use against their new powers," she answered.

She unsheathed her sword from the leather wrapped neatly around her small frame. BOOM! Another green cannonball hit the wall. The vibrant shaking became more of a challenge to hold your stance.

"Anders, ring the bells of retreat. Everyone needs to enter the castle at once!" she screamed over the sounds of frightened people.

Anders ran toward the bells. BOOM! This time the sound and the shaking was so powerful that part of some buildings fell into the streets below. Anders quickly got up from where he had been thrown and reached for the bells. He grabbed the rope and pulled hard. The sounds echoed through the castle and out into the city. Several times he rang the bells and soon people were swarming toward the castle.

BOOM! Houses collapsed, streets cracked. Each cannonball caused more devastation. Animals were brought into the castle, horses, cows, dogs, cats. Hundreds of people were in the castle now. BOOM! The castle shook violently.

"Please help us!" Cerella begged.

The sound of metal from underneath the castle caught her attention.

"My lady, they've dug a tunnel under the castle," Aminon shouted.

343

"Everyone, withdraw your weapons. We are under attack. We must fight for Mere, we must fight for our families. Send your children and animals higher up in the castle, they are coming from underneath." Cerella raised her sword and she was followed by every armed person.

A thunk from beneath the floor let them know where they were coming from. They circled around the area just as another cannonball hit the protection wall. BOOM! This time the city was almost entirely destroyed. Only a handful of buildings remained standing. The now warriors jumped quickly back into their positions just as a large metal spike came up from the dining room floor.

"Steady!" she whispered. "Wait for my signal!"

BOOM! The sound of screaming children could faintly be heard. There was an ear-piercing shrill from outside. A flash of light, as bright as the sun, settled momentarily over the city.

"The wizards have come!" a small boy around the age of twelve yelled from the stairwell. "There are dozens of them!"

"Steady, we are under attack here now!" she yelled at the people now lowering their weapons.

The floor of the castle was broken and warriors dressed in all silver came pouring out.

"It's the warriors of Diadem!" Aminon yelled.

Sounds of joy were heard throughout the castle. The people of Loch made a path for the warriors to come into the castle. Several ran to their children and comforted them.

"My lady, we've been sent by Avery to aid in the war. What do you know?"

Cerella turned quickly and found herself staring at a large man covered from head to toe in shiny armor. He held out his sword and was trying to carefully bow toward the Duchess. She smiled and through her arms around him. She withdrew herself and cleared her throat.

"I didn't think anyone was coming," she said through tear-filled eyes.

The tall warrior stood cautiously, not knowing what to do.

"My name is Gideon, I'm the Duke of Diadem. I've received word of your need and have come to the aid of Loch."

Cerella smiled again and then turned and walked toward the window. The Duke followed.

"The Umbra have been using green cannonballs to destroy our city. I'm not exactly sure what they are, only that each time they hit the wall of protection they make a large sound that shakes the entire city causing complete devastation. Just look at our city." She pointed out the window at the fallen buildings.

Gideon peered out the window to glimpse the sight she had explained.

"The wizards have only just arrived and caused peace within our walls.

"I'm afraid, my lady, that what you see aren't wizards. It's the sight of a broken spell. Each time a spell is

Alicia Rivoli

broken, it gives the image of wizards to try and confuse the enemy. I'm afraid the war has only just begun."

She glanced again out the window and at her once prosperous city and noticed the gates of Loch being broken down. The cannonballs were no longer being fired and she realized that the war was far from over.

"What do we need to do to help?" she asked the Duke.

"You need to take your people and follow the tunnel. It will lead you to safety. We will fight off the Umbra until daylight. That is when their gateways will close and they will need to be back where the came from. They can only fight in darkness. The tunnel is well lit and you will have no problem there. Take everyone, including your animals. However, I need you to leave all of your guards so they can assist in the fight."

Cerella lowered her head.

"Then who is to protect us if the need arise?" she asked quickly.

"You will be well protected there, not even their cannonballs can enter. Now go at once, here they come." Gideon urged her past the windows and into a large hall.

"My people we must retreat underground. Lord Gideon has made safe passage to safety for us all. Gather everyone and everything you can, we must go at once!"

The people hurried to and fro for only a moment and then lined up waiting to follow their Leader down the tunnel. Cerella gave the guards their instructions and had them say

346

their farewells. She then walked briskly toward the front of the precession and gave one last glance at her beautiful castle.

"My lady, you must go now. They are at the gates of the castle!" Gideon yelled. She waved her arm and then led the way for the two-hundred and twenty people into the lit tunnel. As soon as the last person entered the tunnel, it automatically sealed itself and you could hear the fighting no more.

Gideon stood over the now sealed tunnel.

"It is time, men. We go to meet the Umbra!" The men in shining armor held their swords ready and waited. The doors of the castle burst open and a shot of hot air raced through the castle. The Umbra stood in armor of black with thick swords, shields of black brass, and many were on black horses that were also dressed in black armor. Reider stood in the front of the pack, smiling his black toothy grin. He howled with laughter at the sight of the armor that had prepared to meet them at the door.

"Is this the army that the lady has sent to protect her, ten men with swords and only a few with arrows?" he shouted with glee. "All the easier on us to overtake this dreadful place!"

A horn blew somewhere and outside the sounds of the battle drums could be heard. Gideon watched as the Umbra raised their large heavy swords. A broad smile formed on his face and the warrior next to him held up a small mirror. With a swift movement of his arm a loud ringing of bells echoed throughout the entire castle. The sounds of fighting began to be heard outside of the castle. Reider turned on his black horse and saw his entire army surrounded by thousands of warriors. His eyes shot back to Gideon, the shock still lingering on his face. Reider growled furiously and kicked his horse hard in the side. It lunged forward and raced into the castle toward Gideon.

The warriors that had stayed to assist him thrust their swords toward him, only to be knocked aside. Gideon again smiled, reached out, and grabbed another mirror out of his small pack laying on the floor. Just as Reider was about to strike at him, he held the mirror in the air and faced it toward Reider. A flash of bright light hit his attacker right in the eyes. Reider howled with fury.

"We have a slight advantage over you, I'm afraid. Each warrior carries a wizard or sorceress in these mirrors. Admit it, you are no match for thousands of wizards. You may have the help of shadow, but we have the knowledge and strength of magic."

Gideon raised his sword and slashed at Reider. His sword, however, was met with the sword of the enemy.

Gideon raised his sword toward the sky and again took a swing at his opponent. The blades met again, sending sparks throughout the room. Gideon could feel the sweat pouring down his face as the fight drew on. With each movement, he met the sword of his opponent. Both were tiring and ready to rest, but neither would comply to the others request. The battle continued and the sweat of both men was causing their swords to slip slightly through their fingers. Twenty minutes into the battle, a loud BOOM sounded through the castle. Both fighters withdrew their swords and glanced upward toward the sound. People and Umbra were all staring upward. Gideon glanced down just in time to see Reider bring down his sword. Gideon threw up his own sword, but was a shy late. The Umbra blade dug into his arm, causing a large wound to appear. It throbbed with pain.

Gideon switched his blade to his left arm and they continued their duel. The blood dripped from his torn sleeve and the pain was so terrible that he found it difficult to concentrate on the duel happening between himself and Reider. Battling with his left arm was difficult, but he was almost as powerful with his left as he was with his right. He brought back his sword and twirled on his feet sliding to get a better angle and his opponent. Finally he was able to reach Reider. He made a large cut on his side with the tip of his sharpened blade. Both now wounded, neither cared anymore about the BOOM that startled them moments before.

BOOM! The sound rang again through the castle walls. This time it caught their full attention. Both men glared at one another and ran full force to the opening of the castle to see what made such a sound.

"Gideon, it's Elymas, he's come to our aid!" a knight in armor yelled.

Reider looked up toward the west turret of the castle and saw the wizard standing with a force so great that no one could come near him with their weapons. Gideon watched his opponent closely, waiting for him to attack again, but this time, Reider glared hard at him.

"This isn't over, the kingdom will be ours," he blurted loudly.

Gideon raised his sword and Reider jumped quickly down the steps and ran toward a dark shadow. With only a second's glance, Gideon lost sight of his enemy. He searched everywhere, but he wasn't to be found. He raced back toward the entrance of the castle and found only a few Umbra were left, and most were severely wounded. Gideon raced up the stairs, followed by several other officers and searched the castle; no one was found.

"The entrance to the tunnel, quick!" he yelled at his fellow warriors. They raced back down the stairwell and into the large dining hall where the entrance had been sealed. When they arrived, they found it still sealed and the spell was still protecting the people below. The walked swiftly back toward the entrance and were greeted by Elymas.

"They've all gone, my friends. They disappeared through the shadows of the morning sun. I apologize for my late arrival, I was caught up in the weather," he said.

Gideon embraced the wizard in a firm handshake.

"It's nice to see you again, old friend. Will you be leading us down the tunnel?" Gideon asked.

"Not this time, I'm afraid. I'm needed elsewhere for more protection spells and healing," he answered.

350

"However, before I go, let me heal your arm. I am the wizard of healing, you know." He smirked.

Gideon smiled at him and raised his sleeve to allow the wizard a chance to heal his arm. Elymas was different than he remembered. The last time he saw the wizard was when they led the troops to battle for Nebula with his father. They had arrived only a moment to late and ended up escorting the King and Queen and their two children to safety. Of course, Gideon was just a small fourteen-year-old boy then. Elymas was always with their family since before he could remember. Now his once light brown beard was snow white. His cheeks were a rosy red and his smile was large and full of sparkling white teeth. The clothing he was wearing, they were also white as was every inch of hair on his head.

"Oh my. This is worse than I thought. It seems their blades are tipped with poison. Your arm is in pretty bad shape." Elymas glanced over the wound now black with poison.

"We must get you some more Lillias Holloack right away. You did eat some before, correct?" Gideon nodded.

"A small lad brought some to all of us just before we broke through the barrier below the castle. We each had two leaves," Gideon answered.

"Very good," Elymas replied.

He handed Gideon two more leaves of the black-stemmed plant and gave more to several other wounded soldiers. He ran his arm over each wound and they were

351

quickly replaced by new skin. The throbbing pain receded and the use of his arm was quickly returned.

"Thank you, Elymas, we must now be on our way to the others. We are to keep them well protected. Before we go, what made that loud noise upon your arrival?" Gideon asked.

Elymas smiled. "Thunder. It seems our dear enemy has learned to control the weather. He tried to hit me with lightning bolts, but I was protected by a spell and that is what caused the sound of thunder." Gideon grinned; he had almost forgotten how mischievous this wizard could be.

It was Elymas that taught him how to fight, and how to smile and get attention of every lady in the land.

"It's all about your teeth. If they are yellow and crooked, they will reject you, but if you have bright white teeth, dimples, and a big, happy smile, they will love you." He remembered Elymas's words from his training.

Elymas and Gideon were very close friends for quite some time, but after the war of Nebula, he was sent to train in Alchemy with the other wizards, and he hadn't seen him or even talked with him since. Elymas shook Gideon's hand again.

"Keep them safe, my friend. Jacan has many new tricks up his sleeve." He glanced around at the other warriors, then lifted from the ground and flew north toward the city of Mere.

Gideon waved goodbye and then turned toward his soldiers.

"You have done well. We must re-enter our tunnel and follow the good people of Loch to safety. Follow me!" he shouted over the crowd of armored men.

He walked swiftly back in the castle and found the wounded Umbra still lying on the floor.

"Leave them, their master will return for them," he yelled as he went past. The Umbra watched the soldiers traipse into the dining room. Once they were all inside, the door was closed. The Umbra rose from the positions and their wounds were suddenly healed.

"Come, we must follow them!" a rather large Umbra whispered. They waited outside the dining room door for only a few moments and then quickly pushed the doors open. Swords drawn and ready to fight, they found no one.

"Where did they go?" one black soldier asked his new leader.

"They must have some magic room here somewhere. We need to return to Jacan and tell him our news," the large Umbra growled.

They retreated from the room and in a wink disappeared in darkness.

"That should keep them busy for a while," Gideon told one of the captains as they watched from their small mirror. "I really like having these mirrors, they really do help us see what is just in front of us!"

353

"Do you think we should have left them alive?" the captain asked.

"Of course. We want Jacan to find this tunnel. Little does he know that we have a trap set for him. Do you not remember the orders from the high councilman. 'Let at least one see, so all will follow. They will think it's the perfect surprise.' He was right, did you see their faces? It was complete shock. They had no clue where we could have all gone."

The captain nodded and they both retreated from the entrance and took their places in front of the procession.

****

As soon as the entrance to the tunnel was sealed, Cerella became very frightened.

What if the Umbra or Jacan know about this tunnel? she thought to herself. *Why would Gideon leave us by ourselves in this tunnel with no protection?*

The anger built inside of her like fire. She was left with a few hundred animals, wives, and children. The only protection she had were the few soldiers that refused to leave their families. She marched toward the front of the herd of people and faced her people.

"We must follow the tunnel. Gideon told us this would lead us to safety. I want two of the soldiers to remain in the back of the procession, and then I would like to have the rest form lines up all the way from back to front. I know we don't have many men, so give yourself plenty of room. This tunnel is quite large, so we shouldn't have any trouble making our way forward. When you are too tired, tell the nearest soldiers and they will inform me. We will only stop a couple of times to rest, so make sure you are getting the fluids, rest and most importantly food that you need."

She quickly turned around and grabbed her belongings from a rock. No one really had too much, only a few changes of clothing, enough food and water for three days, a few small blankets, firewood, and weapons. The tunnel seemed very eerie and the small children were frightened to walk by themselves, so their mothers carried them for a ways and then made them walk by themselves. As the crowd began to slow down, Cerella turned and faced them.

"We will rest here for some time. Please make sure you get all you need to continue," she yelled over the multitude of people.

It had been a few hours now by this time, and she suspected that daylight would soon arrive at the now destroyed city of Loch. She imagined the sun rising over the mountains in the distance and sight of the dew hanging from the fragrant flowers. Her eyes were closed as she dreamt of being home, warm in her bed, awaiting her maid-in-waiting to wake her for the day's activities. A faint whooshing noise brought her back to reality. She stood quickly and whipped around to see where the noise had come from. The tunnel was well lit, but the shadows that each light gave caused her skin to crawl. She wasn't sure what could be waiting just around the bend, and she really didn't want to find out. She motioned for a guard to come up and take his post in front of the procession. After explaining the noise to him, he withdrew his sword, grabbed a torch from the wall, and shined it in front of him as he walked toward where the sound was coming from.

The whooshing became more distinct the closer he came. With his sword ready, he jumped around the corner of the cave. A man no taller then his knees was standing there with a small orange bird. The bird's wings were moving swiftly up and down causing the whooshing noise.

"Speak elf, or prepare to die," the soldier said sternly.

The little elf looked at the soldier and smiled.

"Know you not who I am?" the little elf asked.

The soldier didn't move. The sword in his hand was held tightly ready to attack if this little creature decided to make a move.

The elf sighed. "You would think, dear Etten, that Gideon would have given us a proper introduction," he said to his small orange bird.

He looked back at the soldier.

"Lower your sword, I am no harm to you. My name is Ezion, I am your guide to the city of Diadem. Gideon has asked me to lead the Lady Cerella and the people of Loch there for protection," he explained.

The soldier stared at the little elf and with some hesitation lowered his sword.

"What proof do you have of this?" the soldier asked.

Ezion pulled a small trinket from the pouch around his small waist.

"I have the medallion of Mere to show my loyalty toward the Duchess of Loch." He held out his hand and the soldier walked forward and took it from the small elf. The medallion was the symbol of Mere. The sword enlaced in gold shined brightly in the palm of his hand.

"Come with me," he told Ezion.

The soldier sheathed his sword and the two walked together around the corner, toward the procession.

"My lady, I present the Elf Ezion. He claims to be our guide set here by Gideon. He is to take us to Diadem," the soldier explained. "He presented me with the medallion of Mere for Your Highness."

Cerella gave a small curtsey and welcomed Ezion. The small elf pulled a small blanket from his satchel that was hanging from his back and laid it neatly on the dirt floor. Next he pulled out two small pieces of meat. He handed one to Etten and put the other in his own mouth.

"Many thanks for the lady to allow me to sit in her presence. It has been some time since I have been graced with such beauty," he said to Cerella.

Cerella watched her new guide and smiled. Ezion was by far the smallest adult she had ever encountered. Not only was he short, but his appearance was quite different from any that she had seen. He seemed to be made entirely of dirt. His clothing was all brown, and made no noise when he moved.

357

The material seemed quite soft, but he almost blended in wholly with the walls of the tunnel. His hair was also brown, as were his eyes and skin.

"Ezion, how far is it to Diadem? We have many small children, expectant women, and elderly among us, and very little to eat. We only had a short amount of time to prepare ourselves to leave our homes," she asked, taking her eyes from his strange appearance.

"It's only a day's walk. You actually only have a half a day now. You have made excellent time," he said as he took another bite of his meat. "This tunnel splits just around the corner and Gideon was afraid you might take the wrong tunnel and be lost under ground, so he asked me to stay put until you arrived. I'm sorry to have startled you, but Etten was getting mighty board. I forgot his favorite toy, and without it, he seems lost."

Cerella looked at his orange bird. The curiosity rose inside of her, as she had never seen such a bird.

"What type of bird is Etten?" she asked.

"Etten is a fire hawk. He has the capability to start fires," Ezion said proudly.

The bird stuck out his chest as if he knew they were talking about him.

"He's very smart, but also very proud." Ezion laughed.

Cerella gave a small laugh and then stood from where she had sat down to talk to Ezion.

"I think it's time we moved on. I don't like tunnels, especially the shadows that this tunnel gives off."

Ezion rose and quickly folded his brown blanket and put it in his satchel.

"The tunnel isn't what you need fear, my lady, it's what's above us that would frighten you," Ezion answered.

Cerella looked toward the ceiling of the tunnel.

"What is it that should frighten me?" she asked.

"War," Ezion responded.

She gave a sigh, and quickly picked up the blanket and small loaves of bread she had been nibbling.

As soon as the group had cleaned up their area and was ready to leave, Ezion led them around the corner and to the tunnel that faced to the right. This tunnel at first was exactly like the one they had left moments before, but after about a mile it became brighter and if you looked, the wall shimmered with bits of small gold. Of course, the gold was of no value to the people of Mere, as their money was made of natural materials, such as bark and rock. Gold was a source of decoration and power. The more gold and silver your city presented, meant the more powerful the city's army. Loch had only a few bits of gold and silver inside the cobblestone streets and along the city wall, but they were not very well armed. It was always the city of glamour. The rich lived there because of the fine shopping and resources. In the castle itself, there was a room of knowledge. The library was so large you could spend days inside and only get to a few rows. By the looks of this tunnel, however, the well armed city started hours away from the front gates.

"The tunnel is well guarded, we have stations set up about every half mile or so," Ezion explained to Cerella, who was watching as the gold shined in the light of the torches.

"I haven't seen any guards," she answered.

"Of course not. We are so well camouflaged that I don't even see them. That is why we wear all brown. Our clothing is made from the finest sand and is completely silent. The only way you know where they are is if you are the one on guard. They move every day to a new area," he explained.

Cerella looked up toward the soaring ceiling. The size of the tunnel alone was stunning, but to have practically invisible guards, that was amazing.

Ezion giggled. "Don't worry, my lady, they know who we are."

She laughed and let her body relax as they walked on.

Three hours after they met Ezion and continued through the tunnel, they arrived at a wall made only of gold. Ezion took out a small silver pin shaped key and without any force needed, stuck it in the gold. A piece of gold moved and another little elf stuck out his head.

"Ah Ezion, we were told of your arrival in the tunnel. Welcome to you and all of our guests," the little elf said, smiling.

A large gate opened that wasn't there moments before and Ezion led the people into another large room.

"Watch your eyes, it's about to become very bright in here," he yelled to the crowd of people.

A large hole formed in the top of the tunnel and the floor quickly started to rise. Soon they were at the top and found themselves surrounded by beautiful mountains, large thick green trees, valleys, and rivers. There was a town a little ways in the distance with turrets of a castle beaming gold light in the sky.

"Welcome to Diadem! The City of Gold," Ezion trilled happily.

The people of Loch, including the Lady Cerella, were awestruck at this beautiful oasis.

"Where exactly are we?" Cerella asked.

"Why, we are in the Forest of Amorie, my lady. This is the secret of Mere. You can only gain entrance through our tunnels and no one knows of our paradise except Avery, and the King and Queen of Mere, of course," he explained full of smiles.

"This is where you will be staying until other orders are given. We've actually been expecting you for some time and have built homes and stores for your people just beyond that patch of trees to the East."

Cerella grinned from ear to ear. "I don't know what to say. Thank you, my people are in need of some good news."

She gave the elf a hug and then turned to her people.

"Welcome, friends. We have been accepted and welcomed to stay here as long as we wish. These fine new friends have even given us our own homes," she explained happily.

The people cheered and thanked all the elves and humans that had come to greet them. They all walked happily into their new city and found the homes that had been prepared for them. A small version of the Castle of Loch had been prepared for Cerella.

"Thank you. Is there anything I can do for your people in return for your humble and gracious welcome?" she asked Ezion.

"You can come to greet the warriors when they return. I've just been informed that they will arrive a little later this evening," he stated.

"Of course, also I'm sure that this has already been done, but please make sure our many thanks are sent to Avery. He will want to know of our safe return," she answered.

"Indeed, and a messenger has already been sent. Now I think you need to get some rest. I must go and have arrangements made for the banquet tonight." He excused himself with a bow and turned up the path toward the small city only a few hundred yards from entrance of her miniature castle.

Cerella opened the door with her three maids, and her servants and entered a palace of gold. Everything was made of either gold or silver, even the stairway. She went up and found a large door. She pushed it open and found a room made for a queen. Large lush pillows, brightly colored curtains, and big picture windows were only a few things that made her smile. She walked toward one window and found herself staring out over their new city. She smiled and drew the curtains. With a large yawn, she lay down on a feather bed and quickly fell asleep, only dreams of her new life still dancing in her head.

21

Iraad

The valley that the Puzzler had chosen was certainly beautiful. As soon as the doorway shut and Avery and Aden were lost behind it, the valley became clear and open. Nothing blocked the stunning views.

"This is gorgeous!" Chloe gasped.

Jason held his sword ready to fight anything that moved, but he nodded in agreement as she spoke.

"Where do you think we need to go?" she asked.

He moved his head only slightly so that he could see his sister.

"I don't know, I guess we wait," he answered.

Chloe sighed and sat down on the grassy meadow. She picked a white daisy and repeated the childish rhyme in her head.

He loves me, he loves me not. He loves me, he loves me not. She continued plucking the petals from the daisies surrounding her and repeating the rhyme.

"We can't just sit here, we don't have much time. Chloe, ask the Puzzler what he wants," Jason requested.

Chloe put down the stem of the daisy she had just mutated and looked strangely at Jason.

"How?" she asked.

"I don't know, just say something," he answered, still holding his sword ready to attack.

"Um, excuse me sir, I don't know if you can hear me, but what are we supposed to do now?" she yelled comically at the sky.

She and Jason waited patiently for an answer but nothing happened.

"Should I do it again?" she asked her brother.

He shrugged his shoulders. "I don't know. This is completely ridiculous; he can't expect us to just sit here, can he?" he said angrily.

Chloe watched her brother and as she did so, caught a glimpse of something strange in a bush only a few yards away.

"Jason, there is something over there," she whispered.

Jason slowly turned around and gripped his sword tightly around the hilt. He could feel his own heart beating faster as the adrenaline pumped through his body.

"Show yourself! Or I shall come in after you!" he yelled at the bush.

"Peace, Jason, it is I, the Master of all puzzles," the bush answered.

Jason and Chloe both smirked.

"You're a bush?" Chloe asked, giggling.

Jason threw back his elbow from his free hand and nudged her in the ribs.

"Quiet!" he whispered.

"No, my dear young lady, I am not a bush, but am invisible to you and anyone else trying to see me." Chloe listened as the bush talked.

She smiled. "Then show yourself to us, so we may believe you are indeed a man."

"Who said I was a man?"

This time it was the Puzzler who laughed. Jason felt a flash of heat hit the back of his neck and every hair stood on end. Something, or someone, was standing behind him. He gripped his sword even tighter and turned himself quickly around. Chloe grabbed his arm and Jason felt his courage drain from his body. A large black dragon with golden wings stood only a few feet from each of them. Jason held his sword up toward the Dragon and pushed his sister behind him with his other hand.

"Do not be afraid, I'm not the one you need to worry about," the dragon said through heated breath. "My name is Howakhan, I am the Master of all Puzzles. It is I that you seek."

Chloe felt her heart skip a beat as the fear raced through her veins. She felt Jason's muscles tighten as the creature spoke.

"How do we know you are who you say?" Jason asked bravely.

"Only the dreamer is allowed to speak and ask questions. You are only here as a guard and to give her aid," Howakhan answered.

366

Chloe gasped. She didn't know what she was supposed to do. She tried to think quickly.

Avery said to be brave, and things aren't always what they seem, she thought through her mind.

"Show us that we can trust you!" she yelled back at the dragon.

"Very well, I have the medallion of peace, given to me by none other than the King of Mere. If you look closely at my neck, you will notice that one scale is silver and holds the emblem of the en-laced swords," he answered.

Chloe and Jason both looked quickly at the dragon's long scaly neck. Sure enough a large scale, right in the center, was silver and inside was the emblem.

"Very well, Howakhan, what are we here for?" she asked, now feeling the tension leaving slowly from her body.

"To learn, sweet girl, why else. If you can pass the test of the Puzzler, you will become invincible to knowledge and power. Your training as a sorceress will be complete as well as your brother's knowledge of what and who he is in Mere, a great warrior." He gave a large toothy grin.

Chloe and Jason looked at each other in surprise.

"All we have to do is pass your test and we become smart?" Jason asked, astonished.

The dragon lay down, shaking the ground beneath him slightly. He looked carefully at the two young adults standing there frightened of him.

"No, Sire, you will be more quick to learn what is taught to you, but your training is never really complete. The tests that I have prepared for you will be very difficult. If you don't work together and figure out the challenge quickly then you will have failed and the hedge will remain. There are no second chances in my puzzles, so you better think quick. I must be on my way now, it is nearly time for the show. Remember, if you don't use teamwork, then you will fail. Good luck, children."

Howakhan rose back to his feet and spread out his large golden wings. Chloe had never seen anything more beautiful then the dragon right in front of her.

"Wait, where do we go?" Chloe shouted before Howakhan took flight.

"You shall walk toward the Valley of Rivers, the rest will come to you."

With those final words, the large dragon took flight, and rose high in the sky. Moments later, nothing could be seen, not even the glistening gold of his wings.

"Well what now?" Jason asked.

Chloe shrugged her shoulders. "I don't know. He said to walk toward the Valley of Rivers. Do you see anything?"

Jason looked around searching for something that might resemble the valley that Howakhan described.

"There, near the far mountain," Chloe yelled. "You see all the rivers?"

Jason looked at where she was pointing, and saw hundreds upon hundreds of small streams, rivers, and rocky ridged waterfalls.

"Well, let's get going, then," he said quietly as he sheathed his sword and lifted the packs that Avery had given them.

"I can't carry both packs, will you be all right to carry one?" he asked his sister.

"Of course, I'm not a weakling," she said sarcastically.

He smiled at her and handed her the lightest of the two packs.

The walk down the hill they were on seemed endless. The sun started to get further and further into the sky and the warmth of its rays started to withdraw.

"Do you think that we need to make camp here for the night?" she asked, out of breath.

Jason stopped and looked toward the valley.

"I'm not sure we can, we need to get there as quickly as possible," he answered.

She looked at him pleadingly. "I really need to take a break, please, let's just stop and rest for a while."

Jason lowered his pack. "Oh, all right, but only for a few minutes, we really need to keep going."

Chloe took a blanket from the pack she was carrying along with two sandwiches. She wasn't really that hungry, but knew if they didn't eat now, then they probably wouldn't for a few more hours. She handed one of the sandwiches to Jason and they both sat on the blanket.

"What is in this sandwich?" Jason said after he took his first bite.

Chloe took off the top piece of bread and found a skinny piece of some type of dried meat, topped with what seemed to be pineapple slices and smeared with some thick orange goop.

"I have no idea, is it bad?" she asked.

Jason chewed on his rather large bite before answering.

"No, it's great. A little sweet tasting, but pretty good."

Chloe watched him for a minute and then she too took a large bite. At first the taste was exactly what he said, sweet. Then, however, it would rotate flavors. First the sweet taste reminded her of an overripe orange, but now she could taste warmed up honey ham, with a hint of fried potatoes. Before she swallowed the bite, it seemed she was eating a piece of chocolate cake topped with ice cream, hot fudge, and a cherry.

"One bite is an entire meal!" she squealed with delight. "I love this place!"

Jason laughed at her and had already put his sandwich back in its bag with only one bite missing from the corner.

"I'm already completely full, I don't think I can take another bite," he exclaimed.

Chloe nodded in agreement. She too had her fill of ham and cake.

She lay down and rested her head on Jason's lap.

"Do you miss Mom and Dad?" she asked quietly.

Jason looked down at her and gave her a small smile.

"I'm sure they are fine. They weren't in the house when that tornado destroyed it. They are probably searching for us though. I heard Avery tell Aden that the opening to the cave had collapsed, so no one could get through."

Chloe grinned slightly. "I hope you're right."

Jason leaned his back against a rock and searched the sky. This sky was almost the same as the one back in Oklahoma. It was clear blue with a few lazy white clouds slowly drifting by. He shut his eyes and pictured their small little house and smiled. He didn't realize how much he would miss it if they had to move or if something happened to it.

"Jason, do you hear that?" Chloe said quietly.

"Hear what?" he asked, his eyes now open and his heart racing.

"I hear singing," Chloe answered with a whisper.

Jason quickly grabbed his sword and removed it from its sheath.

"I don't hear anything. Are you sure?"

She nodded and slowly rose to her feet. She saw a rock in the distance that was overlooking the other side of the large hill and began to walk toward it.

"Chloe, I don't think that's a good idea," Jason said, quickly grabbing her arm and holding her by his side.

"It'll be fine, the music sounds beautiful," she answered.

Jason released her arm and followed her toward the rock. Chloe climbed up the rock and looked out over the side. The breeze that hit her face was hot and felt a little moist.

371

She searched around and saw a small little creature about the size of a kitten sitting on a chair singing to itself.

"Look, Jason, what is it?" she whispered.

Jason looked at where she was looking, but saw nothing except a grassy hillside hewn with flowers.

"What are you looking at? I don't see anything but flowers," he answered.

Chloe looked at him and then pointed at the tiny creature.

"There, sitting on that chair," she said a bit louder.

Jason still didn't see what she was talking about.

"I'm sorry, Chloe, I don't see anything. Are you sure there's something there?" he asked. This time there was a little question in his tone.

Chloe wasn't sure what to say.

"How can you not see it, it's right there. It's a little black fuzzy creature. It is sitting in a small chair and is singing a beautiful lullaby," she said, aggravated.

Jason tried to see what she was talking about but there wasn't anything there. Chloe grabbed his arm and pulled him down from the rock and walked him over to where she saw the creature.

The little black creature stopped singing and stared at the two strangers walking toward him. It growled loudly and then began to change its shape. Chloe stopped immediately and gasped. Jason, still wondering what she was talking about, kept walking.

"Jason, NO!" Chloe screamed and grabbed his arm.

She pulled him backward and tried to run back up the hillside. Jason, seeing the fear in her eyes, knew that she wasn't just seeing things. It must be one of the Puzzler's tricks. He stood up and faced where Chloe saw the creature, and saw for the first time a large gray dragon. It growled furiously and Jason stood and stared. Chloe ran back and grabbed his arm again, and this time he followed. They jumped back behind the rock they had climbed on minutes before, just as a stream of fire flashed behind them. The dragon roared with fury and spread its large black wings and started running up the hill toward them. Jason held his sword tightly in his hands and with all the courage he had, jumped up and thrust his sword forward toward the dragon's roar. The creature halted and opened its mouth. A stream of fire was released from its mouth and Jason ducked just in time before being engulfed in the flames.

"What are we going to do?" Chloe yelled, trying to be heard over the roar of the dragon.

Sweat poured off of Jason's face and the fear was evident in his eyes.

"You need to do something, Chloe, I can't fend off the dragon by myself. Remember what Howakhan said, we need to use teamwork," Jason said heavily.

"What am I supposed to do?" Chloe yelled back.

The dragon came around the corner of the rock, and Chloe and Jason scrambled to get to the other side. The dragon moved far quicker than they did, however, and beat them there. Jason jumped up and swung his sword, making

contact with the creature's nose. It howled in fury, but
Jason's sword made no marks on the animal; its hard armor
scales protected him. Jason kept trying and Chloe watched,
wondering what she could do to help. Suddenly, Jason let out
a howl of pain. Chloe looked up and saw that his arm had
been cut badly from the creature's large teeth. He fell toward
the ground and the creature opened his mouth to let out yet
another ball of fire. The anger of seeing her brother hurt built
up in Chloe, and she screamed.

She leapt up off her feet and threw her hands forward
toward the dragon. As she did so, a red hot flame shot out
away from her and hit the dragon square in the face. The
dragon reared on its hind legs and roared. Chloe raced over
and put her hand over Jason's large gash. Warmth rushed
through her body and over the wound. The dragon howled
again and Chloe looked up and again shot another flame at
the beast. This time, however, the creature avoided it and
sent one of its own burning flames at the two of them. She
threw herself on top of Jason and the flame bounced off like
nothing happened. The creature grew furious at this and sent
several more flames at them. Each time, the flame was
repelled and the dragon grew more and more angry.

It reared up again and tried to come down hard on its
victims. Chloe grimaced as the power and weight of the
dragon hit her shield. Jason watched his sister and knew he
had to do something. He raised his sword with his other hand
and pulled Chloe away from the creature's second pounce.
She looked wearily at him. He pushed her behind the rock

just as the creature came charging toward them. He raised his
sword higher in the air and raced toward the dragon. Jason
lowered his heavy sword and slashed at the dragon with all
his weight. The sword vibrated heavily in his arms as it hit
the dragon's chest. This time, he gave the dragon a small
wound. Chloe rose to her feet, exhausted from her efforts.
She raised her arms and pointed them toward the dragon. She
focused all her attention on her brother, who was trying with
all his energy to defeat the dragon and protect his sister.

    With each slash of his sword, he caused some type of
wound, but it would quickly heal itself and the dragon would
retaliate with even more anger. He was just quick enough to
move away from the dragon's mouth before it gripped his
legs. He slashed his sword down on the creature's head and
Chloe thought hard of what to do to help her brother. Just
then, the dragon roared with anger and Chloe saw that
Jason's sword was red hot and the dragon's wing stripped
and bleeding. She focused her attention on Jason's sword and
fire shot out of it. He grinned at this new power, and thrust
his sword at the dragon's side. The heat of the sword pushed
its way through the hard scales and entered the dragons flesh.
He pulled it out quickly and the dragon again roared with
fury. It opened its mouth and shot a fire ball toward Jason.
Chloe caused her own flames that she was now throwing at
the dragon to deflect it, just as Jason dropped down to avoid
being burnt.

    The dragon dropped to the ground with a thump and
roared at his two attackers. The wound that Jason had

inflicted on his wing and his side was bleeding furiously. He laid down and began licking his wound and attempting to heal them. Jason held his sword up and began to race forward to finish off the beast.

"NO!" Chloe shouted. "Jason, we have to help him. He's hurt pretty badly, and I think that if we help him he will help us in return. I don't think that he is any more danger to us."

Jason stared at his sister in disbelief.

"He will destroy us if we let him. We must finish the job," Jason yelled.

Chloe shook her head. "I don't think so."

She walked cautiously over toward the dragon. She softly laid her hand on his neck and stroked it softly.

"Please help me?" the creature said quietly.

Chloe backed up quickly and stared at the dragon.

"Please, you are a sorceress, you have the power. Please heal my wing and the wound that was afflicted to my side," he begged her.

Chloe didn't know what to do. Was she really hearing this dragon speak to her? Jason watched his sister carefully.

"I think you are right, Chloe, I think he's harmless now," he said as he sheathed his sword. "Don't worry, friend, we'll do what we can for you," he said quietly to the dragon.

"Thank you, I will be in debt to you if you can heal these wounds." The dragon spoke so softly that Chloe and Jason both had to get closer to listen.

Chloe walked around to the other side of the dragon and saw his wing bleeding blue blood, not red like humans.

"I'm afraid I'm not a trained sorceress. I shall do my best to assist you, but you must promise to help us in return," she said bluntly.

The dragon nodded his head in agreement and Chloe placed her arm on the dragon's snout. She tried to remember what she had done to Jason to heal his hurt arm minutes before. She moved her hand slowly over the side wound first and imagined in her mind what she wanted to be done. The warmth from her body seared through her arm and a small fire formed from her fingertips. The fire licked the blue blood and it sizzled and before long, the wound had been healed. Chloe let out a sigh and felt the energy she had left slowly leaving her body. She wearily moved toward the dragon's wing and did the same as before. This time, however, her body quickly tired and she dropped to the ground.

"I'm sorry, please allow me to rest for a moment and then I'll try again. I know you are in pain, but healing a dragon takes far more energy than healing my brother."

The dragon nodded and put his head down toward her. She stroked his snout and rested her head against him. Jason watched her closely, and was ready if the dragon tried anything. The grip he had on his sword made his knuckles hurt and cramp slightly.

"Jason, will you please hand me a flask of water?" she asked him quietly.

377

Jason rose from where he was watching and without taking his eyes off the dragon, walked briskly over to where the water was and returned moments later. He handed Chloe the flask and sat down beside her. The dragon winced with pain when he caught sight of the sword around his waist.

"Why did you attack us?" Jason finally asked the dragon.

Chloe looked up into the dragon's big eyes and saw pain and sorrow.

"I learned some time ago to shape-shift. Many dragons can do this small trick, but sometimes when our identity is known to those around us we are forced into slavery. I was afraid that you were here to take me away, just like so many others I have known. I was protecting myself," he answered.

"But who would do that to a dragon?" Chloe asked as she stroked his long sullen face.

"A man in black has enslaved many of my kin. Warriors came to our village during the night and took many of the small dragons; even a few large adults were taken away. We tried to fight them off, but they disappeared into the shadows darkness and we never found them again." The dragon's tone was very glum as he spoke.

"That must be Jacan and the Umbra. Avery said that they had a dragon," she said quickly to Jason.

He nodded in agreement.

"You know this man, the man in black?" the dragon said hesitantly.

378

"I've never seen him, but he is a very wicked man. He is trying, as we speak, to destroy Mere," Chloe answered.

The dragon growled. Jason quickly pulled his sword from his belt.

"Peace brother, we are on the same side," the dragon blurted. "Jacan has taken my family away from me, he will pay the price for this terrible sin."

Jason relaxed and resheathed his large sword yet again.

"So you will join us in our quest?" Jason asked.

"If you can heal me, I will become your guide, and your friend. My name is Iraad of Gladican, I am at your humble service."

Iraad bowed his head low toward the ground and Jason followed suit. Chloe smiled and hugged the large dragon. She rose from her feet and immediately began healing the dragon's wings. After several long minutes and even more energy, Chloe had healed Iraad. She dropped to the ground and Jason raced toward her.

"Are you okay?" he asked quietly.

She nodded and closed her eyes.

"She needs to get some sleep, and so do you. The sun fell hours ago. I'll keep watch," Iraad said.

Jason looked at the dragon gratefully and nodded. He grabbed two blankets from their small packs and laid one carefully on Chloe and then covered up himself. The warmth from Iraad radiated through the blankets and kept the two travelers warm.

As the morning sun appeared over the horizon, Iraad stretched his long wings and yawned deeply. The sun, however, was no longer over the mountainous region from the day before; now the land was completely flat. Darkened clouds were forming in the distance, and a cool breeze was blowing in with it. Jason opened his eyes and searched the surroundings. Chloe was also staring wide-eyed at the flat land before them.

"Where are we?" Iraad asked, confused.

Chloe looked at the dragon and then at Jason.

"We are home."

Acknowledgments

Thank you to all those who helped make this possible. Colette, Aubrey, Aaron, Kendra, and Nicole for being the first readers of my manuscript and providing valuable feedback. To my husband Chad for all his hard work and final push. To Danijel Firak, the amazing illustrator that took my book and brought it to life. Also to Christine LePorte, the editor that made my story shine.

CPSIA information can be obtained at www.ICGtesting.com
Printed in the USA
LVOW082346170213

320527LV00001B/53/P